Kennedy Ryan

Swiftly on the Wings of the Wind

I0658434

Alicia Layne Thomason

Illustrated by US Illustrations

This is a work of fiction. Names, characters, businesses, places, and events are either the products of the author's imagination or are used in a fictitious manner. Any resemblance to actual persons, living or dead, or actual events is purely coincidental.

Cover design by Joyce Caberto and iStock.com/JohnnyGreig

ISBN: 979-8-218-65308-8

Printed in the United States of America

Acknowledgments

Thank you to my parents, Dennis and Michelle, for their support of my writing throughout my life.

Thank you to US Illustrations for working on the illustrations.

Thank you to my editor, Julia Hilton, for her edits on this book.

And thank you to God and Jesus Christ my Lord and Savior for giving me the wonderful gift of imagination.

Kennedy Ryan

Swiftly on the Wings of the Wind

Prologue

MAURICE CARR PULLED his truck into his usual parking spot. He didn't shut off the engine; the air conditioner felt too good on his face. He would probably start sweating the minute he stepped out of the truck. Or maybe even sooner because the heat seemed to take over the moment Maurice finally did turn off the engine. No matter. Once he was in his apartment, he could turn on the fan and relax. Heaven knew he needed it after working overtime at the hotel fixing too many malfunctioning air conditioners. The air conditioners weren't the only thing those unruly guests complained about. Increasing rates, the heat—seriously, what did everyone expect? They were in Arizona and May was almost over.

But the complaint that took the cake had come from the guest throwing a tantrum after being told to put on a shirt by the breakfast bar attendant earlier that morning. People complained about the hotel policies a lot, but that one guy's temper probably fueled Arizona's afternoon heat. Maurice had felt so bad for that poor young lady. She was only doing her job.

That man's temper had reminded Maurice of a certain criminal he had known. The ringleader of a gang of bank robbers. A gang Maurice had so foolishly teamed up with years ago.

He wiped his brow as he trudged up the stairs. He came to his apartment and pulled his key out of his pocket. But he hesitated when he noticed a few tiny scratches on his doorknob. Maurice narrowed his eyes. How long had those scratches been there? He shrugged it off and unlocked the door.

Maurice sighed with satisfaction. His living room always appeared so inviting whenever he came home from work. He went to the kitchen.

He looked up when he heard a creak near the pantry.

"Hello?"

Silence. Maurice shrugged. The heat was probably making him hear things. He grabbed the iciest water bottle from the fridge. As soon as he turned on his fan, he plopped down on his couch and took a refreshing gulp of water. He felt better already. What could ruin this moment of much-needed relaxation now?

"I was wondering when you would show up."

1

Maurice jumped. His stomach twisted, and his heartbeat had to catch up with his rapid, shaky breathing when he recognized the man standing in the doorframe of his bedroom.

"Horace Cobb!" he gasped. He glanced around the living room for anything he could use as a weapon. He spotted the poker stick near the fireplace and snatched it up. He pointed it at Horace.

"What are you doing in my apartment?" he hissed.

Horace chuckled. "Is that any way to greet an old friend?"

"You're no friend of mine!" Maurice said. "Not anymore. How did you get in here?"

"Let's say I've got some new friends. One of them is really good at picking locks."

A door creaked open. Maurice spun around. A bulky man was walking out of the pantry and sneering at Maurice.

"Meet Ernesto," Horace said. "He and I ran into each other not long ago. Turns out we've got a similar vendetta."

Maurice faced Horace again. "Both of you get out of my apartment before I make some noise!" he said.

"I wouldn't do that if I were you."

At the same time Horace drew his gun, Maurice was grappled from behind by Ernesto. His arms were pinned behind his back, and he dropped his poker stick. Ernesto shoved his own gun at Maurice's head.

"Raise your voice another decibel and you're history, Carr," Ernesto said.

Maurice tried to control his shuddering breath. "What do you want with me?"

Horace drew near to Maurice. His face was too close for comfort. "Like I said, Ernesto and I have a similar vendetta. Against a certain young lady. You know her, actually."

A queasy realization washed over Maurice. "Not . . . ?"

"Oh, you already know who I'm referring to," Horace said coolly. "Yes, her. Ernesto and I crave some sweets. Just not for our teeth. It wasn't just me and Ernesto who escaped from jail. No. Let's just say that Ernesto and I formed a new team. We're going after the young lady who has ruined us before. And you're going to join us."

"Why would I do that?" Maurice demanded. He twitched his arm, but Ernesto's grip was too strong. He twitched again when Horace laid a hand on his shoulder.

"You yourself went all chicken on me last time the two of us tried to take that girl down," Horace said. "But this time, I'm offering you a chance to redeem yourself."

"I've been redeemed," Maurice snapped. "And I won't do it. I won't help you."

Horace raised an eyebrow. He shook his head and removed his hand. "That's too bad," he said. "I gave you a chance. But now I need revenge against you too. You will watch me get my revenge on your beloved little cowgirl as payback for betraying me."

"And it would do well for you not to resist us." Ernesto's hissing tickled Maurice's ear. "Try anything, and we will cut to the chase and blow your brains out."

Ernesto threw Maurice to the floor. Horace turned away.

"Signal to the others, Ernesto," he said. "I'm going to grab our ropes and stuff. I want Maurice bound and gagged. Can't risk him making noise on our way out."

Ernesto nodded. Still pointing his gun at Maurice, he went over to the window and flashed a laser light.

Panicked thoughts flooded Maurice's mind. What could he do? He had to notify the police somehow! But if he were to get shot now, how would anybody else know what these wicked men were planning? Maurice knew he had no choice but to cooperate.

An idea popped into his head. It was risky. But somebody else had to know what was happening.

He pulled his cell phone out of his pocket. Thank goodness Ernesto didn't take it. He only had seconds to send a text to a friend. A pastor.

The pastor who had led him to Christ when he was still in jail.

He wrote his hurried text.

Being kidnapped. Can't explain now. Call police. Pray. Do not text back or call.

He deleted the text as soon as he sent it. He couldn't risk either Horace or Ernesto seeing it.

"Hey!"

Maurice shot his head up at Horace. He tossed his phone to the side.

"Ernesto, you should've taken his phone away!" Horace said hotly.

"I didn't know he had one on him!" Ernesto shot back. He yanked Maurice to his feet.

Horace snatched the phone. He scrolled through it, then slipped it in his pocket. He pointed his gun at Maurice.

3

"One more sneaky move, buster," he said, "and you'll be the coyotes' midnight snack tonight."

Maurice hung his head.

"Let's tie him up," Horace said. "We need to move quickly."

Maurice didn't struggle. As he was marched out the door with a cloth in his mouth and his hands bound behind his back, he could only pray silently.

Lord, protect me. Deliver me. And most importantly...

He drew a deep breath.

Protect Kennedy Ryan!

Chapter One

Home for the Summer

JUST THE SIGHT of her mother and stepfather's house made Kennedy Ryan feel better. She got out of the car and slammed the door, not taking her eyes off the house.

"Home at last!" Victoria said. "I may be in college, but I'm still soaking up the thrill and relief of summer vacation!"

Marilyn Wilson, Kennedy and Victoria's stepsister, laughed. "Victoria, it was only your first year," she said. "But yes, it is nice to be home again."

Kennedy's smile disappeared. She looked down at her feet. More like it was nice to be away from college and that miserable restaurant job. She had already decided that she was going to look for another job when she and the girls return to Phoenix in the fall.

The front door opened. Kennedy saw her sister Jessica running down the porch.

"Jessica!" Victoria said. She and Jessica locked themselves into a tight embrace.

"You're home!" Jessica said. "It's wonderful to see you all! I've missed you so much!"

Marilyn patted Jessica's shoulder. "We missed you too," she said. "I'm so glad we were able to come home in time to see your high school graduation."

"Totally!" Victoria let go of Jessica. "Seventeen and already graduating high school. But are we surprised?"

Kennedy crossed her arms. No, nobody was surprised that Jessica was graduating from high school before the age of eighteen. Kennedy held in a sigh; if only she had that kind of intellect. Then she wouldn't be struggling in her own college classes.

Jessica turned her gaze at Kennedy. Kennedy forced a smile and hugged her sister.

"So, where are your friends?" Jessica asked.

"Susannah and Rachel?" Kennedy said. "They drove in their own cars. Susannah's staying with her cousin Alec and Rachel's staying with her cousin and her family."

"But won't Rachel go back to Prescott?" Jessica said.

5

"Aw, she wanted to stick around long enough to see your grad ceremony," Victoria said.

Jessica put her hand over her heart. "That's so sweet," she said. "Come on, let's go inside."

The girls went into the house. They were immediately greeted by their parents, Caitlin and Isaiah. Kennedy smiled and went straight up to her mother to give her a hug.

"Welcome home, girls," Mom said. She let go of Kennedy. "How was college?"

Kennedy hesitated. "Oh, not bad."

"Not bad?" Isaiah said. "Is that all you've got to say, honey?"

"Oh, well, it's just that the art and music industry classes were tough. And other things. I mean, I still passed. Just glad to be home."

"Hey, Ken, I think you did great in your classes," Victoria said. "You sounded so good at each and every one of your student recitals. And you're smart, you know that. Just remember all the mysteries you've solved before!"

Kennedy took in a sharp breath.

"Well, I hope you didn't run into any mysteries this year," Mom said.

Kennedy's smile was more natural this time. "None," she said. "I'm happy to say that this semester was mystery-free."

She picked up her suitcase. "Think I'll get settled in."

"Victoria and I should too," Marilyn said.

"Of course," Mom said. "Dinner will be ready soon."

Kennedy, Victoria, Jessica, and Marilyn went upstairs. Kennedy opened the door of her old bedroom. Her bed looked so inviting with its clean sheets and flat, wrinkle-free quilt. The little fan sitting in the window blew its cool air on Kennedy's face, like it was welcoming her back to her old room.

"Need any help, Ken?" Jessica asked.

"Nope, I'm good," Kennedy said. "Thanks, though."

She closed the door behind her and put her suitcase on the bed. She snapped it open and started pulling out clothes. She let her mind unpack the miserable memories of being kidnapped in Starwood City. That way they could float and fade away on their own. Hopefully before dinner was ready.

As soon as she finished unpacking, Kennedy lay on the bed and closed her eyes. Only to open them again with a gasp when the darkness threatened to take her mind back to Starwood City's undertown. With a groan, Kennedy turned on her side. She still had nightmares sometimes.

6

Only a small number of people knew about her terrible experience of being held hostage under Starwood City. Her sisters. Her friends. A couple of counselors. But not her mother and stepfather. Much to her increasingly nagging guilt.

A knock interrupted her thoughts. Kennedy sat up. "Yeah?" she called.

Jessica opened the door. "You good and settled in, Ken?" she asked.

Kennedy stood up. "Yep. All unpacked."

"Sweet. Mom has dinner ready downstairs."

Kennedy, Victoria, Jessica, and Marilyn went downstairs to the dining room. Mom and Isaiah were already seated at the table. Kennedy hoped that the smells of the beef stroganoff and cream of mushroom soup would be enough to awaken some appetite in her.

The girls sat down. Isaiah prayed over the meal before everyone helped themselves.

"So, Jess," Victoria said, "what did you do all spring?"

"Homework, prep for graduation, moped around missing the rest of you," Jessica said. She took a sip of her soup. "Mm, this soup is really good."

"This is my recipe," Marilyn said with a smile.

"Of course," Mom said. "I thought I'd use it for when you came home."

"Hey," Victoria said, "these mushrooms are so good, Mom, I might have to worry if they are death caps."

Mom raised an eyebrow. "I'm not sure I'd use a mushroom by that name."

Isaiah smirked. "I would certainly hope not." He elbowed Marilyn. "We feed people for a living."

"I was kidding," Victoria said. "I learned about mushrooms in my biology class. I wrote a report on the death cap. People who've eaten it by accident say that it's the most delicious thing they've tasted."

"I remember learning about that," Jessica said.

"So, Kennedy," Isaiah said, "did you get into the Phoenix Symphony this year?"

Kennedy shook her head. "Not exactly," she said. "I mean, I'm still on their substitute list."

Isaiah's smile faded a little. "At least you've still got your foot in the door."

Kennedy shrugged. What she really wanted was for her violin skills to be strong enough to yank that door open.

7

"Are you okay?" Isaiah asked. "You don't seem very perky."

Kennedy just stared at her stepfather, wondering what to say, wishing that potential answers didn't lay shut up in her mind.

I'm struggling with my art and music industry classes. I don't understand the business side of art and music. I got a measly 78% on my music industry final. If I'm smart enough to solve mysteries, how come I can't understand a simple introduction to whatever industry class? Is it my autism? Am I slow on the uptake because of my autism? And however can I confess to you that I was kidnapped by counterfeiters?

She held in a groan. What kind of future did she have to look forward to compared to Victoria, Jessica, and Marilyn? Maybe she should just become a detective? No way. What happened in Starwood City had been enough.

"Well," Marilyn said, "our job in Phoenix was pretty awful."

"You mean at that restaurant?" Isaiah said.

"Yes. Kennedy, Susannah, Billy, and I were pretty much each other's supporters. All four of us hated it there. Our boss was not a good supervisor. And some of our coworkers were just mean."

"I'm sorry to hear that," Mom said. "I've heard a few things from Kennedy. It always sounded like it wasn't the best workplace. I'm so glad you're all out of it now."

"So am I," Marilyn said. "I know I don't plan on going back there. Dad, your restaurant is so much more peaceful and pleasant."

"We're looking forward to having you back there, hon. And Susannah applied online for a summer job there too."

"Yeah, she told me. We're looking forward to working in a good restaurant."

"The only good thing about our job in Phoenix was that it paid well," Kennedy said.

"Not enough for the toxic workplace environment that you guys were forced to deal with," Victoria said. "I still remember you coming home that one night all strung up. You know, when your boss yelled at you."

Kennedy kept her eyes away from the concerned looks of her mother and stepfather. The food on her plate suddenly seemed less appealing. She changed the subject. "I heard the town has a new mayor?"

"Yes, and he is excellent," Mom said. "He follows well in the footsteps of David Weston. And Jonathon Shea is our new sheriff. He's doing great."

"I heard that too," Kennedy said. "And Benjamin Hill, he moved out of town, right?"

"He did," Jessica said. "Shortly after New Year's. Jonathon made Robert Swift his deputy."

"I think I heard that too."

"Gosh, how do you know all these things, Ken?"

"Billy's been telling me stuff. His sister kept him updated."

Kennedy hoped her cheeks weren't turning red. They seemed to do that whenever she thought of Billy Weston.

"Oh, yes," Mom said, "his sister. The poor dear. Her belly is so huge."

"So she didn't have her baby yet?" Marilyn asked.

"No, she hasn't," Mom said. "She's approaching her due date. I think Jonathon and Felicity are ready for the baby to come. Felicity wasn't even in church this past Sunday due to morning sickness."

"I'll bet the heat isn't helping her," Victoria said.

Isaiah snorted. "That didn't stop her from going to the grand opening of our new tourist attraction last month. Old Dodge Park."

"Oh, yes!" Jessica said. "We went too. It's a little Wild West town just outside of Pine Lodge. Very close to the bluffs. It's also got a mini-golf course, a swimming pool, and a coffee shop. They had a great turnout for the campground, too. Lots of campers."

"We should check it out!" Victoria said.

"They said I could have my graduation party there," Jessica said. "And very soon, they're going to host Wild West shows. Like high noon gunslinging showdowns."

"And I'm sure that Kennedy would just love to see one of those," Mom said.

Kennedy smiled meekly.

"I can totally picture Kennedy in a gunslinging showdown," Victoria said.

"So can I," Marilyn said. She smiled at Kennedy. "But I was just thinking, for tonight, she should play that song she wrote in her piano class."

Kennedy stared at Marilyn. "What?"

"Sure. It's such a lovely tune. And you played it so well at your last student recital."

"Oh, Kennedy," Mom said, "we'd love to hear it."

Kennedy didn't see how she could back out of this. So right after the family finished dinner and cleaned up, Kennedy went up to her room to fetch her music. She fished through her backpack, partially hoping that she wouldn't find anything in there, therefore finding a good excuse not to play. How could she feel like playing the piano when her gloomy thoughts still plagued her mind?

But she found the folder with her sheet music. She opened it and flipped through the pages. At first, she felt rising relief at not seeing her tune. Then she sighed when she saw the tune at the back of the folder. She reluctantly took the folder to the piano. Her family was already gathered in the living room. She felt all eyes and smiles on her as she sat on the bench.

Kennedy made her fingers fly across the keys. She found herself smiling. Somehow, playing this song—this lively tune that she had written herself—made her feel better. After all, this piano piece received an excellent grade. And an excellent reception from her teachers and classmates when she played it for her last recital. And from her family that very evening when she finished.

"That was beautiful, Kennedy!" Isaiah said. "You say you wrote it? And you played it for one of your student recitals?"

Kennedy smiled. "Yeah," she said. "It was an assignment for piano class."

"What's your tune called, honey?"

"I haven't come up with a title yet. It was just called an original composition for the program. But I got extra credit from Professor Jennings when I played it. He was really impressed."

"Billy was too," Victoria said with a smirk.

Kennedy's cheeks burned. She looked down at her music. "Well, it was nice of him to come to my student recitals," she said.

"He went to every single one," Victoria said. "He basically memorized the recitals that Kennedy would be in. One time he put off overdue homework just to attend one of her recitals. Then he skipped out on part of a class for another one."

Kennedy just shrugged.

"So, what do you think?" Jessica asked.

Kennedy gazed at the mini-golf course. She certainly liked the Wild Western theme. The entire course itself was surrounded by a tall wooden fence. Within the course grounds were the green golf roads, which looked like long green islands against the brown dirt ground. Small log buildings served as holes; at least, their little round doorways did. Statues of covered wagons, cowboys and cowgirls on horses, black bulls, and saguaro cacti stood all over the place.

"It's awesome," Marilyn said.

"Come on, let's get the golf show moving!" Victoria said.

"Yes, I agree!"

The familiar voice made Kennedy's heart skip a beat. She turned around. Billy Weston was walking toward the girls. His friends, Wesley Rudolf and Aaron Connolly, who was Kennedy's cousin, were right behind him.

Kennedy couldn't keep her eyes off Billy. It seemed that every time she saw him, he was more handsome. But he and Wesley had finished college that spring. Kennedy still had one more year left. One entire school year away from Billy made Kennedy wish that she didn't have to return to Phoenix. She noticed Marilyn walking up to Wesley and giving him a hug. Envy filled the pit of her stomach.

"It's the college grads!" Jessica said. She gave Wesley a high five.

"Hey, I'm not a college grad," Aaron said.

"It's too bad you didn't go to GCU, dude," Wesley said. "You missed out on some rad experiences."

"Growing up on the ranch and learning from Dad was all the college I needed," Aaron said. "The rancher's life will always be calling my name."

"And that's all cool, man," Billy said. He looked over at Kennedy. Her stomach fluttered when he tipped his hat at her.

"Hey, Ken," he said, "how goes it?"

Kennedy made herself smile. It was probably an awkward, cheesy smile. "Good."

"Hey, guys, we're here!"

Kennedy turned around. She genuinely smiled when she saw her friends Susannah Anders and Rachel Hamilton walking toward them. Rachel's cousin, Sierra Hamilton, and Susannah's cousin, Alec McFarlane, were right behind them.

"Hey, hey, the gang's all here!" Rachel said.

"Almost," Sierra said. "The Grant twins haven't arrived, have they?"

"Not yet," Jessica said. "I'm sure they're on their way."

"Nicole's not here either," Alec said.

"We can start a game now, can't we?" Susannah said.

"Of course we can," Wesley said, swinging his golf stick.

"You kids can," Alec said. "I'll wait for Nicole."

Kennedy watched Alec leave the golf course. Yeah, he just couldn't do anything without his girlfriend. Kennedy eyed Billy. He, Wesley, and Aaron ran to an aisle.

Kennedy set her golf ball on the ground. She aimed her golf stick and focused her gaze on the little saloon at the end of the aisle.

She gave the ball a nudge. It rolled only a few feet. Not even close to that saloon.

"Kennedy, you have all the authority of a bunny rabbit."

Kennedy scowled as she retrieved her ball. She wanted to concentrate on her game, not on all the nasty things her former coworkers had to spew out. She scolded herself for even thinking about her old job. She was going back to her uncle's ranch. Her boss was going to be her uncle. Her coworkers were going to be Aaron, Wesley, and Billy. She knew they would treat her kindly. She would no longer be a soft doormat for a bunch of jerks to wipe their dirty feet—or more like their dirty mouths—on.

Kennedy hit the ball again with a little more force. But it still wasn't hard enough. Her thoughts wouldn't be swayed from their determination to make her anxious resentments an obsession.

"Hey, Gia? Our boss asked me to tell you that you're doing general cleaning today."

"General cleaning?"

Gia's scowl was etched in Kennedy's mind.

"No way. I'll just watch the cash register."

"But Jorge said—"

"Quit telling me what to do, Kennedy."

Kennedy snatched her ball from the ground and threw it back down. Her muscles became tense as she tightened her grip on the stick. She whacked the ball. It flew further across the aisle, but it still didn't reach the saloon.

"Kennedy! How come you weren't at work last evening?"

Her boss's angry voice rang in her ears, almost as though he was yelling at her right there, right now.

"B-because I had class."

"You were scheduled to work!"

"No, not on Wednesday nights. You said—"

"Don't you ever check the schedule? Do you know how to read? Sheesh, you're going to fail college if you don't learn to use that head of yours!"

Yep. Her boss just changed her schedule on her. At the last minute. And didn't even notify her. Then he had the audacity to yell at her in front of a bunch of customers.

In front of Billy.

Kennedy whacked the ball. It sailed across the ground and right into the saloon's little hole.

"Good show, Ken!" Rachel said.

Kennedy smiled. "Thanks."

She turned her gaze to Billy. He swung his stick, only to let out a defeated yell.

"Dude, you missed the ball again!" Aaron said.

"You're the worst golfer in the history of golf," Wesley said.

Billy smirked. "Look who's talking!"

"Hey, I only missed once!"

Aaron shook his head, but he was still smiling. "You guys haven't changed one bit."

"Admit it, you missed us," Wesley said.

"I know I did," Billy said. "I missed my family too. I was kinda happy when I heard that my sister didn't have her baby yet. I want to be around for that."

Kennedy's smile broadened. She could picture Billy as an uncle. If only she could picture him as her boyfriend just as easily. And without a fluttering heart.

"Oh, Billy," Marilyn said, "you must be so excited. I'm so happy for you. Now remind me, the baby's a girl, right?"

"Yep. I'm afraid to say that they still haven't picked out a name for my niece. I told Felicity to get a move on."

"Tell your sister to name the baby Marilyn," Wesley said. He smiled at Marilyn. "After the prettiest gal in Pine Lodge."

Marilyn's smile spread across her blushing cheeks. She slipped her hand into Wesley's. He twirled her a few times, then he wrapped his arms around her waist and planted a kiss on her cheek. With a sigh, Kennedy turned her gaze back to Billy. Would he ever twirl her the way Wesley twirled her stepsister? Would he ever give her a kiss on the cheek? Did Kennedy even have a chance with Billy? Like Marilyn and Wesley? Or would her autism get in the way of a relationship? Was Kennedy even Billy's type?

"I heard Lloyd Jennings is gonna give a lecture at an art festival in Phoenix," Billy said. He glanced in Kennedy's direction.

Kennedy stared down at her golf stick. An art festival did sound appealing. She would have to find out more. But who would be interested in going with her? She didn't exactly fancy the idea of driving down to Phoenix all by herself.

"Well," Wesley said, "I can tell you that if Kennedy went, Lloyd would give her another safety lecture about the Italy trip."

Kennedy frowned.

"Yeah, Lloyd was always joking about that trip, wasn't he?" Rachel said. "You know, a hostage situation is never funny, but every time

14

Lloyd shared the story in class, you know, about how we got mixed up with the affairs of that art thief in Italy, he always made it sound so hilarious. I have never laughed at a hostage situation. And I was one of the hostages!"

Kennedy felt somewhat dizzy. She had been one of the hostages too. But the situation in Italy hadn't left her traumatized nearly as much as being bound and gagged in Starwood City's undertown did. Her thoughts wandered to Rosa Morelli, a kind museum tour guide whom Kennedy had befriended in Italy. She remembered how Rosa had been kidnapped by the art thief. A sharp ache passed through Kennedy's stomach as it churned. She understood too well the shock and the anguish Rosa must have felt at the time.

"I reckon it's his way of coping," Marilyn said. "And he seems to have gotten over that really well."

"He also says that his wife forbid him from ever going on a faculty-led trip again," Rachel said with a laugh. "He just says that he won't go anywhere with Kennedy."

Kennedy sighed. Her lucky teacher. Actually able to joke about his once-terrifying experiences. Meanwhile, here she was still being haunted by traumatic memories of her terrifying experiences. This wasn't her first time suffering PTSD either. She remembered being edgy after her first mystery against Horace Cobb and his gang of bank robbers. But that case of PTSD? Mild compared to all the torment racing through her mind nowadays.

"Kennedy?"

She looked up. Billy was walking toward her. There went the butterflies in her stomach again, flittering around.

"You've been really quiet this whole time," Billy said. "You okay?"

"Yeah, sure," Kennedy said. "I guess, uh, golf doesn't seem to get on with me."

She prepared to hit her ball. But when she looked down, the ball wasn't there.

"Oh," she said, "uh, where's my ball?"

She turned around in circles, letting out one exasperated sigh. Her eyes rested on the little saloon, jogging her memory.

"Oh," she said, "it's in there. Never got it out."

She smiled sheepishly at Billy. "I'm so scatterbrained."

She instantly wished she hadn't said that. She walked toward the saloon, away from Billy so that he wouldn't see her red cheeks. She knelt and reached into the saloon. But she couldn't feel her ball.

"You need help?" Billy asked.

15

"No!" Kennedy said. "No, no."

She stood up. "I might need a break," she said. "I think I'll check out the arena."

She handed Billy her golf stick. And immediately felt awkward when he lifted his eyebrow at her. Kennedy didn't look at anyone as she hurried out of the golf course and down the black asphalt path to the little town. She stopped when she arrived at an alley in between two small log buildings, but only to take a breath. She then opened the door of the building to her left and went in. It was a little dark, but Kennedy didn't mind. It was perfect for hiding. Hiding from her troubles. From her trauma. From her feelings for Billy.

Her eyes glazed over the small room. She must've come in through some back hallway or something. This room looked like a long storage closet with shelves and boxes lined up against the wall, all of them full of old-fashioned Wild West costumes and props such as lassos, rifles, and even archeries.

Kennedy grabbed a bow from the shelf. She strummed the string a few times. It felt sturdy against her fingers. She put the bow back and looked at the rifles and pistols. Then she opened a drawer filled with little boxes of blanks, though Kennedy noticed that a few of the boxes had labels warning that they carried actual bullets. She also found many metal tubes, which she recognized as silencers for the guns.

"There you are."

With a gasp, Kennedy spun around. Billy stood by the open door. Apparently, she couldn't hide from him.

"Billy," she said. "Hey."

"Hope you don't mind me following you," Billy said. "It's just, that, well, you're tenser than Wesley when he's playing a near-unbeatable level on a new video game."

Kennedy looked down at her feet. "I'm sorry."

"Come on, what's bugging you?" Billy asked. "You can tell me."

It seemed that the longer Kennedy stared into Billy's eyes, the faster her heart beat. She opened her mouth to answer, but she couldn't bring out a sound. How could she tell Billy the truth? The last thing she wanted was for Billy to friendzone her. Or worse, ruin any relationship, platonic or romantic, that she had with him.

I'd almost rather be back at that miserable restaurant job. Or even kidnapped again!

"Was it something we said?" Billy asked. "Oh . . . we were talking about Lloyd, and . . . Ken, did we hurt your feelings?"

16

He frowned, and added in a darker tone, "Is it Starwood City again?"

Kennedy waved her hand dismissively. "It's cool," she said.

Billy shook his head. "It's not cool. You're still struggling with those awful memories, aren't you?"

Kennedy sighed. "Yeah. I guess."

Billy laid his hand on her shoulder. Somehow she kept herself from flinching.

"I just don't get it," she said. "What happened to me and the others in Italy doesn't bother me. I was a hostage then, but that didn't leave me traumatized. But what happened in Starwood City does?"

Billy squeezed Kennedy's shoulder. Her heart felt like it was squeezing too.

"I remember you telling me all about Italy," Billy said. "I remember how impressed I was. That wicked curator guy, uh, what was his name again?"

"Alfonso?"

"Yeah, Alfonso. He just demanded that you guys go with him. But you kept your phone hidden from him. You used your own wits to get yourself and everyone else out of that situation. But in Starwood City, well, I think what happened to you . . . it was more of a shock. You were tied up. And you were all alone. But you still escaped."

Kennedy blinked to keep back the tears.

"Can I help?" Billy asked. "Ease your mind a bit?"

He looked past Kennedy. "Maybe we can check out the little town?"

Kennedy smiled meekly. "Okay."

The twosome went outside. Billy shut the door behind him, then he led Kennedy away from the alley and out into the open. Kennedy's smile grew. So this Wild West arena was to be the main attraction of Old Dodge Park. With only a dozen log buildings that faced each other in two rows, statues of people on horseback, covered wagons, and saguaro cacti, the very real bluffs in the near distance, and no paved roads, this place looked very much like an old Wild Western town. The two friends walked past a big, square-shaped building that looked like a nineteenth-century fort. With its log structure and Arizona's state flag waving above the main entrance, that fort appeared to be right at home. Kennedy saw a horse stable right next to the fort. And the bluffs had a clear and majestic view just beyond the tourist attraction itself. Oh, how those surrounding bluffs provided the perfect Wild West background for this place!

"Just imagine what it'll be like," Billy said. "Aaron told me that they're moving the summer horseback riding classes here. And there will be rides in covered wagons and other old-fashioned carriages."

"I am looking forward to checking it out," Kennedy said. "I heard the employees will be dressed up in costumes and serving tourists in these buildings. You know, like the saloon, it'll have bartenders and showgirls playing live music."

"Yeah! We were just at the saloon, you know, a few minutes ago. In a room in the halls behind the stage. And maybe we'll see someone dressed as a teacher in the schoolhouse, or a preacher in the church."

"And maybe a sheriff in the jailhouse guarding a prisoner or two," Kennedy said. She grinned. This area made her think of her favorite novel, *The Galloping Girls of Pine Gulch*. Written by Marilyn's own mother. Kennedy wondered if the construction crew had that novel in mind when they built this place.

She turned her gaze to the center of the town. "I really want to see those showdowns," she said.

"You mean the high noon gunslinging?" Billy said. "Yeah, that'll be the best part! The highlight!"

Kennedy stared at the other end of the town. She could almost picture herself in one of those showdowns, maybe acting as the brave lady sheriff facing off against an escaped bank robber . . .

An image of Horace Cobb flashed through her mind. Then an image of Ernesto. Then Winifred, and her wicked, gloating grin as she taunted the bound and gagged Kennedy. All of a sudden, the town looked more like Starwood City. Kennedy gasped and shook her head.

"Ken?"

She felt Billy grab her hands.

"Are you okay?"

"Just a flashback," Kennedy whispered. She smiled at Billy. "I'm fine."

She looked down at their intertwined fingers. Her fingers began twitching. Billy pulled his hands away. "Sorry."

Kennedy shrugged. "Let's meet up with the others."

Of course her family had to sit in the pew right in front of the Westons. Kennedy opened her Bible to the passage indicated in her handout. It kept her distracted from looking back at Billy. Well, for the most part. She saw Billy go over to Wesley, Aaron, and Alec.

"How's the mining internship, Alec?" Billy asked.

"Wonderful, as usual," Alec said. "I still love working under Ted Garcia."

His smile faded a little. "Been meaning to ask you, have you guys heard about what happened at GCU yesterday morning?"

Kennedy looked up.

"GCU?" Wesley said. "Dude, tell me you're not talking Grand Canyon University?"

"Hate to say this, but I most certainly am," Alec said. "There was a break-in at the university's science building. Saw it on the news. Meant to tell you while we were playing golf, but I forgot."

Kennedy kept her gaze focused on Alec, but it did little to keep her mind off the knots in her stomach.

"Man!" Aaron said. "It's a good thing you guys graduated and came back here before that happened."

Kennedy couldn't agree more with her cousin. The very thought that the college had been broken into so soon after she finished the spring semester was scary enough. She tried not to imagine the break-in happening earlier. Like when she was still at the university.

"Was anything stolen?" Billy asked.

"I think so," Alec said, "but I'm not all that sure. I don't think those security cameras got a good look at the intruders."

"Hey, now that I think about it," Wesley said, "I read about a couple of jailbreaks a few months ago. One in Phoenix and the other in Tucson."

Kennedy pulled her phone out of her purse. Maybe a game would keep her distracted from the guys.

"I also heard about a disappearance in Prescott," Billy said. "Some guy vanished from his apartment. The only clue the police have is a text message a friend of the guy received. Apparently it was a kidnapping."

Kennedy flinched. Her game wasn't a very good diversion.

That poor man, she thought. *Being kidnapped. How awful! I hope he'll be okay.*

"Kennedy!"

Kennedy turned around. She smiled upon seeing Susannah and Rachel coming toward her.

"Room on the pew for me and Alec?" Susannah asked.

"Hey, of course, girl." Kennedy patted the space next to her. Susannah and Rachel sat down.

"Wish I can sit next to you gals," Rachel said. "But the pew might get crowded."

"Yeah, but your cousin and her family love having you," Susannah said.

"That's true," Rachel said. "Uncle Stan wishes my dad was with us. Misses his brother, he does."

She turned to Kennedy. "You seem more cheerful today."

"More cheerful?" Kennedy said. "Oh, yeah, I guess I wasn't too chipper at the golf course yesterday. Sorry about that."

"Hey, we get it," Susannah said. "College was pretty stressful this past spring. And work too."

"Don't remind me."

"Hello, girls."

Kennedy flinched, but it was only Felicity, smiling at her and holding her hand upon her big, round belly.

"Sorry," Felicity said. "Didn't mean to startle you."

"No, it's fine." Kennedy wondered if Felicity noticed her staring at her brother earlier.

"Felicity, the soon-to-be mom!" Rachel said. She turned her grin to Felicity's belly and held out her hand. "May I?"

"Of course." Felicity guided Rachel's hand onto her belly. Rachel beamed.

"I think I feel something, Fel! Uh, kinda feels like a foot."

"Yes," Felicity said, "I think so too. I'm always feeling her feet. She kicks a lot. I reckon she's just as excited for her birth as I am."

"Then she should get a move on," Victoria said. "We heard that you still haven't decided on a name for the baby. Maybe that's why she's kicking you all the time."

Felicity laughed. "I guess Jonathon and I are just picky that way," she said.

Just then the band began playing. The music director called for the congregation to gather in worship. Rachel ran to the pew where Sierra and her parents were sitting. Kennedy stood up and started singing. She glanced back at Billy. He smiled at her. She whipped her head away and kept her eyes on the screen, forcing herself to pay attention to the lyrics and not look over her shoulder. That was all that was keeping her mind off the handsome young man sitting behind her. After the fourth worship song, the music director told the congregation to be seated. Pastor Cameron walked onto the stage just as the band dispersed to their pews.

"Please turn to Psalm 18," the pastor said. He opened his Bible and notes. He said a short prayer before he began his sermon.

"This psalm's title is *The Lord is my Rock and my Fortress*. Please read along with me. 'I love you, O Lord, my strength. The Lord is my rock and my fortress and my deliverer, my God, my rock, in whom I take refuge, my shield, and the horn of my salvation, my stronghold. I call upon the Lord, who is worthy to be praised, and I am saved from my enemies.'"

Kennedy stared down at her Bible. The last line resonated with her.

"'The cords of death encompassed me,'" the pastor continued, "'the torrents of destruction assailed me; the cords of Sheol entangled me; the snares of death confronted me.'"

Assailed. Ernesto and Winifred had assailed her. Ernesto held her arms behind her and pressed the cloth of desflurane against her nose. Kennedy could still smell the strong scent that had lulled her to sleep. But right now, it wasn't lulling her to sleep. No, it was triggering trauma. And the cords . . . entangled. How could Kennedy forget the moment she woke up to find herself bound and gagged in the dark room, closed off to visitors, in the undertown?

Kennedy shifted a little, ignoring Isaiah's sideways glance. She tried to push away those miserable memories. She forced herself to pay attention to the pastor.

"'In my distress I called upon the Lord; to my God I cried for help. From his temple he heard my voice, and my cry to him reached his ears.'"

The butterflies in Kennedy's stomach simmered. That gag did not allow her to cry aloud. But her thoughts had been crying. They cried a prayer. And those distressed, silent cries reached God's ears. That was when she felt that nail.

"'. . . he came swiftly on the wings of the wind.'"

Kennedy smiled a little. How could she not remember how swiftly God answered her plea for delivery? All of a sudden, she found it easier to listen to the pastor.

Pastor Cameron finished reading the psalm and pulled out his notes. "I'm sure many of us know that the author of this psalm was David," he said. "Some of you are probably thinking that these verses are almost identical to 2 Samuel 22. David addressed the words of this psalm to the Lord when He delivered David from his enemies. We all know the famous story of David fleeing from King Saul, who sought his life in order to prevent David from taking the throne. Who knows how many times this young king-to-be was in danger?"

Kennedy knew the feeling all too well.

"Yet God constantly delivered David. Just as it says in verses 16 through 19, 'He sent from on high, he took me; he drew me out of many waters. He rescued me from my strong enemy and from those who hated me, for they were too mighty for me. They confronted me in the day of my calamity, but the Lord was my support. He brought me out into a broad place; he rescued me, because he delighted in me.'"

Kennedy's smile grew. Yes, God had indeed rescued her in the undertown. And all those other times before. Kennedy had felt like she had been drowning in danger. But every time, God pulled her out of those treacherous situations. Those treacherous waters.

Pastor Cameron finished his sermon and prayed. Just as the band was returning to the stage, Kennedy felt a tap on her shoulder. She met Isaiah's concerned eyes.

"Are you okay?" he whispered. "You seemed fidgety."

"Yes." Kennedy smiled feebly at her stepfather. "I'm fine."

But she knew Isaiah wasn't convinced. Luckily for her, the congregation began singing right then. As soon as the last worship song was done and Pastor Cameron gave the benediction, Kennedy grabbed her stuff and pushed past her sisters and Susannah.

"Hey, what's the big hurry?" Victoria asked.

"Uh, nothing, really."

"Well, come on!" Jessica said. "We wanna show Susannah and Rachel the secret tunnel!"

"Your church has a secret tunnel?" Susannah said in disbelief. Rachel spun around and gaped at Victoria and Jessica.

Victoria laughed. "This place had some recent renovations in the sanctuary and the dressing rooms for the baptismal basin."

"And the remodel guys left a bit of a tunnel right under the basin," Jessica said. "The tunnel connects the two dressing rooms. Let's go check it out!"

A chortle escaped from Kennedy's lips. Jessica may be just about ready to graduate high school, but she was still an energetic child at heart. Just like Victoria. Kennedy, Marilyn, Susannah, and Rachel followed Victoria and Jessica to a door to the right of the stage. Victoria opened it and led the girls to the women's dressing room. They walked past the stairs that led up to the baptismal basin and to a little room.

Victoria pointed at a rectangular hole in the wall. "Behold! The secret tunnel! The remnants of the remodeling of the baptismal above!"

Kennedy sat on the chair next to the window. She had only been in that tunnel once, when it was brand new. Before she had gone to Starwood City. When she still loved the thrill of mystery and excitement.

"That is so cool!" Rachel said. She crawled into the hole.

"Aren't they going to fix this?" Susannah asked.

"I hope not," Jessica said. "All the little kids would be really disappointed! And besides, Pastor Cameron said this tunnel would make good storage."

She and Victoria crawled into the hole after Rachel. Even Marilyn bent down in front of the rectangular opening. She looked up at Kennedy.

"Are you coming?" she asked.

Kennedy shrugged. "Sure."

She crawled into the hole after Marilyn. Her eyes began to adjust to the darkness, allowing her to see her sisters and friends just in front of her.

"A little bit of a tight squeeze, isn't it?" Susannah said.

"Hey, it's a lot roomier than that ice tunnel Jess and I had to crawl through once!" Victoria said.

"And it's bigger than I remember," Kennedy said. Even so, she was so close behind Marilyn that she was practically breathing down her stepsister's neck. She was a little surprised that all six of them could fit in here. She ran her fingers over the scratchy wood of the walls and ducked under a little beam.

Her heart picked up its pace.

"You can see the other dressing room right there," Jessica said, pointing ahead.

Kennedy tore her eyes away from the beam. But the light on the other side wasn't comforting. The beam had captured her attention. Like she had been captured in Starwood City. She tried not to picture herself tied to that beam, but the darkness was igniting the darkest aspects of her imagination. Triggering those awful memories. Not only could she see herself bound to that beam, but she could feel the ropes scratching her wrists.

Kennedy spun around on her knees and clambered back. She stumbled as she pulled herself out of the hole.

"Kennedy!" Marilyn called. "You okay over there?"

Kennedy inhaled. "Sure," she called back. "Just fine."

That was partially true. Being out of that dark tunnel did make her feel a little better.

"Here we are!"

Isaiah pulled the car in front of the house. The familiar sight of Uncle Oliver's house made Kennedy breathe out a sigh of contentment. It felt so wonderful to be back here at Silver River Ranch. She was looking forward to working on the ranch again for the summer.

Everyone jumped out of the car. Only Kennedy lagged behind as her sisters and Marilyn ran onto the front porch. Uncle Oliver opened the door and opened up his arms in a warm greeting.

"Honey."

Kennedy felt a hand grasp her shoulder. She looked up at Isaiah. He was giving her the same concerned look he had given her in church.

"What's wrong, Ken?" he asked. "I could tell that something was bothering you in church this morning."

"I'm okay, really." Kennedy looked at the ground.

"I can tell that you're not okay. You haven't been okay for quite some time, actually. Not just since you got back from college. Before then. Since you got back from Starwood City. I remember how you weren't too keen on talking about the rodeo that you had been so excited to participate in."

Kennedy forced a smile. She wished her stepfather hadn't mentioned Starwood City. "Aw, you don't have to worry about me. Come on, let's catch up with the others."

"We will." Isaiah didn't remove his hand from Kennedy's shoulder. "After you tell me what's the matter."

Kennedy let out a sigh of defeat. "Alright, you win. The thing is, it's just that . . ."

She trailed off. She didn't know where to begin. Not getting into the Phoenix Symphony? Struggling in her classes? Getting only a 78% on her music industry final? Her growing feelings for Billy? The situation of being a prisoner?

The last thought made her heart skip a beat. So did the thought of confessing that very moment. Did she dare?

"Is it college?" Isaiah asked. "You've been really quiet since you returned from college. And I know you're disappointed about not getting into the Phoenix Symphony—"

"It isn't just that."

"Then what is it?"

Kennedy sighed. "My boss and my coworkers at my old job were such jerks. Especially toward me. I feel awful. I was such a doormat at that place. All my boss and coworkers did was walk all over me. And my boss yelled at me for going to class. Even said I would fail college. I kind of wish I wasn't autistic. And . . . well, the truth is . . . I think I have feelings for . . ."

She hesitated.

"Go ahead, hon," Isaiah said gently.

"Billy." Kennedy sighed. "I think I've got feelings for Billy."

Isaiah smiled. "So, sitting in front of Billy and his family was making you fidget in your seat?"

"No!" Kennedy said quickly. "No, it wasn't that. It was . . ."

She hesitated again. "I guess I worry too much."

"I agree with you," Isaiah said. "You are worrying too much. Kennedy, I know how hard it is for you to not feel inferior to your sisters. But you have your own gifts. And you're smarter than you give yourself credit for. You've solved many mysteries."

"Yeah, and those events have left me slightly traumatized, especially since I was—"

Kennedy cut herself off with a gasp. She slapped her hand over her mouth.

"What's wrong?" Isaiah asked.

Kennedy took a breath. There went the memory of the dark and gloomy undertown again. She looked up at her stepfather.

"I owe you an apology," she said, her voice breaking.

"Kennedy." Isaiah grasped her hands. "What's the matter? Why do you say you owe me an apology?"

"Because there's something I haven't told you and Mom. You're right, Isaiah. I haven't been doing very well since Starwood City. Because, last summer, when we went to Starwood City for the rodeo, and I got myself all caught up in sleuthing against those counterfeiters . . ."

Isaiah nodded, nervous anticipation widening his eyes. Kennedy squeezed her own eyes shut and released the tears. "I was kidnapped."

She heard Isaiah gasp.

"Two of the counterfeiters kidnapped me one evening," she said. "They put me to sleep and took me to a place in the undertown that was closed off to visitors. Closed off because one of the tour guides was secretly a part of the counterfeiting ring. I was tied to a post. Gagged. I was so scared, and I was all alone. It shook me up, and I just . . . I guess I lost all my confidence after that."

Kennedy blinked back more tears. There. She said it. She gazed into Isaiah's horrified eyes.

"Y-yes. That does explain a lot." Isaiah squeezed her hands. "Oh, Kennedy, honey, why didn't you say anything to me and your mother?"

"I was too traumatized to talk about it. And my sisters and I just didn't want to scare you and Mom. I'm so sorry."

Isaiah wrapped his arms around her. "It's alright," he said. Kennedy felt his hand rubbing the back of her head. "I get that you might not have been ready to talk about something like . . . like that. I am so sorry you went through that. I'm sure it was horrifying. And the other girls know? And your friends who were with you?"

Kennedy nodded.

"Well, you do know that your mom might find out sooner or later?" Isaiah said.

"I know."

"But that conversation can wait until you are ready." Isaiah wiped a tear from Kennedy's eye. "At least tell me you've been in counseling for this."

"I have been. I've spoken to the college counselor at GCU. And I've met with the local counselor once last summer, just before I left for college."

Isaiah nodded. "How did you get out of it? Um, that awful situation?"

Kennedy smiled meekly. "I prayed. Silently, of course, since I was gagged. That was when I felt a nail in the post. Something overlooked by my captors. I scratched my bonds against that nail until they came undone. And then we had our final battle."

Isaiah smiled. "God has protected you so much. Kind of like what Pastor Cameron was preaching about this morning. As for your other worries, well, if God can deliver you out of numerous dangerous situations, such as being kidnapped, then He can guide you through planning your future. And confessing to Billy how you feel about him."

Kennedy blushed. She gazed at her stepfather. Once in a while, she still thought about her birth father, who had died from meningitis when she was fifteen. Her mother's marriage to Isaiah had initially been difficult for Kennedy. But now Kennedy loved Isaiah as though he were her father. Even now, she felt much better after sharing her problems with him. He was a lot like Kennedy's father. Kind, understanding, and a good listener.

"Come on, dear," Isaiah said, "let's catch up with the rest of the family before they miss us."

His arm was still wrapped around Kennedy's shoulders as they walked to the house. As soon as Kennedy went inside, she was greeted by the pleasant aroma of spaghetti and garlic breadsticks.

"There you are, dear," Mom said to Isaiah. "The rest of us were beginning to wonder where you and Kennedy were."

Isaiah grinned. "Just chitchatting," he said. "Come on, let's sit down, I'm hungry."

Kennedy sat next to her stepfather. Uncle Oliver prayed over the meal, then everyone began serving.

"Pass the breadsticks, please," Jessica said.

Aunt Thelma handed Jessica the breadsticks. "We had a lot of fun at your graduation party," she said.

"I think all of us did," Jessica said. "I'm so glad we got to have it at Old Dodge Park."

"I know," Uncle Oliver said. "I'm looking forward to those showdown performances. I'm loaning out some of my horses to the people running it."

"Really?" Mom said. "Do you expect to make money?"

"Very good money, Caitlin."

"Which horses will you loan out?" Marilyn asked.

"Well, Sunshine for sure," Uncle Oliver said.

Kennedy looked up at her uncle. He smiled at her. "You'll still be able to ride her, Ken," he said. "She's still my horse. But I think she'll do really well at the showdowns."

Kennedy nodded, feeling relieved.

"Speaking of horses, ladies," Aaron said, "we should go riding after dinner."

Everyone agreed with Aaron. As soon as they finished eating, the kids went out to the horse stable. Kennedy went straight to the stall of a beautiful, golden palomino mare.

"Hey, Sunshine!" she said. She nuzzled her head against the horse's snout.

Sunshine nickered happily. Kennedy grinned. She missed her favorite mare. She wondered if she would see Sunshine in Old Dodge Park's shows.

Aaron and the four girls led their horses out to the corral to brush and saddle them.

"Hey, kids!"

Kennedy turned around. Isaiah just entered the corral. He had a brown bag slung over his shoulder and a big smile for Kennedy.

"Thought you kids might need some water." Isaiah opened the bag to reveal a bunch of water bottles.

"I grabbed a few," Aaron said. "But hey, we can always use some extra water in this heat."

Kennedy smiled feebly. She had a hunch that Isaiah's real reason for coming out was to check on her.

"Isaiah," she said, "would you care to ride with us?"

"Yeah!" Marilyn said. "I know I'd love for you to join us, Dad!"

Isaiah grinned. "Just let me pick out a horse," he said. He and Aaron went into the stable. The two of them led out a black-and-white gelding. Kennedy and Marilyn helped Isaiah brush and saddle the horse. In a few minutes, everyone mounted their horses. Kennedy nudged her heels against Sunshine's flanks. The mare took off, running out of the corral and toward the hills.

"Hey, Kennedy, wait up!" Aaron called.

Kennedy tugged the reins. Sunshine slowed to a stop.

"Got a little too excited, I see," Isaiah said.

Kennedy smiled sheepishly. "Just happy to be riding again."

They rode through the hilly pastures. Kennedy listened to the sounds of wrens chirping and woodpeckers pecking at the tree trunks. She and her sisters laughed at the gophers darting in and out of their holes.

"Glad to see you're having fun," Isaiah said.

Kennedy smiled at her stepfather. "Riding has always made me feel better," she said.

"Come on," Isaiah said, "I'll race you to that hill over there!"

His horse took off. Not wanting to be outdone, Kennedy goaded Sunshine to run faster. The palomino mare raced past Isaiah's horse. Kennedy laughed when she reached the hill.

"I made it!" she shouted.

"Yeah!" Isaiah said with a laugh. "Just gloat, why don't you!"

"Girl!" Marilyn exclaimed. "You beat my dad!"

"Just once!" Isaiah said. "Maybe she won't be so lucky next time! To the sunset!"

Kennedy steered Sunshine away from the hill and rode after her stepfather and stepsister.

Chapter Two

The Bear Trap and the Brush Fire

KENNEDY SHOVED OUT another scoop of the smelly hay, then paused to wipe her brow. She was practically swimming in sweat. Maybe she should ask her uncle about installing a fan in the stable. Her uncle would never snap at her for asking for a simple favor. It was such a relief to be back on the ranch, even if it did mean working outside under the heat of the desert sun.

Kennedy grabbed her water bottle. Not only was it warm to the touch, but it was almost empty. Kennedy downed the rest of the water and threw the empty bottle in the trash bin. She made a mental note to grab another water from the house. But first she wanted to finish mucking out this last stall. Even though the nasty odors were making her even more thirsty.

Kennedy finished cleaning the stall and went outside. Immediately the heat beat down on her face. She wiped her cheeks and took hold of the reins of a sorrel mare. Kennedy led the mare over to a trough filled with sparkling water. That water looked so refreshing, despite the fact that it belonged to and was being drunk by the horses. Kennedy's mouth felt drier than the desert.

She fanned her face. Was she beginning to feel a little lightheaded? She returned to the stable, figuring that she needed to sit in a shaded shelter for a few minutes. Then she would go to the house and grab some water.

"Reckon we can tackle some roping games later?"

Kennedy's heart skipped a beat at the sound of Billy's voice. She noticed that she seemed to be startled by Billy's mere presence lately. Even after her pep talk with Isaiah, she still hadn't found the courage to speak up.

"In the evening, when it's cooler," Aaron said. "We gotta ride out to the pastures and check on the cattle in a few minutes."

Kennedy smiled. Riding out to the summer pastures with Billy? Maybe she could ask Aaron if she could take his place . . . no, perhaps not, she was feeling too tired to ride a horse right now. Maybe even a little dizzy. No, no, she was fine. She wasn't about to let a mild dizzy spell keep her away from Billy.

A stumble of her feet interrupted her thoughts. Kennedy yelped as she fell forward. Her face was planted in a pile of hay.

"Ken!"

Kennedy lifted her head. It still made her dizzy. She could barely make out the blurry figures of Billy, Aaron, and Wesley staring at her.

"Hey, you okay, cousin?" Aaron asked as he kneeled.

Kennedy pulled herself onto her knees. But it made the dizziness worse. She rubbed her hands against her cheeks.

"Maybe," she mumbled. She felt too queasy to resist when Aaron pulled her hands away from her face.

"Gosh, Kenny," he said, "are you pale!"

Kennedy felt a twinge of relief in her stomach. At least she knew that she wasn't blushing. She avoided Billy's eyes all the same.

"You've got stuff on your face, girl," Wesley said.

"Yeah, well, I did land in this rotten old hay." Kennedy moaned as she wiped away dirt and hay from her cheeks and lips. She wrinkled her nose. Who knew what else was hiding in that old pile of stinky hay? She just hoped that her face was not as dirty as she worried it was.

"Hey, Kennedy, I think you're dehydrated," Billy said. He kneeled on one knee. Kennedy tried in vain not to squirm when he laid his hand on her shoulder. "I'm gonna run you back to the house. I reckon some ice water and a good break is what you need."

"Oh, no," Kennedy said, "I'm fine."

"Ken, I can feel you shaking."

Kennedy let out a defeated sigh. "Yeah, I do feel lightheaded."

Billy wrapped his arm under Kennedy's. She kept her head down as Billy lifted her to her feet. Just his touch made her feel even more woozy and wobbly. First he had to witness her being bullied and yelled at by her former boss. Now he had to witness her fall facedown into old hay. It seemed that her dizzy spell did prevent her from riding out with him after all.

Kennedy's thoughts wandered to the first time she had met Billy. She had made a fool of herself in front of him back then too. And he laughed at her. That memory alone was enough to increase her nausea and embarrassment.

Though, he wasn't laughing this time. No, this time, he had his arm around her shoulders and his hand on hers as he walked her outside. Not a trace of laughter slipped past his frown, which carried the same concern that filled his eyes.

"Let's get to the house pronto," he said. "I don't want you out in this heat any longer than you need to be."

Kennedy smiled faintly. Suddenly it seemed that Billy's soft touch and the gentle way he held and guided her made her dizzy spell fade away. She might even have an advantage in blushing; it would return some color to her cheeks.

An agonized yelp captured Kennedy's attention. She and Billy spun around. Doing so renewed Kennedy's dizzy spell.

"What was that?" she asked.

"It sounded like the dog," Billy said.

As if on cue, Aaron's border collie, Buddy, came limping around from the back of the barn, whining loudly all the way. Even from the short distance from where she stood, Kennedy could make out a strange silver object on the dog's right leg. Buddy collapsed on his side just as Aaron and Wesley rushed out of the horse stable. Aaron yelled in alarm upon seeing his dog.

"What just happened?" Wesley demanded.

"Dude!" Aaron said. "That's a bear trap!"

Billy let go of Kennedy and rushed to his friends. Kennedy followed him. She sat on a rock while the three boys surrounded the whimpering dog. Just the sight of the blood on the poor dog's leg, which was indeed wrapped in a bear trap, made Kennedy feel even paler.

"What do we do, man?" Wesley asked.

"Hey, Buddy, it's okay," Aaron said soothingly. He kneeled next to his dog. "Wes, you and I will stay with him. Billy, you and Ken go to the house and get my dad."

Billy nodded. He walked over to Kennedy. She let him take her hand so he could help her stand on her shaky feet. Just holding his hand, even for a second, made her heart thump.

"It'll be okay, Ken," Billy said. "Just don't look. You're pale enough as it is."

The twosome made their way to the house. Kennedy found it difficult to ignore Buddy's pained whimpers. She peeked over her shoulder.

"Poor Buddy," she said. "Do you think he'll be okay? Who'd be so careless as to leave a bear trap lying around? They're not even legal, are they?"

"I don't think so," Billy said.

As soon as they entered the house, Billy took Kennedy straight to the couch in front of the fan, which was already turned on. Billy got her a water bottle from the kitchen, then he ran down to the basement. In moments, Kennedy saw Uncle Oliver running out the front door. Billy sat next to her.

"Aren't you going with him?" she asked.

"Oh, I just wanted to ask how you were feeling," Billy said. He looked down at his feet.

Kennedy smiled shyly. She gulped down some water and laid her head back. She listened to the fan's whirring. Its light breeze felt like it was bringing color back to her face. Already her dizziness was fading away. Only to be replaced by worrisome thoughts. If her uncle had an illegal bear trap on the ranch, what might happen? Surely he and all his ranchers knew better!

The front door opened. Uncle Oliver came into the living room. "You two okay?" he asked.

"I'm fine," Billy said. "Um, Kennedy here just suffered a bit of dehydration. Right before we found Buddy. So, what's the scoop, Mr. Connolly?"

"Aaron and Wesley are still with the dog," Uncle Oliver said. "Aaron and I are taking him to the vet. I came here to grab a few old blankets and the pickup."

He removed his hat and wiped his brow. "I'm also going to show the trap to Jonathon and Robert," he added. "How that bear trap got onto my ranch is a mystery."

Kennedy wished her uncle had used a different word.

"I don't own any of those things."

"And there's no way anybody could've bought one from the mall's sports and hunting store," Kennedy said. "That place doesn't sell bear traps. I mean, the sale of bear traps isn't legal in Arizona."

"I'll chat with the other ranchers," Uncle Oliver said. He put his hat back on. "And Kenny, dear, if you're dehydrated, the boys can worry about the rest of the outdoor work. You just rest up and drink plenty of water, okay? Maybe when you feel better, you can help your aunt with chores around the house."

Kennedy nodded gratefully.

Kennedy held the door open. Victoria, Jessica, Rachel, and Sierra walked in single file. The Lonely Pine Eatery looked the same as always whenever Kennedy came home from college for summer.

"It's been a while since I was here," Rachel said.

"Always one of the town favorites," Sierra said.

Marilyn greeted the five girls as soon as they took their seats at the counter. Susannah came out of the kitchen, wearing an apron just like Marilyn's.

"So Mary," Victoria said, "you happy to be back here?"

"Of course," Marilyn said. "I really missed working here with Mom and Dad."

"I'm happy to work here too," Susannah said. "It's so much better than that other place."

She held up her notepad. "So, what'll it be?"

"Some ice cold drinks to start with," Victoria said. "And we want those drinks icier than the South Pole."

Susannah laughed. She and Marilyn took the girls' drink orders and went to the kitchen.

"Hey, girls, what's up?"

Kennedy turned around in her seat. She recognized the tall and lanky man standing next to her as Robert Swift, the town's new deputy. He took off his tan cowboy hat and smoothed out his spiky brown hair.

"Just ordering lunch," Kennedy said. "Hey, congratulations on becoming Jonathon's deputy."

"Thanks, girl." Robert replaced his hat. "I gotta admit, I'm happy to just be a sheriff's sidekick in a tiny tourist town. I never thought I could be a criminal catcher like you, Kennedy."

Kennedy smiled faintly. Marilyn and Susannah came out of the kitchen. Marilyn held a tray full of sodas.

"Here we are," she said as she handed out the drinks. She smiled at Robert. "Hi, Deputy. Can I get you anything?"

"I'm ordering lunch to go for me and the sheriff," Robert said. "You can help these ladies first."

He smiled shyly at Susannah. "Don't mean to butt in and distract the waitresses."

"Deputy," Kennedy said, "any updates on that bear trap?"

Robert shook his head. "Jonathon and I talked to your uncle. He said he spoke to his ranchers. Doesn't sound like any one of them ever bought a bear trap."

Kennedy felt a few thumps against her chest.

"Ken told us about that," Marilyn said. "How is Buddy?"

"He's actually doing pretty well," Kennedy said.

"That's good to hear. So, are you ready to order?"

Kennedy picked up the menu, but before she could order, a man stomped out of the kitchen. He focused his glare on Marilyn. Kennedy gawked at him. Who was he?

"Hey, you, chef's girl," the man spat at Marilyn, "when are you gonna help me in the kitchen?"

Kennedy stole a glance at Marilyn, who just sighed.

"I'll help you," she said, "as soon as I finish taking orders."

The man turned his glare to Kennedy. Gazing into those cold gray eyes behind those thick glasses made waves of déjà vu pass through Kennedy's mind. But surely Kennedy would've known if he was a resident of Pine Lodge. She wouldn't forget that oily black hair tied up in a short ponytail and thick black beard on that pointy chin.

"More like wasting time chitchatting," the man said.

"Sir," Robert said, "she wasn't wasting time. She was going to take these ladies' orders when you so rudely interrupted her."

The man scowled at Robert. "Who asked you?" he said.

Robert showed the man his badge. "Remember who's deputy around here."

The man rolled his eyes. "Just deputy, mind you," he growled. He marched back into the kitchen.

"Sorry about that," Marilyn said.

"Who was that guy?" Victoria asked.

"That would be our new coworker, Roman Hughes."

"He's new in town," Jessica said. "He got an apartment just a few days before the rest of you came home. I don't see him around much."

"Doesn't seem like he's a great coworker," Kennedy said.

"I'll admit, he isn't." Marilyn groaned. "For the most part, coming back here has been nice. But Mr. Roman there is just like some of our old coworkers at that miserable restaurant."

"Oh yeah," Susannah said, "he does bring quite a bit of gloom to this place. He takes a lot of smoke breaks, even when he shouldn't be. Our other coworkers don't like him either."

"I think Dad regrets hiring him," Marilyn said. She gave the deputy a small smile. "Thanks for standing up for me."

"Don't mention it," Robert said. "If I could arrest people just for being rude, he'd be the first one I book."

"Aw, cheer up, everyone," Victoria said. "Marilyn, we know your dad. He won't tolerate that guy's nonsense for long. I'll bet you that very soon everything will be back to the nice normal we all know and love. Besides, you've got your date with Wesley to look forward to."

The pink hues that appeared on Marilyn's cheeks almost matched the bright red color of her hair. "May I take your orders, please?"

Kennedy put her menu down. Envy made her appetite fade away. As did the lingering déjà vu that came from Roman Hughes.

Kennedy removed her apron and hung it up. Unloading the dishwasher was her last chore for the evening. She poured herself a glass of ice water and took a big gulp. Oh, that was so refreshing.

She went up to her room. She flipped the fan on, downed the rest of her water, and let herself plop onto her bed. The fan felt so good; just watching the cool air blow on her blonde curls from the side of her vision made Kennedy feel like a pretty princess. Though not as pretty as Marilyn. Envy knotted at Kennedy's stomach. Marilyn had been absent at dinnertime, courtesy of her date with Wesley.

Kennedy looked out the window. She couldn't help but admire the view of the golden sunset shining its rays on the bluffs. She sat up. It was such a beautiful evening outside. Why waste it?

She left her room. The hall was quiet except for the hums of fans behind closed doors. Kennedy went downstairs to the living room.

"Where are you going?"

Her stepfather's voice was almost drowned out by the fan, but Kennedy still heard him. He was sitting on the couch, staring at his tablet.

"Just outside," Kennedy said. "Thought I'd go to the hills."

Isaiah lifted his head. Kennedy saw that worried look in his eyes again.

"By yourself?" he said. "You're okay with that?"

Kennedy shrugged. "I won't go far."

Isaiah smiled. "You know you're safe here."

He straightened up. "But," he added, "if you feel scared, just text me. I'll come out after you."

Kennedy smiled. "Thanks. I will."

She went out the door. She jogged around the house and toward the towering sandstone hills. Normally she didn't wander into the bluffs when it was getting dark, but the evening air felt so good. Yes, the fan in her room still would've been cooler. But the heat wasn't too bad.

Her gaze wandered to the afterglow in the west. Those gold and orange hues seemed brighter here in the hills than the view from her room. Kennedy crossed her arms. Marilyn and Wesley were probably enjoying this sunset. Why, they could be riding out into the sunset together right now. Kennedy could only wish that Billy was here to enjoy it with her.

The black shadows of the towering rocks caught her eye. Kennedy tried to keep her gaze away; she didn't need to picture Ernesto or Winifred or Horace Cobb creeping out of them.

Kennedy pulled her phone out of her pocket. Should she text Isaiah? She didn't want him to feel that he needed to baby her. But then again, he did truly care for her.

Rustling made her spin around. Kennedy's wide eyes were fixated on a bunch of bushes.

More rustling. Kennedy whirled around again. Her eyes grew wider. Maybe she should text Isaiah. But her quivering hands fumbled with her phone, and she dropped it. She picked it back up just as she heard more rustling. Then something that sounded like a faint footstep.

Kennedy's eyes scoured the ground. She snatched up a long stick and held it as though it were a sword.

"Who's there?" she called.

Silence. Kennedy stepped closer to the bushes. They were still now. She was probably being too jumpy. Maybe whatever she heard was just a small animal, like a jackrabbit or a gopher or a raccoon. Hopefully not a rattlesnake.

A smoky odor permeated the air. Kennedy sniffed and coughed. The odor grew worse with every passing second. She twirled on her heels. And her heart raced up to her throat.

Bright orange flames burned on a sagebrush.

Kennedy held in a gasp. The flames seemed to climb higher and higher. She could feel the heat of both the air and the fire on her face, but she was frozen on the spot. What should she do?

Wait, duh, she had her cell phone clasped in her hand! She swiped the screen and dialed 911.

"Emergency services."

"It's Kennedy. There's a sagebrush on fire near my house! Uh, you know, Isaiah Wilson!"

"Right. The fire truck's already on its way, Kennedy. How serious is the brush fire?"

Kennedy continued talking even as her family came running to her side. She heard her mother and Isaiah yelling at Victoria and Jessica to stay back, then she felt Isaiah pulling her by her arm. Kennedy let him steer her away. Glancing over her shoulder, she saw Mom hugging Victoria and Jessica. She could already hear the sirens in the distance. The fire truck arrived in just a few minutes. The sheriff's car was right behind them. Firefighters scattered. Very soon, the fire was put out. The firefighters splashed buckets of water all over the ground.

"Okay," one of the firemen called, "that's good!"

"What happened?" Isaiah asked. "How did that fire start?"

"That's what we're hoping to find out," the fireman said.

Jonathon followed a few of the firefighters around the area. But the golden glows of their flashlights didn't seem bright enough for them. Kennedy could hardly see anything herself. After fifteen minutes, Jonathon approached Isaiah and Kennedy.

"It's getting too dark to make a thorough search," Jonathon said. "We'll come back tomorrow morning to continue the investigation. So this area will be off-limits to everyone for a while."

"Understandable," Isaiah said. "Thank you, Sheriff."

"Of course," Jonathon said. "The firefighters think you were lucky. With this heat, even in the evening, that fire could've spread. It might even have caught onto your house."

Kennedy's stomach churned.

"It seems that God has protected us tonight," Isaiah said. "Thank you again, Sheriff."

He nodded at Kennedy. "Come on, honey," he said, "let's head back to the house."

Kennedy let her stepfather take her hand.

"By golly, that was something!" Victoria said.

"Yeah, talk about lucky!" Jessica said. "You just wait until all our friends hear about this!"

Beep!

Kennedy stopped. She whipped her head around. Her gaze went up to the bluffs.

"What was that noise?" she said.

"What?" Mom asked. "I didn't hear anything."

"Neither did I," Jessica said. "What did you hear, Kenny?"

"Sounded like a car horn," Kennedy said.

"It might've been the fire truck or Jonathon's car," Victoria said.

"Your sister's probably right." Isaiah squeezed Kennedy's hand. "You should come back to the house and relax, honey."

Kennedy nodded. As she followed her family away, she stole one more glance over her shoulder at the sagebrush.

Chapter Three

Reliving Traumatic Memories

THE SAGEBRUSH STILL appeared to be singed. Kennedy squatted beside the little black branches. She poked one but pulled her finger back; it was hot to the touch.

It's okay. It's got to be hot because of the summer heat.

"Couldn't wait for me, huh?"

Kennedy jumped to her feet. She gave Jonathon a sheepish smile. "Just looking."

Jonathon chuckled. "You've always been the detective," he said as he squatted next to the sagebrush. Kennedy took a step back.

"Morning, Sheriff!"

Kennedy turned around. She saw Isaiah, Deputy Swift, and two firemen walking toward her.

"Did you find anything?" Isaiah asked.

"Just got here," Jonathon said.

Isaiah grinned at Kennedy. "Wonder why you're out early," he said.

Kennedy rolled her eyes, but she still smiled. She and her stepfather followed the sheriff and firemen as they strolled around the area. One of the firemen knelt by the sagebrush.

"I just don't get it," he said. "There's no indication that the weather could've started the fire last night. I know it's crazy hot out, even at night, but that's typical for Arizona this time of year."

"I know what you mean, Russ," Jonathon said. He bent over and dug into the sagebrush. "Hey, what's this?"

Kennedy ran over to Jonathon's side. A little burnt cigarette lay in his palm. Kennedy's eyes widened.

"I found a Smoker Gold cigarette," the sheriff said. He held out his hand to show the cigarette to Russ.

"Yeah, looks like it's been used," Russ said. "But also lying out for hours. Maybe this is what caused the fire?"

"What?" Kennedy gasped. "But you said the fire could've set our house ablaze, and nobody in town would be so careless."

"You'd be surprised," Jonathon said. He chuckled. "Don't you worry, I'm not saying anyone in Pine Lodge is an arsonist. But we do get

40

complaints about people and tourists buying cigarettes and leaving them here in the hills."

Kennedy couldn't smile. Her thoughts were swimming. Or more like drowning in rising waves of anxiety.

"I will look into this," Jonathon said. "Warn people not to be so careless. Guess our investigation is done."

"Thank you, Sheriff," Isaiah said. Kennedy felt him pat her shoulder. "Let's go inside, dear. I'm sure your mom is almost done cooking breakfast."

Kennedy turned to her stepfather. "Isaiah," she said, trying not to let her voice shake too much, "we are okay, aren't we?"

Isaiah gave Kennedy an encouraging smile. "Why wouldn't we be? The cigarette is gone. Oh . . ."

His smile disappeared. Concern replaced the cheer in his eyes. "Ken," he said, "don't be afraid. I'm sure it's nothing. Lots of people in Pine Lodge buy Smoker Gold cigarettes and come to the bluffs for a smoke. This isn't the first time a brush fire's been started because of a negligent smoker."

Kennedy smiled feebly. She did trust her stepfather. But the worries in her mind wouldn't let her be fully convinced.

Kennedy watched Jessica walk onto the stage and hug Mom and Isaiah. She looked so cute in her shining black graduation gown.

"Welp," Victoria whispered, "that marks the last Ryan girl to finish up high school. We're all adults now. Well, sort of. I mean, Jess is still seventeen."

Kennedy shrugged. "At least she'll do well in college," she muttered.

"Say what?"

"Nothing."

Kennedy followed Victoria, Marilyn, Susannah, and Alec out of the auditorium. Parents with eyes filled with tears of pride and joy were hugging graduates. A line was forming at the tables. Kennedy spotted Jessica, Mom, and Isaiah near the front of the line.

"Jessica!" Victoria called.

Jessica turned around and waved. Victoria ran toward her, Kennedy, Marilyn, Susannah, and Alec at her heels.

"Congrats, little sister!" Victoria said.

"Thanks!" Jessica said.

Mom wiped her eyes. "My four girls," she said, "all grown up."

Isaiah wrapped his arm around Mom. "Remember not to fill up on too much cake, ladies," he said. "We're still treating our family to our restaurant."

Just then Rachel, her cousin Sierra, and the Grant twins Cora and Carrie ran over and huddled Jessica into a group hug.

"We're so happy for you, Jess!" Sierra said.

"Thank you!" Jessica said.

Kennedy turned her attention to the table. Her eyes glazed over the cakes for a small piece.

"Hey there, Ken."

She turned around. Rachel was standing right behind her.

"Hi, Rachel," Kennedy said. "Thank you for coming to my sister's graduation ceremony."

"Of course," Rachel said. "It was great."

She lowered her voice. "How are you doing, Ken?"

Kennedy shrugged. "Hanging in there," she said. "Wish you could stick around a little longer, Rachel."

"Me too. But it's about time I head home to my parents. I'll be leaving in a few minutes. Just wanted to say hi to you. And Ken, if you need a friend to talk to, don't hesitate to give me a call."

Kennedy smiled and opened her arms. Rachel embraced her.

"Um, hey."

Kennedy let go of Rachel and looked behind her. Billy was standing there, smiling shyly at her.

"So sorry to butt in like this." Billy nodded at Rachel. "You must be heading out, I guess?"

"Yep," Rachel said. She grinned. "Kennedy's all yours."

"Say what?" Billy said. "How did you know I wanted to talk to her?"

Kennedy felt her heart flit. Rachel turned her broadening grin to her.

"Just my intuition," she said. She elbowed Kennedy's arm. "I'll see you guys soon."

Kennedy watched Rachel leave. Then she turned to Billy. However shy his smile seemed, Kennedy was certain that her own smile was even shier.

"So," Billy said, "um, how does it feel, knowing that your youngest sister just graduated?"

"A little weird," Kennedy said. She tucked a curl behind her ear.

"Yeah, I know the feeling. It's how Felicity and I felt when I graduated high school. Now she's married and pregnant."

Billy looked down at his feet. Kennedy stared at her cake.

"Question for you," Billy said.

"Yeah?" Kennedy looked expectantly at Billy.

"Um, maybe we can go over here, where it's not so noisy."

Kennedy followed Billy to the doorway of the auditorium. He opened his mouth but closed it again.

"Go ahead," Kennedy said.

Billy's timid smile returned. "Well," he said, "you know that in Phoenix there's that big art festival?"

"Oh, yeah. You and the guys mentioned it at the golf course the other day. Lloyd is giving a lecture there, isn't he?"

"Yeah. It's a pretty big event. And I was wondering, well, if you'd like to go with me. To the festival, I mean. We can say hi to Lloyd and listen to his lecture. See all the artwork on display. And the Phoenix Symphony will be performing *Pictures at an Exhibition* at the end of the event."

Kennedy bit her lip. If only she could be playing with the Phoenix Symphony at this event. But it only took seconds for her heart's joyful fluttering to overcome her disappointment. Billy had just invited her to go to this event with him!

"So it'll be just the two of us?" she said. She could feel her cheeks turning red. "In Phoenix?"

"Sure. It'll be kind of a day trip. I mean, you don't have to if you don't want to."

"No!" Kennedy said. "I mean, yes!"

She grinned. "Yes, Billy, I'd love to go with you."

A relieved grin spread across Billy's face. "Hey, awesome!" he said. "The event is not this weekend, but the next. I thought I'd cheer you up."

"Cheer me up?"

Now Billy was blushing. "Uh, what I meant was, you just seemed so down in the dumps lately. Like since we came back from college."

"You're right about that," Kennedy said. She looked at her cake, which she still hadn't touched. "Yeah, I guess I have been a bit stressed lately. I do want to go to the art festival with you, Billy. I reckon I might need something nice like that. I'll talk to Mom and Isaiah later. About the art festival. They'd be happy to let me go with you."

She paused. "Isaiah knows, by the way."

"Knows what?" Billy asked. "Oh. About you . . . I mean, er, what happened in Starwood City?"

Kennedy nodded. "He noticed my stress, too. He insisted I talk to him. I couldn't help it. I confessed."

She smiled. "He was so understanding, Billy. He's been so encouraging to me since I told him. But I haven't told Mom yet."

"You tell who you feel you're ready to tell," Billy said. He patted Kennedy's arm, making her heart flutter once more. He did not remove his arm even as Kennedy lifted her hand to toy with her curly hair.

"Kennedy!"

Kennedy looked over her shoulder. She saw her mother waving to her.

"Looks like my family's ready to go." Kennedy nodded at Billy. "Thank you for the invite. I'll look forward to the festival."

Billy smiled. "Me too."

Kennedy sprinted over to her family. She was somewhat relieved that Billy wouldn't be seeing her blushing face anymore. But boy, if his goal was to make her feel better, then he sure aced it! Now she couldn't stop grinning all the way to the Lonely Pine Eatery. The only thing that wiped the grin off her face was seeing Roman Hughes at the counter when she and her family entered the restaurant. Much to her surprise, he smiled and waved at them.

"Good afternoon!" he said. "Congratulations to Jessica. I'm assuming the graduation ceremony was good?"

"Very good, Roman," Isaiah said. "We're here to celebrate."

"Sounds good." Roman picked up some menus and walked over to the round table at which Kennedy and her family were sitting. "I'll serve you. Drinks?"

Kennedy eyed Roman. He was certainly being friendly all of a sudden. She and Marilyn exchanged confused smiles, then they gave him their drink orders. Roman closed his notepad and went to the kitchen. He returned with a tray full of drinks.

"Any appetizers I can start you with?" he asked. "Soups or salads?"

His eyes twinkled. Kennedy had to hold in a snicker; she may have met Roman only once before, but already just seeing him in such a good mood was interesting.

Or causing uncomfortable flutters in her gut, thus making it easier for her not to snicker. That déjà vu was back.

"I'd like a Caesar salad," Isaiah said.

"A salad does sound good," Marilyn said. "But I don't know which one to choose."

Roman smiled at her. "I would recommend the new Italian spinach and mushroom salad," he said.

"That sounds delicious, but so do these other salads . . ."

"I would insist. That spinach and mushroom salad is very good. If you haven't tried it yet, you should."

"Alright, Roman, you've convinced me. I'll order it."

Roman's smile grew as he scribbled on his notepad. "Does anybody else want to try the spinach and mushroom salad?"

"Nah, I'll have a soup," Victoria said. "Menu here says that your new salad has chickpeas and dijon mustard. Sorry, but those are just not my fave condiments. I'll have a Swedish meatball soup and a ham sandwich."

Roman scribbled orders on his notepad. It didn't take him long to return with the soups and salads. He set them on the table in an almost eager manner.

"Enjoy your meals," he said. He returned to the kitchen. Kennedy stared after him as she sipped her soup.

"Hey," Marilyn said, "I'm not tasting any mushrooms in my salad."

"Well, I am," Isaiah said, "and oh my goodness, these are really good mushrooms. I see why Roman insisted that you try it."

Marilyn chuckled. "He must've gotten our salads mixed up, Dad. But that's fine, this is still good. I'll just eat your salad, and you can eat mine."

Isaiah laughed. Kennedy glanced back at the kitchen. She thought she saw Roman giving them a nervous look. But he rushed behind the doorway before Kennedy could get a closer look at his face.

"Are you okay, honey?"

Kennedy turned to her stepfather. She forced a smile. "I'm good," she said. Then her smile grew. "I've got something I should mention to you and Mom. Billy invited me to an art festival. It's in Phoenix."

"Oh, yes," Isaiah said, "I saw the ad on Facebook. It made me think of you."

He grinned from ear to ear. "And you say that Billy invited you to go with him?"

"Yeah." Kennedy looked down at her plate. "It'll be our day trip. We'll see my teacher, Lloyd Jennings."

"Oh, Kennedy," Mom said, "I'm so happy for you. You and Billy will have a great time."

"Yes, indeed," Isaiah said.

No matter how much she was blushing, Kennedy couldn't take her eyes away from her stepfather's encouraging smile.

"Well," Marilyn said, "it's evening, and we still don't have any plans for dinner."

"Of course not," Victoria said. "I'm still stuffed."

"Yes, I was thinking that big lunch we had would be our big meal for the day," Mom added.

"I understand," Marilyn said. "I won't make anything for dinner if no one's hungry."

Isaiah sighed and plopped down on the couch. "No, no, honey, I'm not hungry," he said. He leaned over the armrest and put his hand on his forehead.

"Dad?" Marilyn said. "Is there something wrong?"

"Oh, I'm just not feeling too well all of a sudden. Maybe I ate too much at lunch, or I might be somewhat overheated."

Kennedy couldn't help but notice her stepfather's pale face. "Maybe I can get you some water?" she said.

Isaiah smiled at her. "That might help," he said. "Thanks."

Kennedy went to the kitchen and filled a glass with ice. Her thoughts wandered back to Roman. It was nice not to have dealt with his bad attitude, but his personality change did seem a little sudden. Maybe it was because he was serving Isaiah, his boss. That made sense.

But Kennedy still couldn't figure out why Roman seemed so familiar to her.

Just as she turned off the faucet, she heard Isaiah running to the bathroom. Then the unpleasant sound of him throwing up. Kennedy cringed as she walked into the living room. She and Jessica exchanged nervous looks.

"Golly," Victoria said, "just what we need right after Jessica graduates. The stomach bug."

"He'll be alright, won't he?" Kennedy said.

"Of course," Jessica said. "If it's just the stomach bug, he'll simply need a day to rest and get better."

"Yeah, I guess, but I just hate seeing our dad get sick. You know, since . . ." Kennedy trailed off.

Now Jessica frowned. "Yeah," she said softly. "I know what you mean, Ken."

A twinge of guilt hit Kennedy. How could she inadvertently remind Jessica of their own father's death right after she graduated high school?

46

After a minute of miserable noise, Mom was helping Isaiah up the stairs to their bedroom. Kennedy followed them, the glass of water in her hand.

"Honey," Isaiah said, "I think I should sleep on the couch tonight. I don't want to keep you up all night."

"Really?" Mom huffed. "You think I'm going to make my sick husband sleep on the couch? Certainly not. You're sleeping in here, dear. I will get a towel and a bucket for you. You know, just in case. And some water and saltine crackers."

"I've got water right here, Mom," Kennedy said. She put the glass on the nightstand. "Mom, Jessica's got that double bed. Maybe if Victoria slept with her, you can sleep in Victoria's room."

Mom smiled. "I'll talk to them," she said. She laid her hand on Isaiah's forehead. Her smile vanished. "Gosh, Isaiah, you must have a fever. You're burning up."

The churn in Kennedy's stomach almost burned her. She stared at her mother with wide eyes. Her anxiety must have shown, because Mom gave her a smile.

"I'm sure he'll be fine, Ken," she said. "Thank you for the water. I'll get your dad a wet washcloth for his forehead. Let's just let him rest, okay?"

Kennedy nodded. She stole one last worried glance at Isaiah as she left the room.

Sunlight streamed through the window. Kennedy blinked and yawned. She probably slept in long enough. Heaven knew she needed it after allowing her anxiety to make her get up twice during the night just to check on her stepfather. Both times she had seen him sleeping soundly with the soothing hum of a fan blowing on his face.

The first thing Kennedy did when she got out of bed was tiptoe to her parents' room and peek inside. Isaiah was lying in bed, staring at his phone. Marilyn was sitting at his feet with a glass of water. Isaiah looked up at Kennedy and smiled.

"Good morning, hon," he said. Kennedy smiled a little. He did sound better.

Marilyn turned around to face Kennedy. "Good morning," she said with a smile.

"Hi, Dad, Marilyn," Kennedy said. She took a step forward. "How are you feeling, Dad?"

"Better," Isaiah said. "Nausea's gone and I haven't thrown up again. I still took the day off work, of course. At least I know that your

47

mother will be taking care of the Lonely Pine today. But I just told Marilyn that I won't eat breakfast. I'm still not too hungry."

"I can make you and your sisters something," Marilyn said to Kennedy. She stood up.

"That'll be fine," Kennedy said. She breathed out a sigh of relief. "I'm glad you're feeling better, Dad."

"I just hope nobody else in the family gets the bug," Isaiah said. He grinned. "Or anyone else in town, for that matter."

"As far as I'm aware, nobody else in Pine Lodge has gotten sick," Marilyn said. "You might be the first case, Dad."

"And hopefully the only case." Isaiah turned his smile to Kennedy. "I hope you don't get sick, Kennedy. Not when you and Billy are planning a day trip to Phoenix."

Kennedy's cheeks warmed a little. She shared her stepdad's feelings. She would sooner face off with another criminal than let a virus hinder her date with Billy!

"Oh, yes," Marilyn said. "I'm so happy for you, Ken. I'm sure you and Billy will have a great time."

Kennedy turned to the hallway. "Come on, Mary," she said, hoping her cheerful voice didn't sound too fake or sappy, "let's go downstairs and cook ourselves some breakfast. And uh, feel better, Dad."

She couldn't keep herself from smiling.

The wooden basement was dark due to lack of windows.

It wasn't a basement. It was Starwood City's undertown.

She was in the room haunted not by a pair of ghosts, but by a gang of counterfeiters. And her kidnappers.

Kennedy sat with her back against the wooden post. The tight ropes scratched against her wrists. The soaked gag in her mouth prevented her from making a sound. She struggled. Her wrists and feet refused to move. Where was that nail?

Sudden footsteps echoed down the hall.

Kennedy gasped. Her eyes flew open. She thought that she could still hear receding footsteps. At least she couldn't feel the scratchy itches of the ropes anymore. But her body still wouldn't move a muscle.

Her eyes flitted to the window. Just seeing that window assured her that she was safe in her own bedroom and not a bound and gagged prisoner in that undertown.

Her arms finally jerked from under her pillow. Kennedy let out a groan. Sure. She may not be tied to a post right now, but that nightmare knew how to leave her with momentary sleep paralysis. As though the nightmare itself wanted to bind her.

Kennedy smacked her dry lips. Maybe some fresh, cool water would help her get back to sleep. But when she opened her door and saw the dark hallway before her, she hesitated.

Stop it, Kennedy, she admonished herself. *It's your home.*

The windows gave her some comfort as she tiptoed down the hallway. But she hesitated again when she came to the stairs. She gazed down the black stairwell. Her mind wanted to think of those stairs as leading to the undertown. Kennedy forced herself to go down the first step. So far, so good. She held her breath and went down the rest of the stairs. She breathed a quiet sigh of relief when she came to the living room. The light of the lampposts outside streamed through the window, letting her relax a bit.

Kennedy went into the kitchen. She flipped on the light, which quickly became another form of relaxation against the darkness, and took a small cup out of the cupboard. She opened the fridge and grabbed the water pitcher. She filled her cup. The cool liquid soothed her dry lips and mouth.

"Who's there?"

Kennedy nearly dropped her cup as she spun around. She relaxed when she saw Isaiah leaning against the doorframe.

"Dad!" she said. "You startled me."

Kennedy smiled a little. She felt that she needed a bit more counseling. Surely Isaiah wouldn't mind giving her a few minutes of comfort, even in the middle of the night. Now that she thought about it, maybe it was his footsteps she heard earlier when she woke up from her bad dream.

"Dad," she said, "I came down here for some water. It's just that I had a nightmare. About being imprisoned in the undertown."

"You did?" Isaiah whispered. He slowly pushed himself straight up, only to stumble toward the counter.

"Dad?" Kennedy said. "Are you alright?"

Isaiah's only response was a shaky breath that he seemed to struggle with. He clutched his stomach with his right arm. "I'm sorry." He looked up into Kennedy's eyes. "I'm in pain. Water?"

Kennedy stared at her stepfather. He couldn't be sick again, could he? He recovered from his illness just the other day. He had even been well enough to go back to work.

Now that he was under the light, Kennedy noticed the sickly yellow color in his eyes outside of his irises where his eyes should've been white. His face was the same yellow color.

"Dad," she said, "you don't look well at all. You said you wanted water?"

Isaiah lifted his left hand to scratch his neck. "Itchy," he murmured. "And so much pain."

He tightened his arm around his stomach. He stumbled again. Kennedy dropped her cup. Luckily, Isaiah had grasped the counter before he could fall over.

"Okay, what's the matter with you?" Kennedy demanded. She put her hands on Isaiah's face but quickly pulled back. "Dad, your cheeks are as hot as a summer afternoon!"

Isaiah lifted his face. "I'll sit down," he said, "and rest. You tell me about your nightmare, my dear."

Kennedy took a step back. His voice was so raspy. What was wrong with him? What was with this sudden delirium?

Isaiah straightened up. He smiled weakly at Kennedy. She smiled back. But she didn't even get a second to process any relief. Isaiah's eyes rolled to the back of his head. He moaned.

And collapsed onto the floor.

"Dad!"

Kennedy fell onto her knees next to her stepfather and shook his shoulder. "Are you okay? Wake up!"

No reply. He just lay there.

"MOM!" Kennedy bellowed. "Mom, come down quick!"

Doors slammed upstairs. Rapid footsteps thundered down the stairs. Mom ran into the kitchen. Victoria, Jessica, and Marilyn were right behind her.

"Isaiah!" Mom shrieked.

"Dad!" Marilyn turned her horrified eyes to Kennedy. "Oh my gosh, what happened, Kennedy?"

"I don't know!" Kennedy said. "I came down here for some water, and he was here too. He seemed so confused. Then he just fainted!"

Mom bent over and pulled Isaiah onto his back. His eyes were still closed. His breathing was low and labored.

"One of you girls call the ambulance!" Mom cried. Victoria dashed out of the kitchen and up the stairs. In moments, Kennedy heard her frantic voice.

"It's Victoria at the Wilson house. My stepdad just fell and he's not getting up!"

Kennedy felt like she had sleep paralysis again. But this was no nightmare. She was wide awake, and standing frozen right where she stood, clutching Marilyn and Jessica, watching her mother slap Isaiah's face in a vain attempt to rouse him. She was only broken from her trance when Jessica pulled away from her and ran to the front door. A small crowd of EMTs barged inside the house. Kennedy and Marilyn stepped back to let them into the kitchen. Two of the EMTs, who Kennedy recognized as Liam and Carlos, kneeled beside the unconscious Isaiah.

"Mr. Wilson?" Liam said loudly. "Can you hear me?"

Isaiah's head didn't even twitch.

"Unresponsive," Liam said. "He looks like he has jaundice."

He ran his hand over Isaiah's head. "He's got a fever."

Carlos took hold of Isaiah's wrist. "I'm not feeling a pulse," he said in an urgent tone.

Helplessness overcame Kennedy as she watched the EMT's haul her stepfather onto a stretcher and carry him out the door, all the while doing chest compressions on him. Familiar bad memories began to fill her head.

Memories of her own father's illness.

Her family was going through that nightmare all over again.

The waiting room was eerily quiet. Of course, it was the middle of the night, but for Kennedy, the silence was just too suspenseful.

She couldn't believe it. She simply couldn't believe it. Her stepfather was ill. She wished she knew exactly what he was ill with, but it was certainly serious enough to bring the ambulance over.

Tears stung her eyes. First her father. Now her stepfather.

But at least Isaiah's still alive, she thought. Not reassuring. Forcing optimism was futile.

She noticed the receptionist giving her a sorrowful look. Kennedy gave her a polite nod. The receptionist had been glancing at Kennedy and her sisters several times since they had entered the waiting room.

She looked over at her sisters. Victoria and Jessica sat next to each other. Victoria was gazing at her phone, but judging by the sad look in her eyes, Kennedy guessed that she wasn't paying that much attention to her Facebook scrolling. Marilyn was standing in front of the window. Even from several feet away, Kennedy could make out Marilyn's teary-eyed reflection in the window. She blinked. She knew exactly how her stepsister was feeling.

Her gaze wandered from Marilyn to the piano just a few feet away from the reception desk. Part of her wanted to sit at that piano and play something. Maybe her song that she wrote in college. But she didn't have her sheet music, it was the middle of the night, and her nerves would never be calm enough for a decent performance.

"Kennedy!"

She turned around in her chair to face the entrance and widened her eyes. Billy was running toward her. She, Victoria, and Jessica rose from their seats. Marilyn turned around and walked over to them.

Billy ran straight up to Kennedy and grabbed her hands. She hoped he didn't feel her pulse pick up its pace.

"I came as soon as I saw it on Facebook," Billy said.

"What?" Kennedy said.

"That would've been me." Victoria held up her phone. "I know it's after midnight, but Mom told me it was okay to post a prayer request on my Facebook page. Pine Lodge is gonna find out about this as soon as the sun comes up anyway."

"And I saw it," Billy said, "and came right away."

"You were up this late?" Kennedy said.

With a sheepish smile, Billy let go of Kennedy's hands and shrugged. "I tend to stay up late sometimes."

His tiny smile vanished. "So what happened?"

"Well," Kennedy said, "I found Isaiah in the kitchen. Or, uh, I was up because I had a nightmare."

Her heart skipped a beat at the concern filling Billy's eyes. "I just had a dream about my . . . about the undertown. I woke up and went downstairs to get some water. I met Isaiah in the kitchen. I wanted to tell him about my nightmare. You know, because he's been so sympathetic to me about it."

"Wait, Dad knows that you had been kidnapped?" Marilyn said in a hushed voice.

Kennedy eyed Marilyn and nodded.

"So does Mom know?" Jessica asked.

Kennedy shook her head. "Anyway, I didn't get the chance to say anything to Dad about my dream. He was so delirious. His face and eyes were yellow. And then he just fainted. Right in front of me. I screamed for Mom. Everyone came running to the kitchen. Victoria called the ambulance. And here we are."

She closed her eyes to fight back the tears, only to open them again when she felt Billy's hand on her shoulder. She grasped a few of her curls as she gazed into his eyes. The periwinkle blue color of his irises seemed to match the sorrow in his eyes. And in her heart.

"Ken," he said, "I am so sorry."

Billy turned his gaze to Victoria, Jessica, and Marilyn. "For all of you."

Marilyn closed her eyes. Tears streamed down her cheeks.

"Girls."

Kennedy turned around. Her mother was walking down the hall toward them. She raised her eyebrow at Billy. Kennedy and her sisters rushed up to their mother.

"Mom!" Kennedy said. "How's Isaiah? What did the doctors say?"

"What's going on?" Jessica asked.

"Hey, calm down, girls." Mom let out a sigh. "So, girls, the doctors said Isaiah went into cardiac arrest."

"Cardiac arrest?" Marilyn exclaimed. "But Dad's never had heart problems! And his family doesn't have any cardiac history!"

Mom brushed her hand across Marilyn's cheek. "Hey, just calm down, sweetheart," she said.

"Can we go see him?"

Mom lowered her eyes. She wouldn't make eye contact with any of the four girls.

"The doctors are busy," she said. "We'll wait and see what they say later. Now, I want the four of you to go home and get some sleep."

Kennedy stared at her mother. Home was the last place she wanted to be at right now.

"But what are you going to do?" Victoria asked.

"I'm staying here for the rest of night," Mom said. "I will let you know what's going on when I come home."

"I can take them home, Mrs. Wilson," Billy said.

Mom nodded. "Thank you, Billy," she said. She gave each of the girls a hug. "It'll be okay, dears. Don't worry. Just pray."

Mom turned to leave. Kennedy couldn't stop herself from grabbing her mother before she could take a few steps forward.

"Mom," she whispered, "do . . . do you think . . . ?"

She couldn't bring herself to finish her question. But her mother seemed to catch her drift.

"I don't know if Isaiah will die," she said quietly. Her eyes became red with tears. She stroked Kennedy's hair. "Just pray."

Kennedy ran her own hand through her hair a few times as she watched her mother disappear back down the hall. She was broken from her trance when Billy tapped her shoulder.

"Come on," he said, "let's get going."

He paused. "Kenny," he said, "look, about these nightmares of Starwood City . . . I mean, have you seen your counselor since you came back to Pine Lodge? Maybe I can give you some money for a session?"

Kennedy turned her eyes to the window. "I'm not worried about what happened to me in Starwood City right now," she said. "My thoughts are on my stepfather now."

"Of course, of course," Billy said quickly. "I'm sorry, I didn't mean to be insensitive."

"Oh no!" Kennedy looked back at Billy. "No, Billy, I didn't mean for you to think that. You made a sweet offer. Thank you. But I'm more worried about Isaiah right now."

"I get it, Ken. I know this isn't the first time you . . ."

Billy trailed off. His cheeks turned pink. "I . . . I'm sorry. Hey, let's get going. Oh, Ken, feel free to call me with any updates."

Kennedy followed her sisters and Billy out the door. She glanced over her shoulder at the waiting room, as though hoping to see her mom and stepdad walking down the hall and announcing that everything would be alright after all.

Kennedy trudged into the hospital room. Somehow, she was fifteen years old again. Not that her age mattered. No, all that mattered was seeing her father lying under the white sheets of the hospital bed, a breathing tube on his nose and mouth and a wet washcloth covering his eyes.

Kennedy stood next to her mother, Victoria, and Jessica. Wait, where was Marilyn?

Who was Marilyn?

Kennedy's tearful eyes flitted back to her father. The nurse turned her sorrowful gaze to the family.

"I am truly sorry," she said. "There was nothing else we could do. The meningitis was simply too much for him. At least you can say goodbye."

The nurse lifted the washcloth. Kennedy's eyes widened.

The man lying there was not her father Miles.

It was Isaiah.

Then Kennedy saw Marilyn walking around the other side of the bed. She closed her eyes as more tears spilled out.

When she opened her eyes, Kennedy saw that she was lying in her own bed, in her own bedroom. Her eyes were no less tearful in reality than they had been in her dream. Her bad dream. The second bad dream she had that night.

Kennedy looked at her alarm clock. It was only three in the morning. She sighed and rubbed the tears from her eyes. If only the entire thing—seeing Isaiah collapse in the kitchen, the ambulance, sitting in the waiting room—had also been a simple nightmare.

Kennedy sat up. All those terrible memories were making her slightly nauseous. She took a deep breath. If only she was at the hospital, near her stepfather's side, with her mother to comfort her, instead of here in her room, feeling helpless. She sat on the floor in front of her fan. The cool air helped make the nausea fade away.

More tears suddenly spilled from her eyes. Kennedy gasped and stood up. The nausea threatened to return. She looked at her bed and tried not to picture it as Isaiah's hospital bed.

Kennedy's eyes wandered to the bookshelf. Her favorite Wild Western novel, *The Galloping Girls of Pine Gulch*, sat on the top shelf. That novel had been the last birthday present Kennedy received from her own father before he succumbed to his illness. With a loud gasp to help her suppress the urge to scream, Kennedy grabbed the book and shoved it on the bottom shelf. Then she sat on her bed and covered her eyes as she wept.

God, she prayed, *I lost one father. Please don't take Isaiah too!*

Chapter Four

The Mushroom Caper

DAYBREAK SEEMED TO take forever. But it wasn't long after the first rays of dawn appeared that Kennedy heard the front door opening downstairs. She jumped out of bed, not feeling tired at all despite how poorly she had slept and rushed out of her room. She met Victoria, Jessica, and Marilyn in the hall. The four girls paused just long enough to exchange nervous looks, then they ran downstairs. Kennedy saw her mother sitting on the couch.

"Mom!" Marilyn said. "How was the night at the hospital? How's Dad?"

Mom looked up. Kennedy squirmed when she noticed the tears in her mother's eyes.

"Girls," Mom said, her voice shaking, "the doctors said your father's liver is not doing well. They referred him to a liver specialist in Prescott."

A wave of dizziness made Kennedy sit down.

"I'm planning on going to Prescott myself," Mom added. "I know you girls will want to come too, so we need to make plans to leave."

"Now?" Victoria said. "Mom, you should get some sleep."

Mom yawned. "That's what the doctors told me," she said. "I'll go to the Lonely Pine this afternoon to make arrangements. Kennedy, you should call your uncle and let him know what's going on."

Kennedy returned to her room and picked up her cell phone. She scrolled through her contact list, looking for her uncle's name, only to hesitate when she came across Billy's name. He did say to call him with updates. Should she call him right now? He might still be sleeping. She wouldn't want to disturb him. But he wouldn't mind, would he?

She tapped Billy's name and held the phone to her ear.

"Kennedy, hi."

Kennedy's breathing shook when she heard Billy's voice. At least he didn't sound grumpy.

"Billy," she said, "I'm sorry to call you this early."

"Don't be sorry, Ken," Billy said. "What's the scoop?"

"Well, Mom said the doctors are referring my stepdad to a liver specialist in Prescott."

"A liver specialist? What's wrong with his liver?"

"I don't know, but apparently, it's not doing great. So Mom is planning to take us to Prescott."

"Golly, it must be hard." Billy paused. "You wouldn't mind joining me for lunch at the Lonely Pine Eatery? We can talk some more."

Kennedy blushed; she was glad she was just on the phone with Billy and not standing in the same room with him.

"Yeah," she said, "Mom's going there anyway. Thanks. See you then."

Kennedy hung up. She slowly scrolled through her contact list, hardly paying attention to the names. Billy's support made her feel shy. A good kind of shy.

Kennedy tugged at the reins, pulling Sunshine to a stop. She wiped beads of sweat from her forehead. Her fingertips brushed against her soaked bangs. Kennedy fanned her face. If only her mouth was soaked too. She reached for the water bottle in the satchel that was attached to the saddle. There wasn't very much water left, and it wasn't as cold as Kennedy would have preferred, but it would have to do. She didn't want to get dehydrated again. The last thing her mother needed was another sick family member.

Kennedy had called her uncle earlier that morning. Even though he had given her the day off, he was more than happy to let Kennedy come to the ranch just to ride Sunshine. Kennedy felt so hypocritical coming to her uncle's ranch for a simple horse ride and not to work, but her uncle insisted that the other ranchers would do just fine without her help.

Of course, the morning heat and whether or not she was working on the ranch were the least of her problems. Would Isaiah be alright? What was wrong with his liver?

Sunshine nickered. Kennedy combed her hand through the mare's mane. "You're thirsty too, aren't you?" she said. "Come on, let's go to our favorite creek."

Sunshine began moving again. She trotted toward the hills. Already Kennedy could hear the refreshing flow of the creek. She steered Sunshine so that her horse followed the path of the creek. When Kennedy and Sunshine arrived at a shady area under some trees, Kennedy dismounted and led the horse to the edge of the creek.

"Drink up," she said.

Sunshine just looked at Kennedy with drooping eyes. It was as though the mare could sense Kennedy's worries and sadness. Kennedy smiled feebly and ran her hand over Sunshine's neck. Her mind wandered back to the time when her family first moved onto this ranch. Riding Sunshine had given Kennedy so much peace. Her smile grew; maybe riding Sunshine was a good idea.

Sunshine lowered her head to slurp the creek's cool water. Kennedy wandered into the shade and sat down. She plucked at a few blades of glass and blinked back the tears.

Sunshine came over to her and nuzzled her snout against her hair. Kennedy smiled up at the mare. "Ready for another ride?"

The mare nickered. Kennedy stood up and climbed onto the saddle. Just as Sunshine took off into a trot, Kennedy felt a faint breeze blow against her curls. She smiled; that breeze felt good on her face.

Sunshine picked up her pace. So did the wind. Kennedy held onto her hat. She wanted this moment to last forever. To simply forget all her troubles and fly swiftly on this wind.

All too soon she arrived at the corral behind the horse stable. Kennedy rode Sunshine through the corral's gate and slid off the mare's back.

"Come on," she said, taking the reins, "you've been riding in the heat long enough."

She led Sunshine over to a trough filled with clear water. Sunshine lowered her nose into it.

"Howdy, honey!"

Kennedy turned around. Uncle Oliver and three of his ranchers were entering the corral. Kennedy smiled a little and waved at them. As soon as her uncle approached her, he wrapped his arms around her.

"Did you enjoy your ride?" he asked.

Kennedy let go of her uncle and nodded. "It was good. Hey, thank you for letting me come just to ride Sunshine."

"Of course," Uncle Oliver said. "I understand that you need the day off work, but not the day off riding your mare. You must do whatever you can to calm your nerves. Nobody minds."

The other ranchers gave Kennedy sympathetic smiles as they surrounded Sunshine.

"I am glad you got to ride your favorite mare today," Uncle Oliver said. "Kennedy, dear, this is awkward, but today's the day that I send Sunshine to Old Dodge Park."

Kennedy's heart thumped a little faster. She had forgotten about Sunshine being loaned out to Pine Lodge's new tourist attraction. "But they haven't started their showdowns yet," she said.

"No," Uncle Oliver said, "but they want to look at all the horses they'll be using."

He patted Kennedy's shoulder. "But Sunshine is still mine," he said. "And yours. She'll be back right here, on this ranch, for you to ride. Why, I'm sure the folks over at Old Dodge Park wouldn't mind letting you ride her over there if you wanted."

Kennedy smiled. Yes, Sunshine was leaving the ranch. But only the ranch, and only for a short time. At least she wasn't losing her favorite horse forever. But Kennedy still felt lonely watching the three ranchers lead Sunshine and other horses out of the corral. Her sisters' horses, Shadow and Snowflake, were staying behind. So why couldn't Sunshine stay?

"Hey, Ken!"

Kennedy turned around. Her smile returned when she saw Billy running out of the stable.

"I thought I heard your voice," Billy said. "I thought you were off today."

"I let her come to ride Sunshine," Uncle Oliver said. "She needed it."

Billy nodded with understanding. "That's cool."

"Yeah," Kennedy said, "Sunshine had certainly brought me a lot of joy when I first moved here." She held in a sigh. "But I won't be riding her on the ranch for a while now."

"Yes, she's going to Old Dodge Park today," Uncle Oliver said. "And I should catch up with the guys. See you kids later."

Kennedy watched her uncle walk out of the corral. Part of her wished that he would just bring Sunshine back around.

"I'll bet you'd love to see that mare perform in Old Dodge Park," Billy said. "You know, maybe you can even ride her during a performance."

Kennedy chuckled. "I would enjoy that."

"How's your family?" Billy asked.

Kennedy shrugged. "We're okay."

She forced herself to look at Billy in the eyes. "You know I said we're going to Prescott soon, right?"

Billy nodded.

Kennedy sighed deeply. "So . . . I don't . . . I don't think I'll be able to go to that art festival in Phoenix."

Billy lowered his eyes. "Yeah," he said, "I get it."

Kennedy winced at the disappointment in his voice.

"But that's okay."

She looked back up at Billy. He was smiling at her. "You need to be with your family," he said. He touched Kennedy's arm. Her heart fluttered. "And I'll be by your side too."

"You mean it?" Kennedy said.

"Of course I do. I'm your friend." Billy smiled shyly. "Are we still a go for the Lonely Pine today?"

"Yes, we sure are," Kennedy said. "Oh, I told Mom about it. Us going to the Lonely Pine. I hope you don't mind, but my family will be there too. And so will my cousin, Uncle Oliver, and Aunt Thelma."

"Aaron already told me," Billy said. "I get that your mom and uncle will want to talk. Wesley, Aaron, and I will be there."

Kennedy pulled her phone out of her pocket and looked at the time. It was a good excuse to get her eyes away from Billy's. And to lower her blushing face.

"We should probably leave in an hour?" she said.

"Sounds about right. I'm almost done with my chores, Ken. Then I'll wash up a little."

Kennedy paused. "Do you need any help?"

Billy shook his head. "You came here to relax, Ken. I'm just fine. But I guess I won't stop you if you really want to help me."

Kennedy figured that just five minutes of helping Billy with his chores wouldn't hurt. It might even help take her mind off her stepfather and her mare. She went to the stable to get a shovel, making a mental note not to let herself faint of dehydration in front of Billy again.

As soon as Kennedy and her family entered the Lonely Pine Eatery, Susannah rushed out from the behind to the counter and greeted them.

"Hello!" she said. "Anything new, Mrs. Wilson?"

"Nothing about my husband, Susannah," Mom said. "I do need to speak to the rest of the staff. Oliver and Thelma will be here soon too."

"And Susannah?" Marilyn said. "Thank you for covering my shift today."

"Anytime!" Susannah said. She gave Marilyn a hug. "I'm so sorry about your dad. I hope he gets better."

Marilyn sniffled. "Me too."

Kennedy lowered her eyes. She ignored the sorrowful looks of the other customers. She didn't feel like talking to anybody, even as her sisters and Marilyn accepted condolences from people.

Her gaze fell upon a picture of a cowboy riding a horse at night. She held in a sigh. That picture brought back the memory of her first meeting with Maurice Carr. It was a time when Kennedy was still upset about having moved to Pine Lodge. Maurice was one of the first people who made her feel welcome. He was a man who had reminded Kennedy of her own father. Maurice had become a father figure to her. And she lost that father figure when he had betrayed her.

She just hoped that she wouldn't lose her stepfather too.

The bells on the door jingled. Kennedy saw her aunt, uncle, cousin, Billy, and Wesley enter the restaurant. Billy walked straight up to her. He stood in front of her, his eyes flitting all over the place. Kennedy found it hard to meet his eyes too. It was easier to watch her uncle embrace her mother.

"Hi, Ken," Billy said. "You gonna be okay?"

Kennedy shrugged. "Only if Dad will be okay."

Aaron patted Kennedy's arm. "Come on," he said, "let's find a table. Lunch is on me and the guys."

Kennedy and her sisters followed the three boys to a couple of tables. Kennedy wasn't hungry, but she didn't want to refuse her cousin's offer. She hoped that Susannah would wait on them. But it was Roman Hughes who came out of the kitchen and approached their table. At least it seemed that his polite side would be active today; he gave the four girls a sorrowful look.

"Heard about your dad, ladies," he said. "Mighty sorry to hear that. He's a good boss."

Kennedy gazed at Roman. Why did he look so familiar? Out of the corner of her eye, she noticed that Billy was also staring at Roman with a confused look.

As soon as Roman took the kids' drink orders and returned to the kitchen, Mom headed to the counter. From the corner of her eye, Kennedy caught sight of her mother's puffy red eyes. She stared after her mother as she, too, disappeared into the kitchen. Just watching her mother's sorrow brought back the guilt of keeping her kidnapping experience from her. Kennedy knew that eventually she would have to confess that to her mother. But how could she without Isaiah by her side?

Susannah came out of the kitchen and went to their table. Kennedy smiled up at her.

"Hey, Susie," she said. "You taking our orders?"

"Sorry, no," Susannah said. "I just wanted to say hi."

She bent over to hug Kennedy. "I'm so sorry for you. You and your sisters are going through this all over again."

Kennedy nodded solemnly.

"*Ahem.*"

Susannah straightened back up and stared wide-eyed into Roman's cold gaze.

"I was waiting on these customers," he said.

"Dude, she wasn't trying to take over waiting on our table," Wesley said. "She's a good friend of ours. Let her say hi."

Roman nodded. His gaze softened. "My misunderstanding, Susannah," he said.

Susannah's only response was a nod of her own. She rushed back to the kitchen. Kennedy scowled at Roman. Just what was his deal?

Roman held up his notepad. "Have you kids decided what you would like?" he asked.

"I'm really not that hungry," Marilyn said.

"Understandable. Perhaps I can interest you in something small? Like a salad?"

"Well, now that you mention it, I never did get to try that spinach and mushroom salad you recommended the other day. I think I'll take that."

Roman smiled as he scribbled on his notepad. "Anyone else want to try that salad?"

"No, I just want some soup," Kennedy said.

Roman's smile waned. He took everyone else's orders and left the table.

"You know, guys," Aaron whispered, "I kinda wish it was Susannah who waited on us instead of that guy."

"I know, right?" Victoria said. "Maybe when Dad gets better and comes home, he can give that dude the pink slip."

"If he gets better," Kennedy muttered. She sighed when she noticed Victoria's eyes droop. They all remained silent until Roman came back with a tray of soups and salads.

"If you kids want anything else," he said, "just let me know."

"Thanks," Wesley said.

Roman went into the kitchen just as Mom and Susannah came out. They approached the kids' table.

"Susannah and I made a few arrangements," Mom said. "I still have to talk to a few of the staff members."

"When will we go to Prescott, Mom?" Jessica asked.

"Hopefully tomorrow," Mom said. She walked around the table to stand behind Jessica's chair. "The hospital called me and said they're already transferring Isaiah to Prescott. We'll still need to get a hotel—"

"*Marilyn, don't eat that!*" Victoria squealed.

Kennedy jumped out of her seat. Gasps erupted as Victoria whacked Marilyn's salad bowl off the table. Marilyn leapt to her feet and gaped at her spilled salad. Victoria stood up too, glaring at the salad. Kennedy and Susannah exchanged shocked looks.

"Victoria!" Mom said. "What's gotten into you?"

"Those mushrooms!" Victoria pointed a shaky finger at the floor. "I recognize those mushrooms! Those are death caps! Only the most poisonous mushroom in the world!"

Kennedy felt Marilyn grasp her elbow, as though she were seeking protection from her. A horrified silence fell over the dining room, almost instantly replaced by chairs scraping against the floor and nervous chatter as several customers started spitting out their own food onto their plates and getting up from their tables.

"Alright, alright!" Mom shouted, waving her hands. "Please calm down, folks. We'll take care of this matter right away. I need a cleaning crew over here!"

Susannah dashed to the kitchen. In moments she and a few other employees rushed out to the dining area with a cleaning cart. Susannah collected the mushroom bits and put them in a small plastic bag. Mom ran into the kitchen. When she came back out, she announced that the restaurant was being closed indefinitely for a health inspection.

Kennedy ran up to her mother. "Mom, what is going on?"

"I wish I knew, dear," Mom said. "Look, why don't you and your sisters go home for lunch? Your friends may go with you. I've got to collect names of people who may have eaten anything with mushrooms recently. I'll be home shortly."

Kennedy, her sisters, family, and friends left the restaurant, as did many of the other guests. She didn't say a word the entire drive home. She and her sisters met the rest of their party at their house. Kennedy held the door open as everyone went inside.

"Well, that was something!" Aaron said.

"Yeah, man," Wesley said. "I hope you're not going to order us anything with mushrooms, Mary."

Marilyn chuckled feebly. "After what just happened at the Lonely Pine? Wouldn't dream of it."

"But how did poisonous mushrooms get into the Lonely Pine?" Aunt Thelma asked. "They don't grow in Arizona, do they?"

"No, mostly on the east coast," Victoria said. "Though, they can also grow in California."

"Who cares where the heck they grow?" Wesley said. "It's a dang good thing you recognized them, Vic!"

"Yes, indeed." Marilyn grasped her neck.

Kennedy stared at her stepsister. Her eyes grew wide as she remembered. The day of Jessica's high school graduation, Marilyn had ordered the Italian spinach and mushroom salad. Isaiah had ordered a Caesar salad. But they had gotten their salads mixed up.

So Isaiah had eaten the salad with the mushrooms.

"Vic, Jess," she said, "what happens when a person eats a death cap?"

"Well, the first symptoms are a lot like the stomach bug," Jessica said. "The victim then feels better, but by then, the liver is being damaged, and then . . ."

She trailed off. Her eyes grew large.

"Didn't Dad have those exact symptoms just a few days ago?" Victoria said. "On the day you graduated high school?"

"But he felt better," Marilyn said.

"Which should've been a red flag!" Victoria said, pounding her fist on the table. "A person eats the death cap, gets symptoms that seem like it's just a stomach bug or flu or whatever, feels better later, but the toxins are still doing their damage!"

"To the liver!" Jessica said. "And the doctors said that Dad's liver was in bad shape!"

"But when did Isaiah eat death caps?" Uncle Oliver asked.

"Right after Jessica graduated, we went to the Lonely Pine for lunch," Kennedy said. "Dad and Marilyn each ordered a salad. Marilyn got some sort of mushroom salad. They ate each other's by mistake. Isaiah ate the mushroom salad."

"But how did death caps get into the restaurant in the first place?" Marilyn demanded.

"I'm not sure," Kennedy said darkly, "but what if they were meant for you?"

Marilyn went pale. "But . . . who'd want to poison me?"

"Yeah, why would anyone want to hurt your family?" Billy asked. "What makes you think that at all?"

"Hey!" Wesley said. "Remember when Alec told us at church that Grand Canyon University had been broken into? I looked it up when I got home that day. Mushrooms had been stolen from the university's science building!"

Kennedy felt her stomach flip. Could the theft at GCU and the poisonous mushrooms found in the restaurant be a simple coincidence? No, her hunch told her that was wishful thinking.

She remembered something else.

"Just nights ago, there was a brush fire near our house. And then before that, there was a random bear trap on Uncle Oliver's ranch!"

"Yeah, that's right." Aaron exchanged nervous looks with his parents.

Kennedy's heart accelerated. "We know the fire was caused by a cigarette, right?" she said. "And we don't know anyone in Pine Lodge who would be so careless like that unless . . ."

"The person was not simply being careless," Jessica said, "but left that cigarette on the ground on purpose?"

A queasy feeling washed through Kennedy's head. She had to sit down. Who in Pine Lodge would want to hurt them?

The front door opened. All eyes looked to the living room. Mom and Susannah came into the kitchen.

"Hello, everybody," Mom said. She frowned when she saw the bare table. "Haven't you had any lunch yet?"

"No," Kennedy said. She took a deep breath. "Um, what's the story on the Lonely Pine?"

"The place will be closed for a while," Susannah said. "Your mom let me come here to eat, but I guess we'll be waiting."

"We're sorry, Mrs. Wilson," Billy said, "but, well, we got to talking, and we came to some unsettling conclusions."

Kennedy almost wished Billy hadn't said anything, but she knew her mother might've figured out the details too. So she told her mother about all their suspicions, from the bear trap on Uncle Oliver's ranch, to the brush fire, the salads and how Marilyn and Isaiah had gotten them mixed up, and the robbery at Grand Canyon University.

Mom's face went pale. "Kennedy," she said, "do you honestly think someone is out to harm our family? But why would anyone in Pine Lodge do something like that?"

"Nobody in town," Billy said darkly, "but we all know that Kennedy has stopped many criminals in the past."

All eyes turned to Billy. Kennedy couldn't deny that he was right.

Mom sighed. "That makes sense," she said. "I have always known solving those mysteries was too dangerous."

"No kidding, Mrs. Wilson!" Wesley said. "I still remember when poor Kennedy had been kidnapped by those counterfeiters in Starwood City—"

Kennedy gasped. She quickly gestured her hand across her throat. "Ixnay, Wesley!" she hissed.

It was too late. Mom stared at Kennedy with wide eyes full of shocked horror. "I'm sorry, what?" she said stiffly.

Kennedy facepalmed her forehead. Wesley gaped at her. "You didn't tell your mom that you had been kidnapped and held hostage in Starwood City's undertown?" he said. He tapped his finger on his chin. "Okay, that does make sense."

"This is news to me too," Uncle Oliver said. He gave Aaron a stern look.

An awkward silence fell. Kennedy hid her face in her hands and moaned.

"Kennedy Miriam Ryan!" Mom said abruptly. "Why didn't you tell me about this?" Her eyes glazed over everyone else. "Why didn't anyone tell me? My own daughter being kidnapped!"

"Because I did not want you to panic," Kennedy said. "Look, I obviously got out of that alive, right? I'm here, safe and sound."

"But for how much longer?" Mom demanded. "If what you and your friends are saying is true, Kennedy, then you are in grave danger. I'm calling Jonathon."

Mom marched out of the kitchen. Everyone else exchanged awkward glances. Wesley gave Kennedy an apologetic look. She just waved her hand at him.

"She probably would've found out eventually," she said. "I mean, Isaiah did."

"Your stepdad knew but not your mom?" Wesley said.

"Hey, it was our secret," Aaron said. "I didn't even tell my parents."

"Yes, I can confirm this," Aunt Thelma said.

"Guess I didn't get the memo," Wesley said.

Guilt flooded Kennedy's mind once again. She knew what she had to do. She rushed out of the kitchen and found her mom sitting in the living room, dialing on her cell phone.

"Mom?"

Mom looked up. "I have to call the sheriff, Kennedy," she said.

"I know that." Kennedy sat next to her mother. "But at least let me apologize to you first."

Mom's expression softened. She put her phone down and wrapped an arm around Kennedy. "I don't suppose Isaiah knew?"

Kennedy hung her head. "He found out recently," she said. "Shortly after I came home from college. He noticed how stressed I was. He insisted I talk to him. I tried to get out of it. And it just, uh, slipped."

She turned tearful eyes to her mother. "I am sorry, Mom. I didn't really want to keep secrets from you, but I was . . . I was just so traumatized from being kidnapped. I couldn't talk about it. I had a hard enough time talking to my counselors."

Mom tightened her grip around Kennedy. "Do you think you can talk about it now?"

Kennedy sighed. "I was out roaming the campgrounds one night, thinking about my mystery regarding those counterfeiters. Two of them, Ernesto and Winifred, ambushed me. They put me to sleep. When I woke up, I was tied to a post in the undertown. Tied and gagged."

Mom inhaled sharply and squeezed Kennedy. "Oh, honey!"

"But I prayed," Kennedy added. "Silently, due to my gag. It still worked. I discovered a nail in the post. It was a useful little tool to get me untied."

Mom smiled. "Thank God for that nail," she said. "Thank God for constantly protecting you."

She cradled Kennedy's hand in her own. "And just as God showed you that nail," she said, "now we need to trust Him to show us what to do next. It will be okay, sweetheart."

Kennedy smiled weakly. She hoped her mother was right.

Chapter Five

The Mugshot

KENNEDY WATCHED JONATHON scribble on his notepad. Everyone had gathered in the living room as soon as he walked through the front door. Kennedy stole a glance at her mother, who smiled warmly at her.

"So," the sheriff said, "you think someone was trying to poison Marilyn at the Lonely Pine Eatery the other day?"

Kennedy nodded. She gulped. She didn't want any tears in her eyes now. Not in front of everyone.

The doorbell rang. Mom opened the door, revealing Pastor Cameron Shea.

"Hi, Dad," Jonathon said. "I was wondering when you were coming."

Pastor Cameron smiled at his son. His tone of voice was still solemn. "Of course I'd come. How could I ignore a phone call like the one I got from Caitlin?"

His sympathetic eyes rested on Mom. "I know this isn't the first time you've had a sick husband."

Mom's eyes welled up with tears. "No," she whispered.

Kennedy inhaled. This wasn't the first time in her life that a pastor had visited her family to pray for an ailing father, either.

Mom motioned to a chair. "Have a seat, Cameron."

The pastor sat down and opened his Bible. "I wish I had a chance to visit your husband in the hospital," he said. His eyes wandered from Mom to Kennedy, then to Victoria, Jessica, and Marilyn. "It must be difficult for you. All of you."

You can say that again, Kennedy thought. She lowered her watering eyes.

"Let me say a quick prayer," the pastor said, "then I'll let my son continue asking his questions."

Kennedy squeezed her eyes shut. She barely listened to the pastor praying. Her worries were too distracting. When the pastor finished praying, Kennedy looked back up at Jonathon.

"Okay," Jonathon said, "so, Kennedy, do you know of any potential suspects?"

Kennedy eyed Pastor Cameron. He raised his eyebrows in confusion.

"Possibly any of the criminals she's brought down to their knees," Wesley said.

Now Jonathon raised an eyebrow. "I haven't seen any of those criminals since we busted them," he said. "They'd have to be stealthy to sneak into Pine Lodge. Any of you kids might have even recognized them. And where would they have gotten a death cap?"

"Wait, what exactly is going on?" Pastor Cameron asked.

Kennedy watched Wesley lead the pastor into the kitchen.

"We think the death caps came from GCU," Billy said. "You know, Grand Canyon University."

"Oh, yes," Jonathon said, "that makes sense. Their science building had been broken into recently."

Kennedy felt her stomach twist. It was bad enough that her own university had been broken into. Now it seemed that some of her old enemies were the perpetrators.

"And who served your family?" Jonathon asked.

Kennedy paused. "Roman Hughes," she said. "The Lonely Pine's new waiter."

"And new in town," Marilyn added. "I always got the feeling he didn't like me."

"But enough to try to poison you?" Aaron said. "Why would he try poison someone he only knew for a few days?"

A new thought flashed through Kennedy's mind. She leapt to her feet. "Unless it wasn't only a few days! Marilyn, did Roman Hughes ever seem familiar to you?"

Marilyn stared at Kennedy. "Actually, yes," she said. "But I couldn't figure out why."

"He was familiar to me too!"

"Ditto!" Billy said.

Jonathon's frown became even more serious. "Is there any chance we can question this Roman Hughes?" he asked.

"I doubt it," Mom said flatly. "Roman left his shift early today. Right before Victoria discovered the death caps in Marilyn's salad. I never liked working with him. Constantly taking smoke breaks and neglecting his work. He probably sucked up more of those Smoker Gold cigarettes than he washed cups—"

"Mom!" Kennedy said. "Did you say Smoker Gold?"

Mom stared at her. "Yes," she said. "Why?"

"It was a Smoker Gold cigarette that had been found the morning after that brush fire!"

"You mean the brush fire close to our house right here?" Victoria said.

"And my husband is the only one in town experiencing any food poisoning at all," Mom added. "If Roman is the man who put the death caps in our salads, he did so very carefully. As if he wanted to poison our family and nobody else."

"Okay," Jonathon said, "all these events that we're talking about, they can't just be mere coincidences. We have at least three people in this room who thought Roman looked familiar. Why else would he look familiar unless he was one of your past enemies?"

He closed his notepad. "Guess I'm going to need everyone to come to the station with me. We still have mugshots of your old enemies. Maybe you kids can look through them and see if any of them look like Roman."

"Can you try to catch him, Sheriff?" Mom asked. "He left the restaurant early today, and I tried calling him, but he didn't answer."

"Then he may have already fled Pine Lodge," Jonathon said.

Kennedy groaned. She hated the thought of one of her old nemeses running loose in her hometown.

Jonathon and Robert each laid a pile of papers on the table. "Be careful with these," Jonathon said to the kids.

Kennedy was the first to reach for the papers. And just her luck, the first one she had to grab was a mugshot of Horace Cobb. Just staring into those cold eyes made her cringe. The fact that it was just a photograph and not reality was hardly comforting.

"By golly, Cobb's uglier than I remember."

Kennedy eyed Billy. She had to smile a little at his snarky remark. She watched everyone else sort through the papers.

"Hey, look who I've got," Wesley said. "Ol' Maurice Carr."

He laid the paper on the table. "He obviously can't be Mr. Hughes. Even with a disguise, the dude would've been recognized by everyone all at once."

Kennedy gazed longingly at Maurice's familiar face on the mugshot. She remembered the bond they had shared. His fatherly attitude toward her. And how he just threw it all away. And then felt guilty. Guilty enough to actually save Kennedy from a gunshot from Horace. Even in his mugshot, his face and eyes held guilt and sadness instead of the typical resentment of an arrested criminal. Kennedy remembered that she had forgiven him enough to send him a Christmas letter.

Mom's cell phone ringing distracted her from Maurice's mugshot. She watched her mother leave the room with her phone, then she turned her focus back to the pile of mugshots. She grabbed several papers held together with a paper clip. She recognized these people as the cattle rustlers who had once invaded her uncle's ranch. Octavia, Abner, his half-brother Grey, Maverick, Earl.

Kennedy's eyes widened at Earl's face.

"Jonathon," she said, "do you have another copy of Earl's picture here?"

She held up the photograph for Jonathon to see.

"Yeah, I do," Jonathon said. He squinted at Kennedy. "Do you think he's our man?"

"Maybe, but I wanna test something first. That's why I need a spare copy. Oh, and a black marker."

Robert fetched a black marker and a spare mugshot of Earl and laid it in front of Kennedy. She took the cap off the marker but hesitated.

"You don't mind if I write on this?" she asked Robert.

"Nah, not at all," the deputy said.

Kennedy drew a thin beard and glasses on Earl's face. Then she colored his hair black and added to its length.

It gave her the result she wanted.

Jonathon snatched the paper. "Kennedy, you're a genius!" he said.

He held up the mugshot for everyone else to see. Gasps of recognition erupted from the table.

"Yep, that's Mr. Roman Hughes alright," Wesley said. "Or should we say Earl?"

"So our suspicions were correct!" Billy said.

The freckles on Marilyn's paling face made her look like she had a disease. "And to think that he was my coworker," she whimpered.

Kennedy inhaled sharply. Her thoughts began screaming thanks to the Lord for keeping her stepsister safe.

"Okay, so now we know that Roman Hughes is actually one of the cattle rustlers," Jonathon said. "It makes you wonder if any of those other rustlers are nearby as well."

"Yeah, they might be," Aaron said darkly.

"But my ranch hasn't had any problems with disappearing cattle," Uncle Oliver said.

"They might be too focused on revenge." Kennedy couldn't keep her voice from shaking. "Against us."

She turned concerned eyes to her mother just as she came back into the room. Mom was smiling, showing that she hadn't heard anything. Kennedy almost envied her mother's ignorance.

"Kennedy, guess what?" Mom said. "I got a call from your friend Rachel Hamilton's mother. Rachel had seen your sister's Facebook posts and all her updates. Her mother asked our family to stay with them instead of in a hotel. She insisted that their house is big enough for all of us. Isn't that sweet?"

Kennedy could barely smile. Yes, it was sweet of Rachel to jump right in to help her family in their time of need. But would Rachel's family be safe?

Jonathon took hold of Mom's arm. "Mrs. Wilson," he said, "we came upon an interesting conclusion while you were on the phone. It turns out that Roman Hughes was actually Earl, one of the cattle rustlers who had been on your brother's ranch a few years ago. He was in some sort of a disguise."

Mom's smile was swept away as her face turned pale.

"What are we gonna do now?" Victoria asked.

"Well," Jonathon said firmly, "this settles the matter in my mind. Earl must've slipped out of town after he tried to give Marilyn the salad with the death caps. After two failed attempts, I can't imagine he'd stick around. I might have to ask for information from GCU about their recent break-in. They could have footage I can try to look at."

He looked at Kennedy. "You and your family are going to Prescott, right? I'll plan on sending Robert with you. I want to make sure you and your family have plenty of protection."

"But what about Rachel's mom?" Kennedy asked.

Jonathon nodded at Mom. "I don't want to pose any safety risks to Rachel's family," he said, "but you might as well take up their offer. They live close to the country, right? It might be better to stay out of a hotel and therefore the public eye as much as you can. But that doesn't mean that you can't see your husband in the hospital. And like I said, Roman Hughes, um, Earl, has fled town."

"And you want me to go with them?" Robert asked.

Jonathon nodded. He then pulled Mom, Uncle Oliver, and Robert aside. Aaron went with them.

"I wish I can go with you, Caitlin," Uncle Oliver said, "but if those cattle rustlers are back, then I might need to keep an eye on the ranch."

"And there might not be enough room in the Hamiltons' house anyway," Mom said.

"But I will go," Aaron said. "I will keep an eye on my aunt and cousins, Dad."

Kennedy stared at her cousin. His dad smiled at him.

"Maybe you should," he said.

"I wouldn't mind," Mom said. "I want Kennedy to have extra protection. Jonathon, did you know that when she and all the others went to Starwood City for the rodeo last summer, she had been kidnapped by those counterfeiters she solved a case against?"

With a soft groan, Kennedy slapped her hand over her forehead. Did her mother have to tell everyone?

"No!" Jonathon sounded surprised. "I wasn't aware of that!"

"Only those of us who went to Starwood City with her knew about that," Aaron said. He sighed heavily. "Look, Dad, the reason I didn't tell you and Mom about my cousin's kidnapping was because I wanted to respect her. I figured it was her place to confess when she was ready. And Aunt Caitlin, I'm certain that Marilyn, Victoria, and Jessica were quiet for the same reason."

Mom nodded. She turned her understanding eyes to Kennedy and smiled. Kennedy looked down at her knees. But she could still feel everyone else's eyes on her.

"And that is why I am going with you too," Billy said.

Kennedy gaped at him. "What?"

"Sure. Why not? I'm your friend. I'm going to stick right by your side."

"And me," Wesley said. "You know what? Me, Aaron, and Billy can stay in Gunnar Smith's apartment in Prescott. We might need to watch over our old friend anyway, because if those cattle rustlers are back for revenge, Gunnar might need to watch his back like the rest of us. He was involved in the cattle rustler case too, you know."

"Yeah, you're right, Wes." Kennedy stood up. "You'd better call Gunnar and tell him everything."

She turned to her mother and the sheriff. "And yes, I will be glad to have Deputy Swift come with us."

"Then it's settled," Jonathon said. "And don't worry, Ken. I think that after all those failed attempts on your family, it's possible that Earl and the other criminals may have simply fled Pine Lodge. You should be safe with your friends in Prescott. But we'll take extra precautions all the same."

Chapter Six

Hospital Drama and a Daring Escape

MOM PARKED THE car in front of the Hamiltons'. Kennedy got out of the car. She had never been to Rachel's house before. It was a nice two-story house with light green siding, light brown trim, and a porch to match that trim. Ground level windows indicated a basement. Kennedy looked behind the house. She saw horses grazing on the grass within wired fences. Just beyond those fences were nothing but rolling green hills.

If only her first time here was for a pleasant visit instead of the current drama.

The front door opened. Logan Hamilton stepped out of the house. He approached Mom and shook her hands.

"I'm glad you got here safe and sound," he said. "I trust the drive up here was good?"

"Uneventful," Mom said. "Another car will be coming here shortly. Alec McFarlane and Deputy Robert Swift."

"Good," Pastor Logan said. "Our trailer is ready for them. Come on inside."

Kennedy and her family followed the pastor into his house. She was glad to see curtains covering the windows in the living room, the dining room, and the kitchen.

Kennedy heard running footsteps coming from the stairwell. She saw Rachel rush into the living room. Her mother was not far behind her. Rachel and Kennedy wrapped each other in a tight embrace.

"I heard everything from Dad," Rachel said. She let go of Kennedy. "I know it's not the best of circumstances, but it sure is nice to have you here."

Kennedy smiled. "Glad we could come," she said. "We're all very grateful to your family."

"And your cousin Sierra says hi," Jessica added.

"Sweet," Rachel said. "She and her parents are doing okay in town, I hope?"

"They're just fine."

Mom shook Mrs. Hamilton's hand. "Thank you for letting us stay here," she said. "I really do hope that it'll be safe for you and your family."

"We will make it work," Mrs. Hamilton said.

"Speaking of safe," Victoria said, "Alec, Susannah, and Deputy Swift just got here."

Kennedy peeked out the window. Sure enough, she saw a suburban pulling up next to her mother's car. Deputy Swift got out of the driver's side. Alec and Susannah got out of the back. Pastor Logan went outside. He shook Alec and the deputy's hands, then he helped the three of them bring their suitcases into the house.

"Are you sure that you and Alec will be okay in the trailer?" Pastor Logan asked Robert.

The deputy nodded. "We're armed," he said. "And we will take turns with night watches. As long as we're careful and keep an eye on our surroundings, we should be okay. Now everyone go get settled in. I want us to have a brief meeting in ten minutes."

"We prepared the rooms in our basement," Mrs. Hamilton said. She took Kennedy and her family downstairs to a cozy den. A sofa with a pull-out bed stood next to a fireplace. A second sofa, a dark brown easy chair, and a dark green beanbag also surrounded the fireplace.

"You will have the sofa bed, Caitlin," Mrs. Hamilton said. "I hope it'll be okay for you?"

"Yes, it'll do nicely. Thank you."

Mrs. Hamilton led Kennedy, Victoria, Jessica, and Marilyn down a hall, where there were two bedrooms and one bathroom.

"Two girls can have each room," Mrs. Hamilton said. "And Rachel is setting up a bed in her room upstairs for Susannah. I'll see you upstairs."

Kennedy and Victoria went into their room and began unpacking. Kennedy looked up at the window. She felt safer just seeing the dark crimson curtain covering it. Hopefully the security at the hospital where her stepfather was currently at was strong.

Kennedy's phone vibrated in her pocket. She pulled it out and looked at the screen. Billy was calling.

"Excuse me a second," she said to Victoria. She swiped her screen and went into the bathroom so she could talk privately.

"Billy," she said. "How's it going?"

"So far, so good," Billy said. "Are you doing alright? Did you and the others get to Rachel's house okay?"

"Yes, we're all here and getting settled in." Kennedy paused. "Billy, do you think you, Aaron, and Wesley will be safe at Gunnar's apartment?"

"Now don't you worry about us, Kenny. Gunnar's got our backs, and we've got his. He even said that the apartment security is great. We still might take turns keeping watch at night. I'm just glad that Robert's gonna be close to you."

"Me too. But Billy, really . . . you didn't have to come."

"Kenny. I wanted to come. I am going to support you."

Kennedy smiled timidly.

"Kennedy?"

Kennedy poked her head out of the bathroom. Rachel was coming down the little hall. Kennedy excused herself from Billy and put her cell phone against her chest.

"Oh, sorry to interrupt your phone call," Rachel said, "but Robert's ready for us upstairs. And Marilyn's uncle and cousin just arrived."

"Okay." Kennedy held her cell phone back up to her ear. "Hey, Billy, I gotta go. We're gonna go over some stuff with Robert, I guess."

"I get it," Billy said. "Be seeing you, Ken. And stay safe."

Kennedy hung up. Part of her feared for Billy. She almost wished he didn't come. She couldn't bear the thought of him getting hurt. But another part of her was glad to have his support.

And just to simply have him by her side.

Kennedy, her family, and Rachel went upstairs. Marilyn ran up to a man whom Kennedy recognized as Edward Wilson, Marilyn's uncle and step uncle of Kennedy, Victoria, and Jessica. Standing next to Uncle Edward was his daughter Darcy. Marilyn, Darcy, and Uncle Edward wrapped each other in a group hug.

Kennedy, Victoria, and Jessica sat on a couch with their mother. Rachel, Susannah, Marilyn, and Darcy sat on the floor. Robert plopped himself onto an easy chair. Pastor Logan, his wife, Uncle Edward, and Alec sat on four chairs that they pulled from the dining room.

"Alrighty," Robert said, pulling out his notebook, "first things first—"

"Pardon me for interrupting," Pastor Logan said, holding up his hand, "but I think it would be appropriate if we prayed first."

The deputy smiled. "No hard feelings," he said. "To be fair, I agree. Will you lead us?"

The pastor nodded. Everyone bowed their heads. Kennedy squeezed her eyes and hands shut. She still had to force herself to keep the tears at bay.

"Heavenly Father," the pastor prayed, "we come to you this evening to lift up our friends, the Wilsons, to you. We thank you for bringing them and all their friends safely to our house tonight, and we pray for the continued safety of every one of us in this room. We lift up Isaiah in the hospital. That you will touch him with your mighty healing. Please give peace, comfort, and safety to Caitlin, Marilyn, Kennedy, Victoria, Jessica, Edward, and Darcy. Bless our evening and time together. Amen."

Kennedy looked up at the pastor. She blinked, still hoping to keep away any tears.

"Thank you, Pastor Logan," Robert said. He again held up his notebook. "First off, everyone, please understand that this is not witness protection. Thank heavens we don't need that complicated business despite everything that's been happening recently. But that doesn't mean we're taking any chances with our safety. Sheriff Jonathon and I have already contacted the police department in Prescott and told them everything, so they are on the lookout for our suspects and any other suspicious activity. I'll keep in constant contact with them."

Kennedy shuddered. She had a horrible feeling that Earl didn't pull off his job alone.

Robert turned to the pastor and his wife. "Keep all doors and windows locked at all times," he said. "I would also advise that you keep all curtains closed too. And everyone, keep any weapons that you have at your bedside at night. And never go anywhere alone. Any of you."

He eyed Kennedy. She knew what the deputy was thinking. She glanced over at her mother; she had the exact same look in her own eyes.

"Alec and I will be staying in the trailer just outside," the deputy said. He nodded at the pastor. "We thank you for letting us use that trailer. We will keep it locked up tight and we will take turns at night keeping watch."

"I plan to keep a nightly watch myself," Pastor Logan said.

Robert looked over at Uncle Edward. "How do you feel in your hotel, Mr. Wilson?" he asked.

"The hotel is good," Uncle Edward said. "Darcy and I have a room on the first floor close to the front desk. And the hotel is not far from the police station."

"Good," Robert said. "I spoke with Gunnar Smith earlier. He says that he, Billy, Wesley, and Aaron have everything under control at his apartment."

"I still can't believe everyone insisted on coming," Mom said. "It is so dangerous."

"Maybe that's why they came, Mom," Victoria said. "The more people we've got watching our backs, the safer we might be."

"I checked with security at the hospital," Robert added. "Your husband is in good hands, Mrs. Wilson."

Mom smiled meekly.

"One more thing," Robert said. "We have one other person in the loop. Nicole Hawkins. She is Alec's contact. Nicole heard everything, of course, and she will be dividing her time between her job as a ranger at the Yavapai Creek Wilderness and being here with us. And since she is a ranger, I am glad to have that extra support."

Kennedy smiled. She agreed with Robert's line of thought.

"What are tomorrow's plans?" Rachel asked.

"Well, Mrs. Wilson and her daughters will go to the hospital," Robert said. "And so will Mr. Wilson and Darcy."

"I'll go with them," Pastor Logan said.

"Me too," Rachel said.

"I don't mind Mrs. Wilson and her daughters having friends with them when they visit Isaiah," Robert said, "but let's not go to the hospital in big groups. I will stay here and watch the house while the first group is at the hospital."

Kennedy's stomach twisted. She did want to go to the hospital with her family. But she wasn't ready to go through any of this horror again.

Just seeing a couple of security guards made Kennedy feel safer to simply walk down the hallway. It was also a relief to see that nobody else seemed to be suspicious characters.

"We're almost at the ICU," Mom said. "Don't forget to turn off your cell phones."

Uncle Edward held the door of the ICU open. He waved his hand to usher everyone in. Kennedy almost hesitated. She was nowhere near ready to see her stepfather in the ICU. Marilyn had to give her a gentle push forward.

It seemed that as soon as Kennedy and her family stepped into the ICU, the quiet gloom that permeated the atmosphere took over Kennedy. Not that much could add to her own gloom.

"Caitlin Wilson?"

Kennedy whipped her head around. A nurse stood right in front of her mother and uncle. Mom nodded at her.

"Your husband is right over here," the nurse said.

Kennedy's eyes glazed over the waiting room. Much to her relief, she didn't see anyone that appeared to be paying attention to her mother.

Mom and Uncle Edward began to usher everyone forward. Kennedy glanced back at the doors. She still couldn't see Billy or any of the other boys outside. She reminded herself that they would be here, that she would meet them right here at the ICU. She knew that Billy would come just to be with her. At least, she hoped so.

Everyone followed the nurse to a little room behind glass walls. Kennedy saw her stepfather lying in that bed, connected to a ventilator, a breathing tube covering his nose and mouth. The nurse opened the door, then she glanced at Mom.

"The room is small," she said, "and your husband is still sleeping. I suggest that only a few of you go into the room at a time."

Mom nodded. She smiled at Kennedy, Victoria, Jessica, and Marilyn. "Let's go in," she said.

Kennedy only took one step forward before she hesitated. She stood, frozen on the spot, only able to move again when Jessica nudged her forward. The four girls followed Mom into the little room. Kennedy held in a sharp breath. Seeing her stepfather lying in the bed, basically on life support, his breathing abnormal and almost silent . . . it was too much. Kennedy lowered her watery eyes. This déjà vu was even worse than those frightening familiar feelings she had felt around Earl while he was in his Roman Hughes disguise.

"Isaiah?" Mom said softly. She placed her hand on her husband's arm. The only response she got from him was a twitch of his fingers.

"He hasn't been very responsive," the nurse said.

Kennedy cringed. She remembered how her own dad had become less responsive too as his illness had grown worse. Tears filled her eyes. Same with Mom. How well Kennedy recognized that watery anguish in her mother's eyes. The mournful fear Kennedy had seen many times when she was fifteen.

But there was another fear in her mother's eyes. A fear that hadn't been present the previous time. When her own father had been sick, it was just ordinary meningitis. He pretty much died of natural causes. But Isaiah? His illness was a potential murder.

"We do have some news that we want to share with you," the nurse said. "We've concluded that your husband needs a partial liver transplant."

Kennedy gaped at the nurse. There went her heartbeat on its racetrack again. Why, if her heart beat any faster and harder against her chest, she might need a heart transplant.

"We are working on finding a potential donor," the nurse said. "But we haven't had much luck yet."

Marilyn bursting into tears made Kennedy whirl her head around. She stared after her stepsister as she ran out the door. She made her way to the door but stopped when Mom grabbed her shoulder.

"Maybe you should let her be alone for a few minutes," Mom said.

Kennedy shook her head. "Please, Mom," she said, her voice breaking, "I know how she feels."

Mom let go of Kennedy. "Yes. Of course, honey."

Kennedy left the room. She felt a little bit guilty for having an excuse not to gaze at her gravely ill stepfather. She saw Marilyn sitting on a bench next to Rachel and her father. Kennedy walked over to them and squatted in front of Marilyn. She placed her hand upon her stepsister's. Marilyn opened her teary eyes to look into Kennedy's.

"You know how it is, huh?" Marilyn said with a sniffle.

"I sure do," Kennedy said. "Me and Vic and Jess."

Rachel stood up. "So," she said, "how is Isaiah?"

Kennedy sighed as she too stood up. "Barely conscious."

Rachel laid her hand on Kennedy's shoulder. "It must be so hard on you, girl. I remember you telling me about your own dad."

Kennedy nodded. She blinked, but the tears refused to be held back. "Oh, Rachel," she sobbed, "I don't think I can go through this again! I cannot lose my stepfather too!"

She wrapped her arms around Rachel. She felt her friend's hands patting her back. She also heard Victoria and Jessica crying. Kennedy longed to go to her sisters and comfort them. But she just didn't know how.

"Hey, hello!" a familiar voice called. "Kennedy, Marilyn?"

Kennedy and Rachel let go of one another. Kennedy smiled a little when she saw Nicole Hawkins walking toward them. Much to her delight, Billy, Aaron, and Wesley were with Nicole. Wesley rushed right over to Marilyn and helped her to her feet. She led Wesley to Isaiah's room.

Billy went straight up to Kennedy. "Hey," he said, hardly meeting her eyes, "I'm sorry me and the guys weren't here sooner. Gunnar insisted on making sure that his apartment was secure. I don't blame him, of course. He dropped us off here. He wanted to be here too, but he had to go to work. We just met up with Nicole in the waiting room."

"It's fine," Kennedy said. "It's great that Gunnar's keeping your safety in mind. Besides, I knew you'd come."

"Of course I would." Billy tucked one of Kennedy's curls behind her ear. She felt herself blushing. Then again, she probably already had been blushing and just didn't notice because of her tears. Strangely, she didn't mind Billy seeing her tear-streaked face.

"How's your stepdad?" he asked, his voice barely a whisper.

Kennedy closed her eyes, letting more tears stream down her cheeks. "He needs a partial liver transplant," she said. She heard Billy's soft moan. She let go of Billy and crossed her arms. Billy gave her final pat on the shoulder, then he walked toward Isaiah's room. Rachel stood next to Kennedy and laid her hand on her shoulder. Nicole stood just a few feet away from them with a weak smile and sorrowful eyes. Kennedy's thoughts went back to her first meeting with Nicole. The young Native woman had prayed for her then.

"How about I read some Scripture?" Pastor Logan said. He set his Bible on his lap and opened it. "I'll read from Psalm 18, verses 16 through 19."

Kennedy raised an eyebrow at the pastor. Funny how he should choose verses from that psalm, given that Pastor Cameron had recently preached on that very same psalm.

Kennedy and Rachel sat next to Pastor Logan. Nicole sat next to Kennedy and wrapped her arm around her just as the pastor began reading. "'He sent from on high, he took me; he drew me out of many waters. He rescued me from my strong enemy and from those who hated me, for they were too mighty for me. They confronted me in the day of my calamity, but the Lord was my support. He brought me out into a broad place; he rescued me, because he delighted in me.'"

Kennedy stared down the hall. Those words resonated with her. Just like they had during Pastor Cameron's sermon. Making her think once again of the time when she had been a prisoner in the undertown in Starwood City. But for some reason, that memory didn't seem so scary right now. God had watched over her and delivered her. Would He deliver her from her enemies now, and deliver her stepfather from his illness? Which was a result of poisoning from her enemies? Thus delivering Isaiah not only from his illness, but from the enemies as well?

What had Pastor Cameron said? His sermon seemed like it had been so long ago. Oh, yes. Pastor Cameron had mentioned how God delivered David from his enemies.

He came swiftly on the wings of the wind.

Kennedy smiled a little. She felt Rachel's hand pat hers. A gesture that was all the more comforting.

"I remember that psalm, Dad," Rachel said. "You read it to that man in jail. You know, that man you led to Christ."

Pastor Logan's faint smile lasted only a second. A nervous melancholy filled his eyes, and he looked down at his Bible. Rachel frowned too.

"Oh Dad," she said, "I'm sorry. I didn't mean—"

"It's alright, Rachel," the pastor said gently. "You didn't offend me. I just felt like I needed to read these verses right now."

His eyes glazed over his Bible. "One of my favorite psalms."

Kennedy glanced from the pastor to Rachel. Rachel seemed to have noticed her inquisitive look.

"Dad does prison ministry sometimes, you know," she said. "A few years ago, he befriended . . ."

She trailed off and fixed her eyes on the wall.

"Go on," Kennedy said.

Rachel didn't meet Kennedy's eyes. "Um, a prisoner," she said. "After some Bible studies together, Dad led that man to Christ. He got out of jail while we were in Starwood City."

"That's wonderful," Kennedy said. She still noticed the sad look on the pastor's face. She was tempted to ask him more about this former prisoner. Something about this man was obviously troubling Pastor Logan. But she didn't think such a question would be all that appropriate.

"Doctor! Get over here, quick!"

Her mother's scream made Kennedy's blood freeze. She spun around and dashed toward Isaiah's room, Nicole and Rachel right on her heels. But they didn't even get to go into the room. Mom was shooing Billy, Marilyn, Victoria, Jessica, and Wesley out just as a doctor and two nurses were running into the room. Kennedy was startled to see Victoria and Jessica in tears. Marilyn's hands covered her entire face.

"What's going on?" Kennedy demanded.

Wesley ran his fingers through his spiky hair. "Kenny," he said, "it's not looking too great. Your stepdad's vitals were really going down."

Kennedy brushed past Wesley, intending to peek into the room, maybe even force her way in. But then her mom came out and a nurse shut the door. Kennedy pressed her nose against the glass wall. The doctor adjusted Isaiah's breathing tube. A nurse was feeling his pulse, then she pointed to the monitor, speaking in an incoherent but urgent voice.

Then her mother grabbed her shoulder and pulled her away from the glass. Mom wiped her red and puffy eyes. Somehow, she managed a weak smile. "We should just let the doctors do their work, Kennedy," she said.

"But what is going on?" Kennedy asked. "I want to know!"

Billy grabbed her shoulders. Kennedy didn't even bother to shake him away; his touch was the only comfort she had right at the moment.

"Your stepfather's vitals just went down," Mom said.

"More like plummeted," Victoria muttered through choked sobs.

Mom sighed. She gave Victoria a hug. "Girls," she said, "it's going to be a long while before you can see Isaiah again. Maybe you should go back to the Hamiltons' for the evening."

"What about you, Mom?" Jessica asked.

"I'm going to stay a little longer."

"What?" Kennedy said. "No, Mom! I don't want you to be alone!"

"I won't be alone," Mom said. "This hospital's got staff and plenty of security."

"And she'll have me as well."

Kennedy saw Uncle Edward walking toward them. He put his hand on Mom's shoulder. "I should stay by my brother," he said.

"I'll stay a little longer myself," Nicole said. "I can give your mom a ride back to Rachel's house when she is ready. And Darcy and Mr. Wilson back to their hotel."

"But don't you have your ranger work?" Victoria asked.

"I'm off tomorrow," Nicole said. "The superintendent and I made some negotiations. He's really understanding. Now you girls run along. Your mom and I will keep you updated."

Uncle Edward turned to Darcy. "You should go with your cousin, honey," he said. "She needs you right now."

Darcy grasped Marilyn's shoulders and gently steered her down the hallway. Pastor Logan, Rachel, Victoria, Jessica, Billy, Wesley, and Aaron were right behind them. Kennedy reluctantly followed them. She stole one last glance over her shoulder at the glass walls of her stepfather's room.

"Why do I have to cook dinner again?"

Maurice heaved a silent but heavy sigh. Here came another meal-prep argument from Winifred and Octavia. Even if he wasn't held captive and tied to the bedpost, he would run away from the trailer just to get away from the constant squabbling.

"Because cooking is your job," Octavia snapped.

"Oh, please, don't you two go through this again."

Maurice looked over his shoulder at Abner Munoz. The former cattle rustler was glaring at the two women. When Abner noticed Maurice staring at him, his scowl deepened.

"You knock off your little thing too, Carr," he growled. "You should know that I ain't gonna fall for that long, sad face with those puppy dog eyes."

Maurice turned his face away. The evening when Horace and Ernesto had abducted him right from his own apartment and brought him to their hideout, Maurice had been greeted with yet another nasty surprise: Abner Munoz. For a split second, Maurice was almost relieved to see a familiar face, a man who had once lived in Pine Lodge and worked on the Smith family's farm. But right away Maurice chided himself for such foolish thinking. Unlike himself, Abner was no prisoner. Maurice had known about Abner's turn to crime. And his capture by police when he and his gang of cattle rustlers had the audacity to turn their business onto Oliver Connolly's ranch. Maurice couldn't help but smile a little; he knew it was Kennedy who had exposed those rustlers.

And why they had agreed to a revenge scheme against her. That thought was enough to turn his smile upside down.

From the corner of his eye, Maurice saw Abner meander to the bedside. Maurice returned Abner's sneer with a scowl.

"It's too bad you had to go soft, Maurice," Abner said. "I do reckon that you would've made a fine gangster with the rest of us."

"I feel guilty enough as it is," Maurice said.

"Oh, is that so?" Abner leaned against the wall and slipped his hands in his pockets. "How guilty? Guilty enough to try to go back to Pine Lodge and grovel before all your former friends? Don't chance it, that's my advice. I've got no inclination to go back, so why should you? Besides, who's to say they'd welcome you back to their little town with open arms?"

Maurice lowered his eyes. *That might be the only thing you and I agree on, Abner.*

"That's enough chitchatting," Abner said. He glared at the women. "I think I'll go on a patrol of my own while you two ladies, er, debate on who is going to make dinner. And you'd better have dinner ready when we all get back. We're as hungry as bears now. Don't make us turn into a gang of hangry bears."

Abner stomped out of the trailer. He slammed the door behind him.

"Well, it's your turn to cook," Winifred said to Octavia. "I cooked every single meal for the lot of you yesterday."

"I quit cooking for everyone since your husband wouldn't shut up!" Octavia said. "Always complaining that your meals are better than mine! So I told him that if his wife is such a wonderful cook, then she should take over."

"And you get to sit on your rump all day! How convenient for you to use watching the prisoner as an excuse!"

Maurice smiled when the two women glared at him. "One of you just get something going for dinner," he said. "I'm hungry too. The lunch you served me was hardly enough for a baby bear, and it's very tedious sitting here tied to this bedpost all day."

He wriggled his wrists, only to wheeze a little bit at the burning stings of the ropes scratching his skin. How was he able to still feel anything in his hands? How were they not numb by now?

"Deal with it," Winifred said icily. She sneered at Maurice. "At least I know that you can't escape. Unlike your precious little Kennedy did when Ernesto and I had kidnapped her."

Maurice slumped. Kennedy. That poor young lady. No matter how dire his current situation was, over the past several days, he had been more worried about Kennedy than he had been for himself. All he could do was pray silently multiple times each day that God would deliver him and keep Kennedy and her family and friends safe.

And so far, his prayers for Kennedy seemed to have been answered. Maurice had heard about the bear trap Maverick and Earl set on Oliver Connolly's ranch. But simply hearing about a plot was nothing compared to the horror of being forced to sit in Earl's pickup, bound and gagged, watching the brush fire from afar.

Seeing Kennedy right there.

Maurice remembered being able to smile despite his gag when he saw the firefighters quench those flames. And with the temper tantrum that he had thrown in the driver's seat, Horace had accidentally bumped the horn. Unfortunately for Maurice, that measly little honk went unnoticed. Horace held his gun on Maurice to ensure that he caused no further ruckus. Then, shortly after the fire department left and Kennedy and her family went back to their house, Horace quietly drove away in angry silence while Maurice silently praised the Lord. His only disappointment was the lack of his deliverance when the sheriff had been so close.

Even more horrifying? The day when Earl had told Horace about the death cap mushrooms in Isaiah Wilson's salad. Horace had thrown another tantrum about Isaiah eating the mushroom salad and not Marilyn or Kennedy. But Earl had pointed out that the girls losing their stepfather could simply be another element of their revenge plans. Horace's only response was to snap at Earl to make sure that either Kennedy or Marilyn ate the last remaining death cap bits. Maurice had lost sleep that night, worrying about the girls and praying fervently for God to protect them and their family. He even neglected to pray for his own deliverance. Much to his relief, Earl's next report was that the death caps had been discovered right before Marilyn had a chance to eat them and the Lonely Pine Eatery was closed down. Earl was too scared to do any more spying. But Grey knew how to keep an eye on the online world of Pine Lodge. Ever since the news of the very ill Isaiah being transferred to a hospital in Prescott, Horace had been busy making new plans.

"Say," Octavia said, "Winnie, maybe we should cut a little slack for poor Maurice here. He can cook."

Maurice gaped at Octavia. Winifred glanced from him to Octavia.

"Is that a smart move?" she asked. "We'd have to untie him, you know."

"I know that," Octavia snapped. "I'm not stupid. Look, we want dinner ready for the men when they come back from their patrol, right? We don't want to hear them whine, right? We can let Maurice loose just long enough for him to cook for us, then we will let him eat a little and tie him back up again. The men will never know, not even Mr. Ernesto outside."

"Ernesto wouldn't notice anything if it was under his own nose," Winifred said. "I keep telling Ruben not to give him guard duty."

"I'm missing your point," Octavia said impatiently. "My point is that we don't have to do any cooking. Besides, it's not like Maurice can drug our food. You and your husband don't have any desflurane with you now."

Winifred glanced at Maurice. She shrugged. "Alright," she said. "I am tired of cooking all the time. But before we untie him, let's make sure the door and all the windows are locked. I will grab a gun too."

Maurice faced the wall. He couldn't help but smile a little.

It was now or never.

In a few minutes, Octavia was untying him. He breathed a sigh of relief, only to frown again when he saw how red his wrists were. He began to gently rub them, but even the soft touch of his thumb stung the rashes.

"Well, what are you waiting for?" Octavia said. "Go on, get cooking, or else I'll have to tie you back up."

"If I'm going to cook," Maurice said, "I'd like to get some feeling and circulation back into my hands."

"Whatever you say," Winifred said. "Just don't expect us to give you any ointments. We're not nurses, you know."

She smiled slyly. "Just look at your wrists, you poor man. I wonder if Kennedy's wrists were this red."

Maurice glared at her. Winifred glared back.

"What's your problem? Ernesto and I didn't hurt Kennedy. We just lulled her to sleep, took her to the undertown, and tied her to a post."

"Yeah," Octavia said, "and she still escaped."

She sneered at Maurice. "Unlike you."

"Oh, you think Ruben, Ernesto, and I wouldn't take a few extra precautions?" Winifred snapped. "How that sly young cowgirl ever managed to get away is still a mystery to us."

Maurice shrugged. "I'm just glad she did," he said. "And I hope she gets away again."

Winifred pointed her gun at him. "Enough chatter, buster. Now get to work. It's the only freedom you'll be enjoying. We have burger patties and buns thawed out and a pot of water waiting to be boiled for the hot dogs."

Maurice went over to the griddle. "I used to grill hot dogs and hamburgers a lot." He smiled at Winifred. "Your husband will think you cooked them, Mrs. Messer."

He turned on the griddle and set the patties on top. As the patties sizzled, Maurice's eyes rested on the frying pans hanging from hooks over the stove. Then he watched the grease slide into the little hole into the grease catcher.

Those pans and hot grease? Might be useful.

And so would the pot of water. Already, it was beginning to boil.

Winifred and Octavia sat down. Maurice glanced at them from the corner of his eye. Winifred still had the gun. What else might be a good distraction?

The hissing of the patties gave him the answer. He ambled over to the little fridge and busied himself with digging through the shelves and drawers for some condiments, lettuce, tomatoes, and onions. Then he pulled out an unopened bag of hot dogs. He sniffed the air. Never in his life had he thought that the aroma of burning hamburger patties would bring him so much hope.

"Carr!"

Maurice casually looked up at Winifred. She was glaring down at the griddle. Maurice could almost hear her glare sizzling more than those patties.

"Don't let these burgers burn, you idiot!"

"Sorry, ma'am." Maurice took his stuff from the fridge and set it all on the counter. "I just have to throw these dogs in, then I'll check on the burgers. Oh, hey, is this big ol' pot dirty?"

"Excuse me? You're using dirty dishes?"

Maurice shrugged. He lifted his hand over the pot. Even the steam stung the rashes on his wrists.

Perfect.

"Guess I'll have to dump this water and get a clean pot."

Maurice picked up the pot.

He tossed the boiling water at Winifred.

Her scream filled the trailer.

Octavia leapt to her feet. Maurice grabbed the little grease catcher and flung the grease at her face. Octavia screeched as she grasped at her cheeks.

"Hey! Ouch! It burns!"

"Ow, ow!"

"Get it off!"

Maurice's eyes searched the floor around Winifred's feet. She had dropped her gun. Just as he had expected. He snatched up the gun and grabbed a frying pan from its hook. Then he leapt for

92

the door. He kicked it open and jumped out of the trailer, slamming the door behind him.

"What the heck?"

Ernesto had jumped from his lawn chair. He ran toward Maurice, his gun ready. But Maurice was ready too. He fired his own gun just to startle Ernesto. The former counterfeiter yelled in alarm and ducked. It was just what Maurice needed to let his frying pan give Ernesto a good whack across his head.

Ernesto collapsed at Maurice's feet. Maurice bent over and began searching the unconscious man's pockets. He fired a few shots at the trailer door to keep those two ladies from opening it. He finally pulled out some car keys from Ernesto's pocket. Maurice grinned; he knew which truck these keys belonged to.

And that truck so happened to be parked right over there.

Maurice dashed to the truck and hopped into the driver's seat. He punched the lock button before he even shut the door. Just as he started the engine, he saw Winifred and Octavia barge out of the trailer.

He chortled. Too late for those poor cowgirls. All they could do now was jump out of the way as he steered the pickup around. The tires squealed as they raised dust. He drove off faster than any drunk driver could. In seconds, the two trailers were out of sight.

Maurice's shaky breathing became relieved laughter. He rigorously patted the steering wheel. He was probably more giddy than a teenage boy driving home from high school on the first day of summer vacation.

"My Lord and my God," he exclaimed, "thank you! Thank you, thank you for finally giving me a chance to escape! And now, let me know what to do next!"

Well, he already knew what he needed to do next. He had some good information that the police would need to know about as soon as possible. He prayed one more time.

"Please keep protecting Kennedy and her family, Lord."

He pushed his foot down on the accelerator. He heard the wind howling against the windows. As if the wind itself was celebrating his escape with him and cheering him on.

Maurice flew swiftly on that wind to freedom.

The pizzas that Mrs. Hamilton had ordered arrived early. Kennedy made herself eat, wanting to be polite to Mrs. Hamilton, but that afternoon's drama lingered with her, bringing a lack of any appetite.

"What time should we head back to Gunnar's apartment?" Aaron asked.

"When Nicole comes back with Mrs. Wilson and Marilyn's uncle," Billy said. "She wants to follow us there to make sure that we get there safely."

"I reckon that's a good idea," Robert said.

R-R-RING!

Pastor Logan stood up. "Sorry," he said. "That's mine."

He looked at his phone. His eyes grew wide, and his mouth fell open.

"What's the matter, Dad?" Rachel asked.

Pastor Logan didn't answer his daughter. He looked at his wife. "I need to take this call!" he said in an urgent tone.

And with those words he rushed away from the kitchen, swiping his thumb on his phone screen.

"Hello!" he said. "Yes, it's me, Logan! Is it really you?"

Kennedy's heart thumped against her chest. What kind of phone call would get Pastor Logan so riled up? She exchanged confused looks with Robert, Alec, and Billy.

A sigh of relief made her look back at the pastor. He was grinning from ear to ear. "I am so glad that you're okay! Praise the Lord. Tell me what happened."

Kennedy's rising curiosity increased her desire to listen. She had a hunch that everyone else felt the same way. But Pastor Logan descended into the basement, and Kennedy could no longer make out his words.

"Is your father okay?" Darcy whispered to Rachel.

Rachel smiled. She also looked relieved. "I reckon he is," she said. "I'm sure he'll explain everything when he comes back."

"It's got to be his friend who disappeared, honey," Mrs. Hamilton said.

Kennedy's eyes widened. "His friend who disappeared?" she said.

Mrs. Hamilton nodded. Before she could say anything else, Kennedy's attention was drawn back to Pastor Logan's voice. She saw him coming up from the stairwell.

"Y-yes. Of course. I will tell her right away."

His wide eyes bore right into Kennedy's eyes.

"Thank you for calling me. I'll text you her answer as soon as I can. And watch your back. Bye."

Pastor Logan tapped his phone and returned to his seat at the table. But he only sighed.

"Dad," Rachel said, "was it him?"

Pastor Logan nodded, barely looking at his daughter. "Yes," he said. "He escaped from his captors."

A mild wave of nausea made Kennedy drop her slice of pizza. "C-captors?" she said. "Pastor Logan, I do hope you don't me asking, but what is going on?"

The pastor looked right at her. "Kennedy," he said, "Rachel mentioned at the hospital today that I made friends with a former criminal whom I led to Christ?"

Kennedy nodded, her eyes growing wider along with her growing anticipation.

"He wants to help you," the pastor said. "He says that he too is involved in this affair."

"You mean our family affair?" Victoria said. "Like with our stepfather being poisoned and all that?"

"But how?" Kennedy asked. "I don't even know him!"

"Actually, you do know him," the pastor said. "Kennedy, he is Maurice Carr. And he's coming over tonight to speak with you."

Chapter Seven

A Dubious Benefactor

WHATEVER WAS LEFT of Kennedy's already measly appetite was washed away. She pushed her plate to the side. All she could manage was a big gulp of her soda. She felt everyone else's eyes on her.

Robert took Pastor Logan aside to speak to him in private. Despite the temptation to go eavesdrop on their conversation, Kennedy couldn't move herself from her seat. Then Pastor Logan said a hasty goodbye and rushed out the front door.

"Kennedy?" Robert said. Kennedy whirled her head to look at the deputy.

He held up his cell phone. "I'm calling your mom."

Kennedy winced. What would her mother say?

She would find out soon, it seemed. Once he got off the phone, Robert announced that he was picking up Mom from the hospital. And it didn't take long for the deputy to return to the house with her mother, Uncle Edward, and Nicole.

"Kennedy!" Mom exclaimed as soon as she burst through the door. Her eyes darted to the living room. "So he's not here yet, is he?"

Kennedy shook her head.

Mom gripped Kennedy's arms. "Is this wise?" she asked. "Letting Maurice Carr come here to see you? What if he's one of the criminals wanting revenge on you?"

"Please, Mrs. Wilson," Rachel said, "he's not. My dad would insist. And so would I. Maurice is a Christian now."

Mom raised an eyebrow at Rachel. But she didn't get to say anything else. The sound of a car engine outside made everyone turn their gazes to the living room. Rachel ran over to the window and peeked out.

"It's them," she said. "And that's Maurice in the passenger seat, alright."

Part of Kennedy wanted to stand next to her friend and peek through the window too. But she was frozen on the spot.

It was like the front door opening was the sole cause of Kennedy's accelerating heartbeat. Then it had to skip a beat when she spotted the familiar face right behind Pastor Logan.

Maurice Carr smiled weakly at her.

Kennedy's heart thumped faster with every step she took toward the living room. In moments, she and Maurice were gazing into each other's eyes.

"Hello, Kennedy," Maurice said.

Kennedy grasped a strand of her curly hair and inhaled sharply. She opened her mouth. But only a little squeak came out. "Hi."

She lowered her eyes. They fell upon Maurice's wrists. His red wrists covered in fresh rashes. Kennedy's eyes widened; were those rope burns?

"Everyone, let's sit back down," Pastor Logan said. "Oh, uh, Maurice, do you want a few slices of pizza? You must be hungry."

"No thank you, Logan," Maurice said, "the police fed me. I do want to go down to the basement, though. If it's no trouble for you. I would just feel safer down there."

"Of course!" Pastor Logan said. "I understand."

Everybody went downstairs and sat around the fireplace. Maurice sat in front of the fireplace. Kennedy hesitated. Should she sit next to him? She took a step toward him, but then she felt Mom pull her to the sofa bed. Kennedy sat on it with her mother and Jessica.

A cumbersome silence filled the den. Maurice's weak smile went around the circle. First to Kennedy, then to her mother and sisters. To Marilyn and Nicole. To Wesley, Aaron, Billy, and Robert. Even to Alec and Susannah, both of whom were scowling at him.

"It sure is nice to see so many familiar faces again," Maurice said.

Wesley smiled a little. "You won't believe the crazy stuff that's been going on in Pine Lodge since you . . . uh, went away."

Maurice chuckled. "I've been keeping up with the news, my boy."

His timid gaze fell to Kennedy. "Seems like you've had some more adventures these past several years, huh?"

Kennedy shrugged. "I don't really mean to keep chasing after criminals." She groaned. "It's just got me and my family in this terrible situation now."

"I've been in a terrible situation myself," Maurice said.

"Is that why you're here?" Kennedy asked. "How did you know about my stepdad, Maurice? And about what's going on with me?"

Maurice sighed. Fear rose in his eyes. And so did another miserable emotion that was all too familiar to Kennedy: trauma.

"I got out of jail almost a year ago," he said. "Logan led me to Jesus Christ while I was still in jail. When I was released, Logan helped me find a nice apartment and a job as a maintenance man at a hotel. It was wonderful to get a chance to start over with my life. But even after all these years, the shadows of my evil choices have come back to haunt me. Not long ago, I came home from work and was greeted by Horace Cobb and another man named Ernesto in my apartment."

Kennedy sucked in a deep breath. Of course Horace Cobb and Ernesto had to be involved. Horace, the first criminal she had encountered. And Ernesto, one of her kidnappers.

"They kidnapped me from my own apartment," Maurice said.

A shiver tingled Kennedy's spine. Her mother squeezed her shoulders, helping her to relax a bit.

"Horace wanted me to be a witness to his revenge schemes against you, Kennedy."

A wave of mild nausea flew over Kennedy's head.

"Why would that snake care whether or not you saw his revenge plotting against Kennedy?" Billy asked.

"Because I stopped him the very first time," Maurice said. "I was helpless in that moment when Horace and Ernesto were in my apartment. They had guns on me. I only had a few seconds to text Logan and warn him that I was in danger. Then Horace took away my phone. He had me bound and gagged and marched out of my apartment."

Kennedy's eyes widened. Somehow Maurice didn't stutter, but Kennedy could see the painful trauma growing in his eyes.

"What happened next?" Victoria asked.

"I was a prisoner of ten criminals," Maurice said. "They had two trailers stolen from a campground near Tucson."

He held out his red wrists. "I spent most of my time in captivity tied to a bedpost."

Gasps filled the den. Kennedy snapped her eyes shut and whipped her head the other way. The vivid memory of her own red wrists played in her mind's eye. She rubbed her wrists together.

They almost felt like their rope rashes had returned. She felt her mother's comforting arms wrap around her.

"Who were these criminals, Maurice?" Robert asked.

Maurice looked back at Kennedy. "Horace was the leader," he said. "Then there was Ernesto. Oh, Horace's old comrade Mort Kane was also with him. Ernesto had a couple of his old comrades with him too. A husband-and-wife duo named Ruben and Winifred Messer."

Kennedy gulped. There went the nausea again. It was bad enough that Ernesto was coming after her. She didn't want to deal with her second kidnapper too.

"The other five were a gang of cattle rustlers," Maurice said.

"Let me guess," Billy said dryly. "Were the rustlers Earl, Octavia, Maverick, and a pair of half-brothers named Abner and Grey Munoz?"

Maurice nodded. "I recognized Abner," he said. "I hadn't known what had become of him after he left Pine Lodge years ago. Until I read about Kennedy's case against the cattle rustlers on her uncle's ranch in the newspaper."

He sent another awkward smile in Kennedy's direction. "I did like keeping up with the Pine Lodge news in jail," he said.

"Can't imagine you liked seeing Abner again," Wesley said.

"It wasn't a pleasant reunion, I can tell you that," Maurice said. "But then again, even before I turned to crime, I never did get along with Abner."

"Hey, nobody did," Aaron said with a light chuckle. "I can guarantee you that nobody in Pine Lodge misses him."

Maurice let out a feeble chuckle, but the longing in his eyes was still evident to Kennedy. He lowered his gaze to his twiddling thumbs.

"How did you escape?" Kennedy asked, twiddling her own thumb through strands of her curly hair.

Maurice smiled at her. "Today was a low-key day," he said. "Criminals hiding out, me their prisoner. Well, let's just say some laziness on the part of the villains helped me out. The two women, Winifred and Octavia, were in the trailer with me, watching me while the men were out doing their usual evening patrols. The ladies got into a petty argument over who was going to cook dinner. Then they decided to make me cook. I decided to make a little disturbance by letting the burgers burn by distracting myself with digging through the fridge."

A few chuckles escaped from the boys.

"Winifred wasn't happy about me burning the food. And while she was distracted, I grabbed my chance and tossed a pan of hot water on her. Then I threw hot burger grease at Octavia and grabbed Winifred's gun that she had dropped. I snatched a frying pan, just in case I needed an extra weapon. While the women were writhing in pain, I broke through the door and made my escape. I whacked Ernesto across the head with the frying pan. I stole his keys to a pickup and raced to the police station in Prescott. I told the cops everything. They gave me some dinner and let me call Logan. I wish I could've rescued my own phone, but I didn't take the chance. Too focused on my own escape, I guess. Anyway, Logan came for me. And here I am."

Silence filled the den once again.

"That's . . . quite a story, Maurice," Nicole said.

"I can confirm that he had been abducted," Pastor Logan said.

Mom still hesitated. "Well, if you say so . . ."

She turned to Maurice. "So you knew everything?" she asked. "What these criminals were planning, what they did to my husband and everything else?"

"I do," Maurice said. "They stole the death cap mushrooms from Grand Canyon University. Earl disguised himself so he could mingle in Pine Lodge. Grey helped him make a bunch of fake papers and ID's to get a job at the Lonely Pine Eatery. In fact, Horace and I had been watching from a distance when Earl set that fire near your house."

"You were there?" Jessica exclaimed.

Maurice nodded. "At a good distance. But I could still see the entire thing. I hoped that Earl would not attack Kennedy."

Kennedy laid her head down due to increasing nausea. She felt her mother's hand caress her cheek, but that touch didn't bring enough comfort to quell the horrifying thought of Earl having been so close to her. While she was alone. In the bluffs. At night.

"Horace and I were in a pickup," Maurice said. "Its engine was off, and I know there was no way anyone could've seen us up on that cliff from your point of view below."

"Yes," Marilyn said, her voice shaking, "you're right. But you weren't able to come down, I guess?"

"Of course not. I was bound and gagged in that pickup."

Bound and gagged. How Kennedy hated those words.

"And even if you were able to get out," Robert said, "I'm sure that Horace would've shot you."

"That's a risk I would've taken if I could've," Maurice said.

Once again, his eyes met Kennedy's. "You cannot imagine the joy I felt with each failed assault on your family. But I was horrified when I learned Isaiah had been poisoned."

"Where are the criminals now?" Mom demanded. "Are they anywhere near Prescott?"

"Their trailers are hidden in a canyon in between Prescott and Pine Lodge," Maurice said. "I gave the police directions to their hideout."

Mom exhaled a sigh of relief. Nicole stood up and walked over to Maurice. She sat down next to him. He gave her a surprised look. So did Kennedy.

"Maurice," Nicole said, "you've been through a terrifying ordeal. I'm so sorry you went through all that."

Maurice smiled. "At least it's all over now," he said.

Nicole took hold of his wrist. "We should take care of those rope burns."

Maurice gingerly rubbed his fingertips over his wrist. "I'd appreciate that."

"We have some first-aid supplies upstairs," Mrs. Hamilton said. "I'll show you where they are."

Maurice gave Kennedy one last smile before he followed Nicole, Robert, and Mrs. Hamilton up the stairs. Kennedy kept her eyes on him until he disappeared from sight.

"Well, imagine that!" Victoria said. "Maurice is back."

"And for the better, it looks like," Wesley added.

"Is it really for the better?" Mom stood up from the sofa bed. "How do we know that he isn't just baiting us, and leading those criminals to our location?"

Kennedy just stared up at her mother, unsure of whether she should agree with those worries or not.

"Please, Caitlin," Pastor Logan said, "I promise you that he was saved while in prison. I was allowed to visit him many times after his conversion. He even got out of jail early for good behavior. He's been coming to my church since then."

"Yeah," Rachel added, "Maurice and I get along so well. He even said that I remind him of you, Kennedy."

Kennedy scowled at her friend. "You never said anything to me about Maurice going to your church," she said. "Or who he was at the hospital."

Rachel lowered her eyes. Kennedy felt guilty right away.

"I didn't go to my dad's church for very long after Starwood City," Rachel said. "We went back to college in the fall, you know. And I wanted to say something to you. I did, really. But you were so depressed from your trauma about, uh, what happened to you in Starwood City. I figured that I should give you time to heal before I said anything to you about Maurice. Then I just kinda forgot."

"We might have a good reason to trust him now," Billy said. "I mean, he did save us from Horace Cobb the first time."

Kennedy felt like burying her head in her arms. How could she not remember that moment? She could still see it in her mind's eye. Maurice yanking Horace's arm back before he could fire his gun. She couldn't deny that even back then, Maurice had shown evidence of a change of heart.

Pastor Logan pulled out his phone and gave it to Mom. "This is the text he sent me when he was abducted."

Mom looked at the phone. She nodded and handed it back to Pastor Logan. "If you say it's legitimate, Logan, I trust you."

Kennedy meandered over to the stairwell. But her timidity forbid her from going up those stairs. She could hear the running water from the kitchen upstairs. She also heard pleasant voices.

"How does that feel, Maurice?" Nicole asked.

"Much better, thank you," Maurice replied.

"Good. Let's get your hands dried. But don't rub the towel on your wrists, Maurice, pat them."

"I gotcha."

"Oh, Maurice," Mrs. Hamilton said, "I am so glad you're okay and out of that."

"Me too, Diane."

"Our whole church had been praying for you. We were so worried about you."

"I was too." Maurice chuckled. "But I knew the Lord had me in His hands. And he delivered me from my enemies."

Maurice's words resonated with Kennedy. She trotted up the stairs and to the kitchen. Mrs. Hamilton was walking down a hallway. Nicole was patting Maurice's wrists with a hand towel. They didn't seem to have noticed her. Kennedy took a step back, thinking it might be better to just shy away. But then Robert had to glance in her direction and smile.

"Hey, Kennedy," he said, waving his hand toward her, "you can come on over."

Maurice whirled his head around. He grinned at Kennedy. She wanted to wince, but she recognized Maurice's old grin. Not an evil grin of some stereotypical cowboy bandit like Horace. No, this was his playful and fatherly grin that she used to love so much.

Kennedy drifted over to his side. Her stomach felt like a butterfly ballroom. She leaned back over the counter and lowered her eyes so that she was looking at her crossed arms.

"Kennedy."

She forced herself to lift her head and look into Maurice's eyes. His grin had faded to a feeble smile.

"It sure is good to see you again," he said.

Kennedy wondered if her own smile was even feebler.

"Kennedy," Maurice said, "I'm so sorry."

He faced Nicole and Robert. "I am very sorry for betraying Pine Lodge. I should never have joined forces with Horace and his gang."

He looked back at Kennedy. The remorse in his eyes was as clear as Silver River.

"I've heard about all the adventures you've had these past several years," Maurice said.

"All of them?" Kennedy asked.

"All of them. You've been making the news quite a bit, girl. Catching an art thief in Italy, finding ghosts in Virginia City and Starwood City—"

Kennedy let out a soft gasp.

"What's wrong?" Maurice asked.

"N-nothing." Kennedy silently admonished herself for that gasp. But she still couldn't hear Starwood City without her nerves tingling.

"Oh." Understanding came over Maurice's eyes. "I think I know."

Kennedy raised an eyebrow. "Say what now?"

"You dealt with those counterfeiters in Starwood City," Maurice said. "And . . . please forgive me for mentioning this, but three of them were Ernesto and Ruben and Winifred Messer. I do know that Ernesto and Winifred had taken you captive. Oh, Kenny, it must have been terrifying."

"Oh, yes," Nicole said, "it was awful. We were all so worried for her. Billy especially."

Kennedy hung her head. She fought back the tears; there was no way she was letting herself cry in front of Maurice.

She felt his hand on her shoulder. She looked back up at him. Somehow, she didn't flinch. No, his hand had a gentle touch that felt oddly comforting.

"I know what you must be going through," he said. "Being kidnapped? Wouldn't recommend it."

Kennedy's gaze pierced Maurice's eyes. Indeed, in those eyes, she saw anxiety and trauma. Not unlike her own. But behind that anxious trauma, she also saw hints of his former fatherly self.

"Kennedy!"

Kennedy spun around. Billy and Marilyn had run into the kitchen. They stopped when they saw Maurice. He smiled at the two of them.

"Hi, Billy," he said. "Marilyn."

Marilyn twiddled her fingers. Billy held up his hand in a brief wave. "Just making sure we're all good up here," he said. He stood next to Kennedy and patted her arm. That was when the butterfly ballroom decided to finish its intermission.

"We're just fine," Nicole said.

"How's your family, Billy?" Maurice asked.

"We're good," Billy said with a nod. "Dad stepped down as mayor. Passed the torch to another."

"I think I heard about that. And Jonathon Shea is the new sheriff, right?"

Billy nodded again. Maurice turned his sorrowful gaze to Marilyn.

"I'm so sorry to hear about your father," he said. "I've been praying for him every day. What those wicked crooks did to him was terrible."

Tears streamed down Marilyn's cheeks. Then she ran up to Maurice and hugged him. Kennedy's eyes almost popped right out of her face. Maurice looked surprised too, but he just smiled and ran his hand over Marilyn's bright red hair.

"Maurice," she sobbed, "I can't stand this! My dad needs a partial liver transplant, but what if he doesn't get one in time? Oh, Maurice, I just can't go through this!"

"No, of course not," Maurice said. He raised his eyes to look at Kennedy. "I . . . I can imagine that none of you girls can."

Marilyn let go of Maurice. "Are you okay?" she asked.

"Yes, I'm fine, dear. Now that I'm here safe and sound. And getting a chance to apologize to several of my old hometown residents at once. Marilyn, I am very sorry for everything I've done."

Maurice nodded at Billy. "Your dad was a good mayor. I'm very sorry I betrayed his trust in me during my days as one of Pine Lodge's politicians."

Marilyn smiled as she wiped away her tears. "You know," she said, "many people in Pine Lodge do miss you. Me and my dad included."

She nodded at Kennedy. "Even Kennedy."

Kennedy looked down at her feet.

"Maybe you should come back with us," Marilyn said.

Kennedy whipped her head back up.

Maurice hesitated. "I don't know if I'd have the guts to pull that off," he said softly. "But thank you anyway."

"Well, my offer is open when you're ready. I'm sure my dad would agree."

Kennedy opened her mouth to speak, but she was unable to utter a sound. Did she agree with Marilyn's point of view?

Was she really ready to have Maurice Carr back in her life?

Chapter Eight

Good News for Once

PANCAKES, SAUSAGES, EGGS, and boxes of cereal sat on the table. But Kennedy could only stare at the food. The previous evening's events hindered her appetite. So did her lack of sleep.

Pastor Logan had invited Maurice to stay at his house. But Maurice insisted that he leave. He claimed that he didn't want to risk the criminals tracking him to the house. He also said that he wasn't going back to his apartment, a move which everyone agreed with Maurice upon. After some careful consideration, Billy, Wesley, and Aaron decided to take him back to Gunnar's apartment. But as soon as Nicole, Maurice, and the three boys left, Mom had to go on a rant about Kennedy's safety. She had even suggested going to Uncle Edward and Darcy's hotel. Pastor Logan and his wife had to calm Mom down and encourage her to let her family stay at their house. Kennedy's worries about Isaiah's safety in the hospital and an entire gang of criminals showing up at the house during the night—and her worries about Billy's safety—kept her awake.

But nobody had come declaring war on the house. Other than Kennedy's mind, the night had been peaceful.

Those weren't the only anxious thoughts tormenting her appetite. Just knowing that Maurice had been at the house the previous evening made her too scared to eat the food before her, as well as afraid for everyone else who was eating. She knew that she was being irrational. Maurice couldn't have had a chance to lace any food or condiments or whatever was in the refrigerator and cupboards.

Her cell phone buzzed on the table. Kennedy looked at the screen.

"It's Billy!" she said. She jumped up and rushed downstairs. She swiped the screen.

"Billy!" she said. "Are you alright?"

"Yeah, Kenny," Billy said, "we're a-okay. You should've seen Gunnar's face when we brought Maurice to his place! I mean, we called him on the way to let him know, but still! We took turns with the night watches. Maurice cooperated with us. He was okay to let us keep an eye on him. Didn't try anything sneaky. He even helped Gunnar cook breakfast for all of us. Anyway, how are you doing?"

"It's been quiet here," Kennedy said. "Nothing new."

"That's good to hear." Billy paused. "I'd offer to let Maurice talk with you, Ken, but he's on the phone himself. With the cops."

A chill went up Kennedy's spine. "Do they have an update on those criminals?"

"Maybe. Hey, Maurice is off the phone now."

Kennedy's stomach churned. Any chance of an appetite was again ruined.

"Oh, wait, never mind," Billy said, "he just said he's gonna call Pastor Logan."

Kennedy heard another cell phone ringing from upstairs. Then the pastor's voice.

"Maurice, good morning! I trust you and the boys are fine?"

"Maurice just called him," Kennedy said. Relief replaced her stomach's twisting and churning.

"Yeah, I can confirm that too," Billy said. "We'll keep each other posted, Ken."

"Of course. Thanks for calling. Talk to you soon."

Kennedy hung up. She did feel some relief. At least she knew the four boys were still safe. She sat back down at the table.

"How's Billy doing, dear?" Mom asked.

"He says he's just fine," Kennedy said. "He and the others."

"Dad's talking to Maurice right now," Rachel said.

"I know."

Kennedy took note of the pastor's voice as he spoke. He sounded like he had still not gotten over his relief from last night. In fact, he almost sounded like he was simply talking to a dear old friend whom he hadn't spoken to in ages.

The sausages on Kennedy's plate were still warm. And her stomach was beginning to rumble a little. Kennedy took a bite. Her breakfast tasted just fine.

"So, Mom," Victoria said, "uh, is there any chance we can visit Dad later?"

"We will certainly try," Mom said. She patted Victoria's head. "But we still need to be careful. After our surprise visitor last night, I'm not risking any of your girls' safety."

"But Maurice won't hurt us," Marilyn said.

Mom bit her lip. "I understand Logan trusts him," she said. "But those other criminals may be after him. I just don't want them to find you girls . . . well, let me sleep on it."

Those conflicting thoughts sure found a good battleground in Kennedy's mind. Walking through the ICU doors now was a good way to distract her mind from having Maurice Carr back in her life. But on the other hand, having Maurice Carr back in her life was a good distraction from her stepfather's terrible illness.

Wait, was that Maurice standing next to Billy, Wesley, and Aaron at the reception desk right now?

Kennedy held in a groan. Did her conflicting thoughts and emotions really have to converge in reality?

Maurice looked in her direction and smiled. So did Billy. Kennedy didn't know if she was okay with walking up to either of them. It took a push from Marilyn to make her feet move forward.

"Hello, everyone," Maurice said. Kennedy forced herself to look into his eyes. Once again, they held that familiar fatherly look. And a hint of enthusiasm. "Mrs. Wilson, may I ask you something?"

Mom hesitated. "Of . . . of course, Maurice," she said.

Billy gave Kennedy an encouraging smile. "You and your family will want to hear this," he said.

"Yes, I spoke to the boys about it this morning," Maurice said. "You see, last evening, Marilyn told me that her father needed a partial liver transplant."

Marilyn nodded.

"Well, it occurred to me that I should get my liver tested and see if I'm a match for Isaiah."

Mom's eyebrows shot up. "What?"

"Sure," Maurice said. "I'm healthy. My criminal record will not be an issue. At least, I hope not for you."

Mom smiled meekly. "You're willing to do this?" she asked. "If you're a good match, would you really consider donating part of your liver to Isaiah?"

Kennedy gaped at Maurice. His grin only grew.

"I want to try," he said. He turned his eyes to Kennedy, and his grin faded to a simple smile. "It's the least I can do for your family after what I did years ago."

Kennedy couldn't help but let her lips release a little smile.

"I'll be taking my tests very soon," Maurice said. "Doctors had some openings this morning. We'll check my liver and a few other organs like my heart and my kidneys, then we'll get some lab work going."

Mom's smile grew. "Well," she said, "do you suppose you can spare a few minutes to see my husband?"

Maurice's smile faded, but not the hope in his eyes. "You mean it? You wouldn't mind? I . . . I would like to see him."

"Then come with us."

Mom led Kennedy, her sisters, Marilyn, and Maurice over to Isaiah's room. Even before Mom opened the door, Kennedy saw the sad recognition in Maurice's eyes. They all gathered around the bed. Kennedy saw Billy, Wesley, and Aaron standing just outside the glass walls. Billy seemed to be watching her intently. At least watching Maurice stare at her unconscious stepfather was a good excuse for Kennedy to tear her eyes away from Billy.

Maurice sighed and crossed his arms. "Never thought I'd be reunited with Isaiah in this sort of manner," he said. "I remember your wedding, Caitlin. I was already involved with Horace and his gang at the time."

His eyes fell on Kennedy. "But at least that didn't stop me from enjoying your family's celebration."

Kennedy shrugged. She had a hunch that Maurice, even in his then-new team up with the criminals at the time, had probably enjoyed her mother's marriage to Isaiah more than she had. For a long time, Kennedy wished that she had been more cheerful at her mother's wedding.

Even long before this moment.

Maurice turned his solemn gaze back to Isaiah. "Well, old friend," he whispered, "it's me. Maurice Carr. Yeah, me. The guy who thought a gang of bank robbers could help me become mayor of Pine Lodge or something. I put all that behind me now."

Isaiah didn't move. Kennedy doubted that he even knew that Maurice was in the room, his hand resting on the bed.

Maurice's voice began breaking. "You would be so happy to know that I finally found Christ. You mentioned the Gospel to me once, so many years ago, when your dear daughter Marilyn was only a toddler. You invited me to ask Jesus to be my Lord and Savior then. I should have accepted that invite at the time. Then maybe I would not have teamed up with those bank robbers. I would not have gone to jail. Or threatened your daughter and stepdaughters. And cause myself so much regret."

He wiped away a tear from his eye and looked up. "Mrs. Wilson," he said, "is it okay if I pray?"

"Oh, Maurice," Mom said, "of course it is."

Kennedy hardly had time to hesitate. Victoria and Jessica grabbed her hands. Kennedy closed her eyes. She heard Maurice's soft voice.

"Heavenly Father, I lift up my old friend Isaiah to you, and his family. His wonderful family. I thank you, dear Lord, for the chance you have given me to reconcile with Caitlin and her four wonderful daughters. Please, Lord, let Isaiah be healed. Not simply so I can reconcile with him, which you know that I would love, but so that his wife and daughters will not have to lose him. Please do not let Marilyn lose her father like she had lost her mother. And please don't let Caitlin, Kennedy, Victoria, and Jessica walk through this nightmare of losing a beloved family member a second time. In Jesus's name, amen."

Kennedy wiped her eyes as soon as she opened them. They rested on Maurice, whose eyes were every bit as red and wet as her own. Was it just her, or was gratitude beginning to fill her heart?

She loved Isaiah. She so desperately wanted her stepfather to live. But she was keen on the possibility of having her old father figure back.

Just then, a nurse opened the door and leaned forward. She gave Mom a smile, then she turned to Maurice.

"Mr. Carr?" she said. "The lab is ready for you to begin your testing."

Maurice grinned and nodded at Kennedy. "Wish me luck," he said. "I do hope that I'm a good match."

Billy poked his head through the doorway just as Maurice and the nurse left the little room. He smiled at Kennedy. "You've got hope, girl," he said.

"Oh, I hope so," Kennedy said. She watched Maurice follow the nurse to the ICU's exit. But before the nurse could even touch the doors, they flew open, and Wesley came running into the ICU. Maurice and the nurse looked at him in surprise. Kennedy and Billy left the room. They and Aaron hurried over to Wesley.

"What's going on here?" Billy asked.

"I've got bad news, everyone," Wesley said. "Gunnar called me just now. He said that he got a call from his landlord because his apartment was broken into today!"

Kennedy felt sick to her stomach. She, Aaron, Billy, and Maurice exchanged horrified looks. The nurse looked confused.

"Do they know who broke in?" Aaron asked.

"Yeah," Wesley said. "They looked at security footage. And lo and behold, Gunnar recognized the intruder as none other than Abner Munoz."

Maurice groaned and hid his face in his hands. "They've found me," he whispered. Kennedy gazed at him sorrowfully. The anguish in his quivering voice was undeniable. And relatable.

"Didn't you talk to the police earlier?" she asked. "What did they have to say?"

Maurice's fearful eyes met hers. "They said that when they arrived at the place I directed them to, they found no campsite. So the criminals had already fled. Can't say that I was all that surprised when I heard that."

"So we have no idea where those crooks are now?" Mom said. Maurice shook his head.

"I'll call Robert right away," Aaron said. He whipped out his cell phone and raced out of the ICU. The nurse gently goaded Maurice to leave the ICU with her. Kennedy watched Maurice as he and the nurse disappeared from the hallway. Worries filled her mind like a harmful fluid in the lungs. Would he be safe? Would those goons find him again? Or her and her family and friends? If they figured out that Maurice was staying at Gunnar's apartment, could it be possible that they knew about the myriad of guests at the Hamiltons' house?

But when Kennedy and her family and friends returned to the Hamiltons' house that evening, they were reassured to hear from Rachel and her parents that their day was uneventful and nobody had been seen sneaking around close to the house.

"We set up a couple of porch cameras outside before all of you came," Mrs. Hamilton said. "We've been checking them on a regular basis. Nothing unusual. Why, Rachel and Susannah were outside all by themselves this afternoon tending to the horses, and they're both just fine."

Rachel nodded. "It's still pretty dang scary to hear about Gunnar's apartment, though," she said. "I really hope that Maurice and the guys can find another place to stay." She smiled a little. "I also heard from Marilyn that Maurice offered some organ donation services."

Susannah gave Kennedy an encouraging smile.

"Yes, indeed, Rachel," Maurice said, smiling proudly. "I'm hoping to get the test results back soon."

But will those results come soon enough for Dad? Kennedy wondered. *And even if it is soon enough, what if the tests show that Maurice's liver or other organs aren't a good match for Dad? And will Dad be safe?*

She had to sit down with the new wave of anxious thoughts slamming into her mind like a tsunami. If Abner had known that Maurice was staying at Gunnar's apartment, could it be possible that he and the other criminals knew where Isaiah was at the hospital? Would her ill and vulnerable stepfather be safe?

"What are you guys gonna do tonight?" Alec asked.

"That's what we've been asking ourselves," Aaron said. "We voted unanimously that we can't go back to Gunnar's place. And I don't wanna cause hard feelings to Rachel and her folks, but I reckon this house doesn't have enough room for me, Maurice, and the other guys."

"I'm afraid we don't," Mrs. Hamilton said.

"Maybe we could try staying in the hotel where Darcy and her dad are at?" Billy suggested.

"That's not a bad idea," Wesley said. "It might be our only idea now. But I'm not too keen on Gunnar staying at his place all by himself. He mentioned he's got a late shift tonight. I'd just hate for him to go back to his place at ten-thirty at night and find Abner there."

Maurice nodded grimly. "I second that notion, Wesley. In fact, I don't think Gunnar should be alone at all. He also had a part in your kids' case against those cattle rustlers a few years ago, right? Add all that to the fact that Abner and Gunnar know each other personally—"

"And the fact that it was Abner who had broken into that apartment today!" Wesley said. "Yeah, Maurice, you're so right. We can't let our old pal be left to himself."

"So what do we do?" Aaron asked.

Silence was the only answer to Aaron's question. Just then Alec's phone rang. He excused himself and left the living room.

"Hey, Nicole," he said. "Yeah, we're all good so far. Glad no one was at Gunnar's apartment when Abner broke in. What now? I say, honey, are you serious? She said that? And she's sure? But what about her own safety?"

Kennedy and Billy exchanged inquisitive looks.

"Right then," Alec said. "Thanks, baby. Tell your aunt thank you from all of us. I'll tell them."

Alec swiped his phone screen as he walked back to the living room. He smiled at Billy, Wesley, and Aaron.

"Got some pretty good news," he said. "Kind of in answer to tonight's question about you guys. Turns out Nicole's aunt has a little knowledge of our predicaments. Nicole admitted that she's been keeping her aunt updated on everything."

"Nicole's aunt?" Maurice said with a smile. "Hey, would her name be Myra Hawkins, by any chance? And does she live on the Yavapai-Prescott Indian Reservation?"

Alec gaped at Maurice. "Yeah," he said. "Yeah, Nicole's aunt is Myra Hawkins. And she does live on the reservation. How did you know?"

"Because we know her," Rachel said, smiling herself. "She goes to our church."

"Interesting!" Mom said. "And she wants to help us?"

"But wouldn't that put her in danger?" Kennedy said.

"Myra's not afraid, apparently," Alec said. "She told Nicole that she'd be willing to step in if Nicole's friends needed backup. So when Nicole told her about the break-in at Gunnar's apartment, she told her niece to have Maurice and the guys stay at her house. She's got a basement with quite a bit of spare room and her house is in a wooded area on the reservation. She says it's a good hiding place. Nicole also mentioned that her aunt is an assistant kung fu teacher. She insisted too. And Nicole insisted that she stay at her aunt's house too. You know, since she's a ranger."

"Guess that might be our best bet," Maurice said. "We will accept that offer. But we will have to take extra precautions."

"Like when we go to Gunnar's place to get our stuff?" Billy said. "Make sure no suspicious guys are lurking around? And make sure nobody follows us when we drive to the reservation?"

"You got it, son," Maurice said. "Let's get rolling, boys. The sooner we get this out of the way, the better."

Kennedy stared at Billy with wide eyes as he went out the door with Aaron, Wesley, and Maurice. She wanted to follow him. To make sure he would be safe.

"Think they'll be okay?" Alec asked. "It's kinda odd that one of the criminals found Gunnar's apartment so soon after Maurice got away from them, eh? Who knows if being with Nicole's aunt will make any difference for their safety so long as Maurice is with them."

Kennedy cringed.

"Why won't any of you trust Maurice?" Rachel demanded. "He's changed! We keep telling you guys that!"

"You didn't know him before he went to jail," Susannah said.

"But I got to know him later! Me and my parents!"

"Okay," Mrs. Hamilton said, holding up her hands, "let's not get into an argument here. It's pretty much out of our hands. We just have to trust in the Lord to protect Maurice and the boys and that they will use common sense and take advantage of police protection."

Kennedy stood up. "If all of you will excuse me," she said, "I'm going to take a nap."

She rushed to the stairs, probably faster than the guilt and anxiety rushing through her mind. She wasn't tired. How could she be tired right now? A nap was probably the last thing her restless mind would let her do. But she did feel like she needed an excuse, any excuse, to get away from everyone else and focus solely on her own thoughts.

"Kenny, wait!"

Kennedy held in a sigh when she saw Susannah trotting down the stairs after her.

"I hope I didn't hurt your feelings," Susannah said. "I didn't mean to be rude or anything to Rachel. I know that Maurice was good to you before . . ."

Kennedy waved her hand. "It's all fine."

"I just have a hard time trusting Maurice," Susannah said in a lower voice. "Every time I think of him, I think of the time when my cousin was kidnapped."

Kennedy groaned. She plopped down on the sofa bed.

"Oh, gosh," Susannah said, "I'm so sorry! You must really hate that word."

"Sort of." Kennedy kept her eyes on the ceiling. "But, well, you know . . . Maurice wasn't the guy who took Alec away."

"I know that. But, it's just that . . ."

"Yes, I know. He did know about it and he didn't care. I just don't know if I wholeheartedly trust Maurice myself. Despite everything I've seen so far. I mean, yes, he has apologized multiple times, he does seem nicer, Rachel and her parents think he's

116

changed, he's offered his own liver for my stepdad, and I very much recognize the pain, fear, and trauma in his eyes . . ."

Kennedy let her words fade. She looked right into her friend's eyes. "You know that I know how it feels to be kidnapped," she said. "To be a prisoner. It's awful, Susie. You feel so alone and helpless. If that post in the undertown hadn't had that nail, who knows what would have become of me."

Susannah laid her hand on Kennedy's shoulder. "Ken," she said, "even if you didn't have that nail, you still had Billy. Do you think he would've given up at anything to rescue you?"

Kennedy smiled a little. She turned her head away when she felt her cheeks turning red.

"I'll never forget how determined he was to get into that undertown for you," Susannah added. "Nothing was going to stop him from going after you. He wasn't willing to wait for any rangers. He practically begged Lincoln on his knees to let him go down to the undertown. Rachel and the other guys had to run after him the moment Lincoln agreed."

Kennedy's shy smile crept across her lips, almost on its own volition. Her friend was sure making it sound as though Billy was Kennedy's knight in shining armor.

"And Alec knows how you've been feeling lately," Susannah added. "He came down with a bit of PTSD too after his ordeal as a captive. I remember him telling me how he felt. He had to make many visits with a counselor and a therapist for a few months after his experiences. Oh, that does remind me, Kenny, he recently told me that if you ever need a fellow kidnapping victim to talk to, he's open."

"Yeah, that thought has crossed my mind once or twice," Kennedy said. She yawned. It seemed like a nap was a good idea after all. She excused herself from Susannah and went to her room.

The buzzing of her cell phone woke Kennedy up. She let out a little gasp as she sat up in bed.

"Is that your phone?" Victoria asked. She turned over in her bed. "Who's calling at eight in the morning?"

Kennedy leaned over and looked at her phone on the nightstand.

It was Billy.

Kennedy snatched the phone, practically ripping it from its charger, and swiped her screen.

"Billy!" she said. "What's wrong? Are you okay?"

"Hey, hey, calm down, Ken," Billy's voice said. He let out a chuckle. "We're all just fine, girl. Me and the guys, and Nicole and her aunt, and Maurice. We've been good and safe here at this nice reservation."

Kennedy breathed out a sigh of relief and turned a sheepish smile to her wide-eyed sister. Victoria smiled back and let her body slump into relaxation.

"But anyway, I've got great news!" Billy said.

Kennedy's smile grew. "You mean we have good news for once?"

"Yeah, we sure do! Maurice got his tests back this morning and he's a perfect match!"

"He did?" Kennedy exclaimed. "But he only had his tests three days ago!"

"I know, but your stepdad's a top priority patient. And like I just told you, Maurice is a perfect match. His blood work, his liver, everything! He's got the green light to go for a partial liver removal surgery and everything!"

Kennedy's heart felt like it was about to win a big race. She grinned at Victoria, whose eyes appeared as though they were going to pop with eager curiosity.

"Thank you for calling me," Kennedy said. "I appreciate it, Billy."

"Of course, Ken. And you should thank Maurice too. He's gonna donate part of his own liver for your stepdad."

Kennedy's smile faded a tiny bit. "Yes, he is making a big sacrifice," she said. "And so soon after his own terrifying ordeal."

"Exactly. And Ken, I really hope none of you will mind, but we all would like for you and the others to come visit us here."

Kennedy almost dropped her phone. "You mean at Nicole's aunt's house?" she said in disbelief. "On the reservation? But you guys went there because you needed a safer place to hide."

"I know that. And we've got it. Nothing has happened these past few days, Ken, I can promise you that. No nighttime raids on the house, no creepy guys sneaking around, not even one of us getting a spooky feeling of being watched. Why, just last evening, I was out and about exploring the reservation with Nicole and Aaron and the three of us were just dandy. Besides, it might be good for all of us to have a rendezvous and catch up on things. Make more plans, which we might need to do since Maurice and your stepdad are going to a transplant center in Phoenix."

"Well," Kennedy said, "let me talk to Mom and everyone else. I'll text you soon."

"Sounds good." Billy paused. "Ken, I do hope you can come. I know you're scared. Don't blame you. I am too. But the thing is, uh, I just miss seeing you."

"It's only been a few days."

"I know. But . . . even a few days without seeing you was a bit much for me."

Kennedy knew the feeling all too well. Her lips formed a shy half-smile. "I will try my best to come," she said.

"Great!" Billy sounded relieved. "Hope to see you soon!"

She heard a beep. Kennedy lowered her phone and gazed at the black screen. She did miss seeing Billy. But what if all of them going to the reservation was too much of a risk?

"What did Billy say?"

Victoria's eager voice nearly made Kennedy jump. She had almost forgotten that her sister was still there. Kennedy gave her a smile and told her everything that Billy had said.

Victoria screamed and jumped off her bed. She twirled a couple of times. "Oh my goodness! Kennedy! This is way too good to be true!"

Don't jinx it, Kennedy thought.

"Come on, Ken, come on!" Victoria just about ripped the door open. "We gotta spread the news! We gotta tell everyone else!"

Kennedy couldn't help but grin. She ran out of the room too. Victoria had already barged into Jessica and Marilyn's room. She was hugging the two of them. Both Jessica and Marilyn looked a little confused. Even Mom was standing behind Jessica's bed, an awkward smile on her face.

"What's with all the cheer?" Jessica asked.

"Billy called Kennedy and said that Maurice's tests were a positive go for Dad!" Victoria said.

Sudden joy and hope replaced the confusion in Marilyn's eyes. She grinned at Kennedy. "Is this true?" she asked.

Kennedy nodded. She turned her smile to her mother, who had a hopeful smile of her own.

"Let's go upstairs," Mom said. "Breakfast might be ready."

Sure enough, as soon as Mom and the four girls went into the kitchen, they were greeted by the pleasant aromas of pancakes, blueberry muffins, toast, and bacon. Mrs. Hamilton, Rachel, and Susannah were setting the table.

"Good morning," Mrs. Hamilton said. "Oh my, you all look quite cheerful this morning."

"Wait until you hear the news!" Victoria said.

"What news?" Rachel asked. "What's going on?"

"Let's wait until we're all seated," Mom said.

It wasn't long until everyone came into the dining room and got seated. For once, Kennedy's stomach was growling.

"So it seems we have some news this morning," Pastor Logan said. "Do share."

Despite the return of her appetite, Kennedy was more eager to share the good news than she was to eat. She didn't think her spirits could be lifted any more until she saw the glowing joy and reassurance in the eyes and smiles of everyone else around her.

"Oh, now that is wonderful!" Pastor Logan said.

"There is something else," Kennedy said. "Um, Billy wants me to visit him and the others. At Mrs. Hawkins's house."

The cheerfulness in the atmosphere seemed to fade a little. Victoria, Jessica, and Marilyn exchanged nervous glances.

"Can we do that?" Susannah asked.

"Well," Kennedy said, "Billy said that they've been safe. It's been a few days. And he also said that we might need to meet back up so we can make plans since Dad and Maurice's next step will be going to a transplant center in Phoenix."

"That's a pretty good point," Pastor Logan said. "We can talk more about it after breakfast. Let's pray and thank the Lord and ask Him for guidance on our next steps."

Chapter Nine

Terror on the Reservation

NICOLE PARKED THE car in front of a two-story house. Kennedy was glad to see so many trees around the area. Those trees towered over the house and gravel driveway like a small army of leafy guardian angels.

Robert and Rachel parked their cars on either side of Nicole's car. Upon seeing her mother getting out of the passenger seat, Kennedy opened her own door.

"Thank you for the ride, Nicole," Victoria said.

"Of course," Nicole said. "Glad to lead everyone here."

"There's certainly a good crowd here," Rachel said.

"Yes," Nicole said, "so let's get into the house quickly."

The group clambered onto the wide porch. Nicole didn't ring the doorbell or knock. She opened the front door and held it open. She ushered everyone inside. The living room was a spacious area with a loveseat in front of the fireplace, a beanbag right next to the loveseat, and a long couch by the wall.

"Aunt Myra!" Nicole called. "We're here!"

A middle-aged Native woman appeared from the hallway. She gave everyone a cordial smile. She pushed her raven black braid over her shoulder and hugged Nicole.

"I'm glad you're all here," she said, "safe and sound."

"Yeah, the drive here was good," Nicole said. "Everyone, this is my Aunt Myra. Well, uh, some of you probably have met her before."

"Yeah," Robert said. He shook hands with Nicole's aunt. "I vaguely remember you. It's nice to see you again. We appreciate you for taking care of our friends, Mrs. Hawkins."

"Oh, everyone can just call me Myra," Nicole's aunt said. "I will get Maurice and the other kids. Please, everyone, have a seat."

Everyone sat down. Kennedy wondered how happy Myra must be to have this big living room. She could have a party here!

In just a few moments, Myra returned to the living room followed by Maurice, Billy, Aaron, Wesley, Gunnar, and, much to Kennedy's surprise, Gunnar's girlfriend Tiana Flores.

"Whoa," Billy said, "nice crowd."

"We all support our friends," Susannah said with a smile.

"So, Nicole," Myra said, "tell me which one of these fine young gentlemen is your boyfriend."

Nicole smiled faintly. "I'm so sorry, Aunt Myra," she said, "but Alec didn't come with us. He wanted to, but he felt that someone should stay with Mr. and Mrs. Hamilton at their house."

Myra's smile was replaced by a disappointed look.

"But I'm here," Susannah said to Myra. "I'm Susannah. I'm Alec's cousin."

She shook Myra's hand. Kennedy noticed Billy grinning at her. He gave a wave. Her own meek smile made her cheeks burn even more than they already had been. She wanted to go over to him. But then Gunnar and Tiana sat on the couch next to her, and Billy disappeared into the kitchen.

Kennedy let Tiana wrap her arms around her. Gunnar gave her a pat on the back. She smiled at him. When Kennedy and her family first moved to Pine Lodge, Gunnar had often teased her. Kennedy couldn't stand him. She used to wonder why her cousin was friends with him. But their adventures with the cattle rustlers on Uncle Oliver's ranch replaced their rivalry with a strong and cordial friendship.

"It's been a long time, Gunnar," Kennedy said.

"It sure has," Gunnar said. "How are you holding up since Starwood City?"

Kennedy's wince made her smile disappear. Upon seeing the guilty look in Gunnar's eyes, she decided to change the subject. "How is the animal preserve?"

"Going good as always," Tiana said. "So, Kennedy, Gunnar has told me all about your recent adventures."

Kennedy's smile waned. "Yeah," she said, "and now look where it's got us. My stepfather is suffering because of me."

"Say what?" Gunnar said. "No, no, Kennedy, do not blame yourself. You've always done what you thought was right. Those criminals are just being vengeful. But this is not your fault, you got that?"

Kennedy slumped. She appreciated Gunnar's words, but they did little to wipe away the guilt flooding her mind.

Myra and Nicole served their guests snacks, soda, water, and coffee. Maurice took a seat on the couch. His and Kennedy's eyes met, accompanied by feeble smiles.

"So," Kennedy said, "uh, heard you're golden to get rid of part of your liver."

Maurice chortled. "That I am, hon," he said. "Even as we speak, the hospital is prepping Isaiah for transferal to a transplant center. I've spoken to the doctors on the phone this afternoon. I've already scheduled my own surgery."

"Do you feel nervous at all, Maurice?" Gunnar asked.

Maurice turned his smile to Gunnar. "A little bit," he said. "But I'm more than happy to give part of my healthy liver to an old friend in need."

"And we need to make our own plans," Kennedy said. "Uh, Mom might want to talk to you, Maurice."

"Of course." Maurice walked over to the fireplace, where Mom was sitting with Victoria and Jessica. She smiled at Maurice and stood up to shake his hand.

"I gotta admit," Gunnar said, "it's sure interesting to see Maurice making amends with everyone. I never thought I'd see him again."

"I know the feeling," Kennedy said softly.

"Yeah, you do, don't you?" Gunnar said. "You and Maurice used to get on pretty good. Then he broke that bond. Now he might be trying to repair it after all this time."

Kennedy slid her fingers through her hair. "I'm not sure if I'm ready to repair it," she whispered.

"You should try," Gunnar said. "You and I didn't get along so great, remember? Now we're good friends."

"You never tried to help a gang of bank robbers."

"Well, no. But believe me, Ken, I reckon Maurice is mighty thankful to have a chance to reconcile with you. I know I'm glad to be able to support you and your family now. When you first came to Pine Lodge, I was such a bully. I was so heartless toward you even though you had just lost your dad. Even nowadays I have to fight off recurring guilt for my actions. So imagine how Maurice might be feeling now."

Kennedy tried to smile. She had to admit that Gunnar did have a pretty good point. She spotted Billy leaning against the wall, smiling feebly at her.

"It's really no wonder that Maurice wanted to donate part of his liver," Kennedy said. "But . . . well, what if the transplant process doesn't go well?"

"It will." Tiana laid her hand on Kennedy's arm. "It must."

Kennedy's eyes welled up in tears. She blinked a few times, but she was unable to hold more tears back. "Oh, Gunnar, Tiana," she said, "I'm just so scared. I can't lose another parent. It's just like losing my father all over again!"

She broke into sobs. She felt Tiana's embrace. Kennedy wiped her eyes and looked up. Even through her watery vision, she could see many sorrowful gazes coming in her direction. Including Maurice. Including Billy.

Embarrassment burned her tear-streaked cheeks. Kennedy tore away from Tiana's embrace and ran out the front door. She ran down the steps of the porch and stood on the grass, gazing at the hills. She thought she heard the door open.

"Kennedy!"

Kennedy whirled around. Billy was coming down the porch toward her. He rushed right up to her. Kennedy didn't stop him from grabbing her hands in a soothing grip. She closed her eyes and took a breath. She felt a tear slide down her cheek.

"Hey, it's okay," Billy whispered. Kennedy felt the tender touch of his finger wipe away the tear on her cheek. She opened her eyes so that she could gaze into his eyes. His periwinkle blue eyes. Oh, how that blue hue in those eyes matched the color of the Wild Western skies that she used to picture in her mind's eye whenever she read her favorite novel, *The Galloping Girls of Pine Gulch*. And the rivers too . . .

Billy's eyes began streaming a river of tears.

"Are you okay?" Kennedy asked.

Billy sniffled and blinked. "Oh, Kenny, you don't know how much it hurts me to see you in so much pain," he said.

Kennedy raised her finger toward his face but hesitated. Billy smiled and tapped his fingertip on hers. Blushing, she wiped away a few of Billy's tears. Just touching his face made her heart and stomach flitter.

"At least you're surrounded by friends this time," Billy said.

"What?" Kennedy said. "What do you mean by 'this time'?"

Billy heaved a sigh. "I heard what Gunnar said to you," he said. "I share every bit of Gunnar's guilt. I mean . . . last time, when you first moved to Pine Lodge, you . . . you were lonely and sad over your dad's death. And I bullied you. I am still sorry."

"But that's all in the past, Billy," Kennedy said. She gripped his shoulders. "You support me now."

Billy smiled. "Of course I do. Always."

124

He reached for his shoulder and grasped Kennedy's hand. His grip tightened around her hand. She squeezed her palm against his. She didn't ever want to let go.

Billy lifted his eyes. His smile grew. "Would you look at the sunset?" he said.

Kennedy turned around, still clinging to Billy's hand. She also smiled. The sunset was a half-circle of pink, orange, and yellow rays glowing in the sky and casting their rays of faint evening sunlight onto the green hills and through the branches of the trees. Even the few saguaro cacti looked like they were showing off golden smiles at Kennedy and Billy.

A slight breeze picked up, waving the trees a little bit. And it felt wonderful on Kennedy's face. It was like this gentle wind was trying to dry her tears.

Billy reached his free hand for her other arm. "Come on," he said, "it's the perfect evening for a Wild Western waltz."

He suddenly hesitated. "That is, uh, if you're cool with it."

Kennedy's stomach fluttered. That butterfly ballroom was back. And those butterflies were inviting her and Billy to dance with them.

She smiled shyly as she twirled a strand of her hair. "Yes, I'm cool with it."

Billy's smile returned. He and Kennedy awkwardly started moving their feet. Almost right away Kennedy stepped on his toe, but her embarrassment didn't get a chance to rise up in her gut because Billy just chuckled. He raised his arm so she could twirl under it. That twirl felt so wonderful with this breeze.

Billy's grin upgraded to a hearty laugh. He moved his feet faster. Kennedy couldn't help but laugh too as Billy pulled her into a sashay.

Then Billy wrapped his arm around Kennedy's back. She let out a tiny gasp as he lifted her off her feet and began twirling. Her arm encircled his neck. She felt the wind flap through her hair like swift wings, as though the wind itself wanted to waltz along with them.

Billy was right, this evening was perfect. Not too hot, even though it was summer in Arizona, so Kennedy didn't have to worry about Billy's spinning making her dizzy. Oh, how could it have made her even a little bit lightheaded? Only joy was allowed to roam in her head.

Her feet touched the ground too soon. Kennedy and Billy paused their dancing, but not the squeezing of their hands. Billy's enchanting periwinkle blue eyes kept Kennedy's eyes locked onto them, and his enchanting grin made her own timid smile broaden.

And that enchantment was beginning to tempt Kennedy into kissing those lips that surrounded that smile.

But then that smile waned. "Ken," he said, "I feel like such a coward."

"You?" Kennedy said. "A coward? No way! Why on Earth would you even say that?"

"Because I've been hiding my true feelings from you for a long time," Billy said. "Almost a year, actually. Even after you were kidnapped, and we found you safe and sound in that undertown, I still couldn't find the courage to . . . confess. And I'm sorry."

Kennedy's smile came back. So did her stomach's butterfly ballroom, which was being conducted by the accelerating waltz of her heartbeat.

"You don't have to be sorry," she whispered. She let go of Billy's hand to fulfill her fingertips' craving to toy with her curls.

Billy smiled again. He tucked a couple of Kennedy's curls behind her ear and took her hand back in his. "Kennedy, I—"

Rustling in the trees made them spin around.

Kennedy and Billy, still holding hands, stared at the trees before them. They seemed pretty still, though with less sunlight gleaming through the trunks. Kennedy leaned in closer to Billy. Her hand clung to his shoulder.

"Might be an animal," Billy whispered.

"Maybe," Kennedy said. "Wait, what was that . . . ?"

She could've sworn that she glimpsed a tall silhouette dash through the trees.

She did.

That silhouette pounced out of the foliage.

Kennedy screamed. Billy jumped in front of her, his arms outstretched.

The attacker's ski mask did little to hide his angry glare. He raised his right arm, the knife in his hand glinting under the rays.

"Look out!" Kennedy yelled.

She felt Billy's arms around her waist, then both she and Billy tumbled to the ground. The man had missed his lunge, but he was standing over the two of them, sneering.

He lunged again. Billy threw his leg out, giving the man a good round kick in the face. The man yelped and fell on his side. It gave Billy the seconds he needed to scramble onto his feet and jump on top of the man. Kennedy backed away and stood up.

"Billy, be careful!" she shouted.

The man jolted, throwing Billy off of him. Billy was on his back once again with no chance to get up. The man pounced on him, pinning him down.

"*Billy!*" Kennedy shrieked. For a split second, she felt like fainting from the nausea that was suddenly overwhelming her. What could she do? She couldn't let that crook hurt Billy! Wait, the knife. That guy had to have dropped it. But where was it?

She spun around, her eyes scanning the grass for the knife. She spotted it and snatched it up. Then she lunged at the man.

"Get off of him!" she screeched. She slashed the man's arm. The knife cut across a weird mark on the arm.

The man yelled in pain and grasped his arm. He glared up at Kennedy. But Kennedy was too focused on his mark.

It looked like an old burn. In familiar lettering.

The brand of her uncle's ranch.

"Abner!" Kennedy gasped.

The man stood up. He was still clutching his arm, but he gave Kennedy an evil sneer.

Kennedy pointed the knife at him. "Don't come any closer!"

Abner snorted. "You are coming with me, young lady," he said.

But before he could take another step, he was tackled from behind by Billy. Abner let out an alarmed cry as Billy's arm coiled around his neck.

"*What the heck is happening out here?*"

Kennedy spun around. She saw Robert, Gunnar, Wesley, Aaron, and Maurice dashing down the porch.

Abner's horrified eyes shot up at the five newcomers. He broke free of Billy's grasp and fled into the trees. Billy rushed over to Kennedy and embraced her.

"Come on, let's go get him!" Wesley said. He, Robert, and Maurice ran through the trees. Only to come back in a minute with disappointment written all over their faces.

"He got away?" Billy said.

Maurice nodded grimly.

"Who was he?" Aaron demanded.

"A-Abner," Kennedy stammered.

"What?" Gunnar said. "Oh no, don't tell me that you mean Abner Munoz?"

Kennedy could only nod.

Maurice shuddered. "He's found me again."

"Back in the house," Robert said. "Come on. Everyone get back in the house. Now."

The deputy ushered everyone to the porch. He had to push back a small crowd clamoring at the front door. Kennedy let Billy guide her over to the couch. She sat down but didn't loosen her grip on his hands. His touch was her only comfort right now. He sat next to her. So did Maurice, who appeared every bit as frightened as Kennedy felt.

Mom pushed her way through the living room and knelt in front of Kennedy. "What happened out there?" she asked.

Kennedy's voice quivered. "A-Abner, Mom. It was Abner Munoz. He's one of the crooks. He attacked me and Billy."

Mom wheezed. Tiana plopped backwards onto the couch; Kennedy almost thought that she had fainted. Robert ordered Myra to get him a notepad and call the police. Myra grabbed a notebook and a pen from a drawer and gave them to the deputy. Then she disappeared into the kitchen.

Robert opened the notebook. "Kennedy, Billy," he said, "can either of you tell me what happened?"

"Sure." Billy straightened his posture and began telling the story. Robert jotted down his every word.

It wasn't long before sirens could be heard from outside. Mom and Maurice both turned relieved gazes to the window. Robert and Myra went outside to meet the police. Myra came back in with two policemen. And Rachel's parents and Alec. Rachel and Susannah rushed right up to them and hugged them.

Myra looked right at Kennedy. "The police need one of you to show them what happened outside," she said.

Billy ran soothing fingers through Kennedy's hair. "I'll be right back," he whispered. He stood up, but his hand was still on Kennedy's palm. He seemed just as reluctant to leave her side as Kennedy felt. But his hand slipped away from hers and he followed Myra and the two policemen outside. Kennedy watched him until he was out of sight, then she slumped over.

"Hey."

Kennedy met Maurice's kind gaze. He laid his hand on her shoulder. "I'm still here."

Kennedy smiled a little.

"How do you know it was Abner Munoz who attacked you and Billy?" Wesley asked. "His ski mask had to have been blacker than night itself!"

"I saw his arm," Kennedy said. "Remember when he and the other cattle rustlers were on Uncle Oliver's ranch, and we found their campsite where Tiana . . ."

She trailed off and gave Tiana an apologetic look.

"Yeah, I do," Wesley said. "You branded him. He's got your uncle's ranch's brand scarred on his arm. No way I'll ever forget that."

"I'm kind of surprised that Abner came here alone tonight," Alec said.

"What if he wasn't alone?" Mom said.

"He had to have been alone, Aunt Caitlin," Aaron said. "The other crooks would have helped him attack Kennedy and Billy if they had been around. And Abner took off the moment he saw the rest of us."

A few policemen came into the house. Mom, Pastor Logan, and Mrs. Hamilton greeted them. They all stepped out onto the porch. Tiana got up and went to the kitchen. Kennedy caught a glimpse of the fear on Tiana's pale face. She got up too and followed Tiana.

"Are you okay, Tia?"

Tiana turned around. She gave Kennedy a feeble smile. "I guess so," she said.

"It's Abner, isn't it?" Kennedy said. "You must be terrified at the thought of him having been so close to you."

Tiana's eyes welled with tears. "Y-yes. You're right. He was one of the men who had kidnapped me a few years ago."

Sparks of empathy and trauma went off in Kennedy's mind. She couldn't help herself. She walked right up to Tiana and hugged her as tight as she could.

"Tiana," she said, "I really hope you do not mind me saying this, given what you had gone through with those rustlers . . . but, well, the truth is . . . you know that me and Gunnar and the others ran into some counterfeiters down in Starwood City?"

"Yes, I do." Tiana pulled away from Kennedy. "Gunnar told me that you had been kidnapped there."

"Yeah. Two of the counterfeiters, Ernesto and Winifred, carried out the deed. They ambushed me in the campground and put me to sleep. When I awoke, I found myself tied to a post in the undertown, hidden away in some remote room. I was bound and gagged. Thank goodness for that nail in the post. I used it to untie myself. So yeah, I managed to escape, but, uh, I had to go back to counseling."

Kennedy crossed her arms. "I was so scared. Up until that point, I had never been kidnapped. I was usually the one doing the rescuing. Now I know how you must've felt, Tiana."

"And so do we."

Kennedy and Tiana turned around. Alec and Maurice had come into the kitchen.

"Yes," Kennedy said, "both of you had been kidnapped, too, in the past."

"Don't remind me," Alec said with a light chuckle. "Gosh, I will never forget that horrible moment. I was dumped in the woods by my captor. He didn't even take the time to remove my bonds and blindfold. I didn't know where the heck I was until I tumbled over a stump that so happened to have the perfect sharp stick to untie the ropes around my wrists."

He patted Kennedy's shoulder. "My stump, your nail."

Kennedy smiled for just a second. "I still have nightmares about being kidnapped, though."

"Same with me, Ken," Alec said. "Even five years later, my trauma likes to make unexpected and unpleasant comebacks."

"Ditto," Tiana said. "I still think about my ordeal once in a while. I remember how I kept thinking of my parents. And Gunnar, of course. Oh my gosh, even now, I cannot tell you the relief I felt when you guys found me in that trailer."

"All four of us have been lucky," Alec said.

"Indeed," Maurice said. His grave voice matched the fear in his eyes. "I may have escaped, but I'm not out of the woods yet. It seems that my kidnappers are still chasing me."

"And me," Kennedy said, her voice beginning to shake. "I think Abner wanted to kidnap me."

Her whole body began shaking. She didn't want her hunch to be true. The very thought of being kidnapped a second time was too much for her. She pressed her palms against her forehead, but that did nothing to stop her mind's eye from seeing those terrible memories of being the undertown's prisoner once again.

"Girl," Wesley said, "you okay? You look like you're about to have a seizure."

Kennedy felt Maurice's strong grip on her shoulders. She fidgeted at first, only to find his grip oddly relaxing.

"Kennedy," Maurice said, "it's okay. You're safe."

Kennedy lowered her trembling hands. "Oh, Maurice," she whimpered, "what are we going to do?"

Maurice wrapped his arm around Kennedy. "Pray," he said. "I'm still donating part of my liver to your dad. He will be okay. And we will be too."

Kennedy looked up into Maurice's eyes. Behind the trauma that was all too familiar to her, she saw his old fatherly look. And it appeared stronger than the trauma. Kennedy laid her head against Maurice's chest. He ran his palm down her hair.

"You know what this reminds me of?" Maurice said. "Psalm 18."

"Psalm 18?" Kennedy said.

"Yep. Logan read it to me while I was in jail. It just seems to resonate with me right now. You know, because David wrote it. And David used to run away from his enemies all the time."

"Like us."

"Yes. Oh, those verses in my head are such a comfort right now, I might as well just recite them. 'He sent from on high, he took me; he drew me out of many waters. He rescued me from my strong enemy and from those who hated me, for they were too mighty for me. They confronted me in the day of my calamity, but the Lord was my support.'"

"'He brought me out into a broad place'," Kennedy said. "'He rescued me, because he delighted in me.'"

Maurice's smile grew. Alec and Tiana were also smiling.

"There's another phrase in that psalm that I like," Kennedy said. "'He came swiftly on the wings of the wind.' When I was tied up in the undertown, I prayed in my mind for God to help me. Right when I finished praying, I felt the nail. God delivered me so—"

"Swiftly?" Maurice said. "Yes. And my escape was swift."

"My rescue was swift," Tiana said.

"And me finding that stump to undo my bonds was swift," Alec added.

Kennedy smiled. This little counseling session calmed her nerves.

But upon seeing Billy standing in the living room, talking to her mother, Kennedy's nerves started bouncing up again. But so did her smile. The determined look on Billy's face made him all the more handsome. He looked in her direction and smiled. Kennedy blushed as she wandered over to the doorway between the kitchen and living room. Her mind wandered back to the moments before Abner's attack. Those romantic moments when Billy was holding her and dancing with her. Kennedy wondered how close she had come to confessing to Billy that she had strong feelings for him. That she loved him.

Why, oh why, did Abner have to interrupt those romantic moments and replace them with her traumatic feelings?

Billy truly was her knight in shining armor.

"You should tell him how you feel."

Kennedy spun around. Maurice was leaning against the doorway. His smile matched the twinkle in his eyes.

Kennedy didn't think she could blush anymore. "What?"

"I think you know," Maurice said with a chuckle. "I'll tell you the truth. I may have been peeking out the window when it was still peaceful out there."

Kennedy's face began burning.

"But I can also see it in your eyes, Kennedy," Maurice said. "And his eyes too."

He pointed to Billy. Kennedy looked over at him. Billy had just torn his own eyes away from her, but Kennedy thought she caught a glimpse of timid love in his eyes.

The same timid love that she felt for him.

Her heart skipped a beat. Could it be? Maybe Billy truly did reciprocate her feelings for him. Oh, how could she not have seen it? She could solve cases against criminals, figuring out their every move with only a few clues, yet she could not see Billy's feelings? It seemed so obvious now. He had asked her to go to the art festival in Phoenix with him. And then when her stepfather fell ill, he came to the hospital at midnight to see her. He insisted on supporting her, cheering her up, and staying by her side to keep her safe. He had asked her for a dance that very evening. He had picked her up and twirled her. His eyes and smile hid nothing.

And was he not extremely anxious for her when Ernesto and Winifred had abducted her? Anxious enough to break into the undertown for her?

"My stepfather said the same thing," she said to Maurice. "He also thought I should tell Billy how I feel."

"I agree with him," Maurice said. He then frowned. "But we still have other pressing issues that we need to talk about with your mom and everyone else. Abner still attacked you tonight, and that needs to be addressed."

Kennedy nodded. Maurice was right. She eyed Billy once more, then she and Maurice walked over to her mother and Pastor Logan.

Chapter Ten

A Frightening Prayer Vigil

KENNEDY EASED THE door of the horse stall open and stepped inside. Unlike the rest of the stable and even the corral outside, this stall didn't irritate her nose with the odors of old hay and horse droppings. Not a single straw of hay or speck of dirt could be seen on the floor. The two troughs looked like they had been painted with a fresh varnish.

The stall was just like Kennedy's heart: empty. No Sunshine to go out on an evening ride today. Just like yesterday. And the days before. No Sunshine to keep her mind off her anxieties.

After Abner's attack on her and Billy at the reservation, Kennedy, her family, and the rest of their group returned to Pine Lodge. Well, for the most part. Uncle Oliver had insisted that Mom and the girls, including Uncle Edward and Darcy, stay on the ranch. Mom had been worried about everyone's safety as usual, but Uncle Oliver assured her that his ranch had been fine and that as long as Kennedy and her sisters stayed near the house, they would be fine too. The other ranchers had been patrolling the area.

But to Kennedy, it was déjà vu. Living on her uncle's ranch because of her father being in the hospital. And this time, there was danger involved. Kennedy and her family needed a place to stay where their enemies wouldn't discover them.

Would Uncle Oliver's ranch really provide that safety?

Kennedy left the stall and went to the tack room. Might as well try to busy herself with some chores. Sure, it was kind of nice to be working on her uncle's ranch again, but no amount of work could distract her from her constant worries. Nothing could keep her distracted from her constant worries. Kennedy tried everything from chores to playing her piano tune from college. The one time she and her sisters were at their house in Pine Lodge, Kennedy had grabbed her sheet music in the hope that playing the piano would give her some peace. She had her original composition memorized now. But the piano in her aunt and uncle's living room wasn't enough to distract her mind from drowning in anxiety.

The ringing of Uncle Edward's cell phone might, though.

"Hello, Caitlin."

Kennedy rushed out of the tack room. She saw Marilyn and Darcy standing near the door of the stable, both of them with gazes fixed on Uncle Edward. His serious expression renewed Kennedy's nervous thoughts.

"What?" Uncle Edward said.

Marilyn glanced over her shoulder at Kennedy. The fear in her eyes was probably identical to Kennedy's eyes.

"But I thought the transplant surgery was a success."

Kennedy knew it wasn't the boiling hot air that was making her lightheaded.

"Oh?" Uncle Edward turned his worried gaze to Marilyn. "I guess . . . yes, alright. You will be down there for a few more days? I don't blame you, Caitlin. I should go down there. Yes, I know, but he's my brother."

Uncle Edward sighed. "Of course. I will watch the girls, but I will be ready to go down there at a moment's notice. Thank you. Bye."

He swiped his phone, not making eye contact with any of the girls.

"What's wrong?" Marilyn demanded. "Uncle Edward, what is wrong with my dad?"

"A few complications." Uncle Edward stuck his hands in his pockets. "Um, the new liver might need more adjusting."

Kennedy had a hunch that Uncle Edward wasn't telling the whole truth. Just days ago, she heard that her stepfather was resting in an ICU in some hospital in Phoenix after gaining part of a new liver. What was happening now? Was the liver not cooperating in its new body?

Her thoughts wandered to Maurice. He had gotten out of the hospital himself just yesterday. He was already making a good recovery. And his liver did match Isaiah's. So what was happening?

And how disappointed Maurice would be if he learned that his sacrifice may have been in vain!

"Please, Dad," Darcy said, "tell us the whole truth."

Kennedy looked back up. Uncle Edward heaved a sigh.

"Isaiah will be in the ICU for a few more days," he said. "It's possible that . . ."

He trailed off. Marilyn burst into tears. Darcy wrapped an arm around her. Kennedy's eyes watered. She spun around, paying no attention to the queasiness filling her head, and rushed back to Sunshine's stall. She used the stall to run out to the corral.

Kennedy sniffled. Her tears felt hot running down her cheeks. She scanned the corral for Sunshine. Which she knew was futile. Sunshine was in Pine Lodge at Old Dodge Park. Not here to give her comfort.

"Ken."

Kennedy turned around. Billy was standing behind her. His eyes widened with fear, and he dropped the brush from his hand.

"What's wrong?" he asked, grasping her shoulders.

Kennedy choked back a sob. "Uncle Edward got a call from Mom just now," she said.

Billy gulped.

"No, Dad's not dead," Kennedy said quickly. "Not . . . yet."

"But it was a bad phone call nonetheless," Billy said.

Kennedy wrapped her arms around Billy. "Oh, Billy, what will happen to my family if Isaiah does die?"

"I can't say." Billy's whisper was soft in her ear. "But you'll have me."

Kennedy pulled back and smiled at Billy. His blue eyes held that comforting look again. How she loved that look.

Billy took hold of her hands. Her smile grew.

"Alrighty," he said, "I know you don't have Sunshine with you right now, but, uh, maybe I can try to cheer you up?"

"Oh!" Kennedy said. "I'd . . . Billy, don't you still have things to do? Chores to finish?"

"Hey, I can take a short break. And you should too. I'd bet that if your uncle saw you now and heard the news, he'd insist that you take a break."

Kennedy squeezed her hands within Billy's grip. "It's a nice evening out. Just like at the reservation."

"Yeah. But with some safety this time. Come on!"

Billy turned around and took off, pulling Kennedy along with him. The twosome ran out of the corral and toward the hills. The descending sunrays danced upon those hills, adding their golden hues to the bright green grass. The trees and even the bluffs in the distance glowed golden orange against the sky gleaming like a dark sapphire.

Billy grasped her hands. Kennedy squeezed her fingers. She felt their tingle against his palms, and her heart beating fast as she gazed into his eyes. A gust of wind blew past her curls.

Yet, even with her hands in Billy's, she still couldn't help but worry. She and Billy having a frolic in the countryside? She loved the idea. But last time, they had a terrifying interruption. And not to mention that the dirt was still hot from a brutal beating of afternoon heat. What if the heat made her dizzy?

But as Billy stood in front of the sunset, holding Kennedy's hands, all worries seemed to float away. It was as though the sunset that was making Billy glow was taking away Kennedy's worries. Yes, she would be embarrassed if she fainted in front of him, but fainting in his arms would also be kind of romantic.

Billy began moving his hands. Kennedy let him sway her hands with his. Almost immediately after their hands began moving, so did their feet. Kennedy wondered how she and Billy were going to dance in cowboy boots. But at the same time, she didn't care how awkward their dance would be. Just that she was dancing with him again.

Then Billy let go of Kennedy's hand. He didn't let go of his eye contact, though. He slowly placed his left hand on Kennedy's waist. Kennedy glanced down for a second. Then she slipped her left hand up to Billy's shoulder. Their other two hands never came undone.

"Ready?" Billy said, his awkward smile returning.

"Yes. Oh, yes!"

Billy pulled Kennedy into a bouncing waltz. Kennedy could care less if she was stumbling a little bit as they pranced up and down the slope of the hill. She could care less if her own smile was sappy and awkward. Billy's feet were clumsy too. But neither of the two dancers lost their balance.

A breeze began to pick up. Kennedy's smile broadened. It felt so wonderful on her face. It felt so wonderful to be waltzing again with Billy. Waltzing swiftly on the wings of the wind.

No, Kennedy may not be riding Sunshine this evening. But being with Billy was every bit as comforting. Besides, she knew that Sunshine wasn't gone forever. No, Sunshine still belonged on Silver River Ranch. She was still Kennedy's horse. She was simply offering her services to Old Dodge Park for a short time. She would be home soon. In the meantime, Kennedy was enjoying Billy's company, and she was determined to not let her anxieties interrupt this beautiful moment like the last beautiful moment had been.

Though, there was an interruption this time. Kennedy just had to stumble upon a gopher hole and lose her footing as she and

Billy flew down the hill's slope. Billy lost his own footing at the same exact moment. The twosome fell on their sides and rolled down the hill together. Kennedy had to land right on top of Billy's stomach.

Awkward silence petrified her. She was released from that petrification when Billy started laughing. Kennedy laughed too as she moved away. Billy sat up and grinned at her.

"Well!" he said. "Reckon dancing on a hill in cowboy boots may not have been the best idea we've had."

"I don't care!" Kennedy said. She crawled over to Billy and wrapped her arms around him. "It was beautiful!"

She wanted a round two. She didn't care if they stumbled over their boots again. She also wanted to hear a certain confession from Billy. Something he was going to say to her last time, right before Abner's attack. She had an idea what that confession might be. But for some reason, she still didn't dare let her hopes soar too high.

A buzzing noise made her let go of Billy. He looked down at his pocket and pulled out his phone.

"Looks like my sister just texted me." He swiped his phone. His grin came back. "She's telling me that Pastor Cameron wants to set up a prayer vigil at the church tomorrow night."

He looked at Kennedy. "For Isaiah."

Kennedy raised her eyebrows. "It does makes sense for my mom to tell the pastor about Dad right away," she said.

"And my family and the pastor's families are in-laws," Billy added. "It's no wonder the news is spreading fast."

He put his phone down on the grass so he could place his hand on Kennedy's arm. "I'll be with you at that vigil," he said.

"But will it be safe?" Kennedy said. "A prayer vigil? What if something happens like it did at the reservation?"

"Nothing has happened in Pine Lodge or here on this ranch so far," Billy said. "I mean, I know that's what we've been thinking a lot lately, and an attack did happen on the reservation. But we do know that Maurice has been safe at Pastor Logan's house since he got out of the hospital. We also know that your family has been safe here. I can still confirm that Susannah and Alec have been safe in Pine Lodge. And Wesley too."

Kennedy smiled meekly. "Alrighty. We can go to the vigil tomorrow night."

Just the very thought of a prayer vigil for her stepfather made gratitude rise in Kennedy's heart. And as Billy took hold of her hand and helped her rise to her feet, Kennedy's thoughts went back to the time she had first told Isaiah about her feelings for Billy. It seemed so long ago.

It did look like Billy reciprocated those feelings. Didn't it? "Billy?"

He turned around. His enchanting smile had come back. "Yeah, Ken?"

Kennedy opened her mouth to speak. To tell Billy how she felt.

But only silence came out.

Her stomach was twisting, but it was no longer a ballroom of butterflies. More like butterflies fleeing from a hungry bird.

"Thank you for your support," Kennedy blurted out.

Billy nodded. Kennedy kept her smile, but in her mind, she was beating herself up. Two romantic moments with Billy. A bunch of obvious signs that her romantic feelings for Billy were mutual.

She had to be the only chicken to be found on Silver River Ranch.

It wasn't Sunday morning or Wednesday night, but the parking lot appeared to be packed. The moment Kennedy and her family entered the sanctuary, they were greeted by Pastors Logan and Cameron.

"Wow," Mom said, her eyes wandering over to the pews, "we have a good crowd."

"Are you surprised?" Uncle Oliver patted Mom's back. "You pretty much have an entire town supporting you."

Kennedy glazed over the familiar faces. She smiled when she saw Billy talking to Wesley, Aaron, Alec, and Gunnar. Rachel and her cousin Sierra were sitting with Tiana Flores and Susannah on the pew behind the boys. Kennedy also saw her former music teacher Nadia Powell, her former horseback riding teacher Alan Barnes, Deputy Robert Swift, Nicole, and Jonathon.

She also spotted Felicity talking to Maurice.

Kennedy lifted an eyebrow. Why was she surprised? It only made sense for Rachel and her parents to bring Maurice. He didn't look too bad for a guy who just had part of his liver removed, but unlike the very pregnant Felicity, Maurice was sitting down.

Felicity's eyes met Kennedy's. She waved. Maurice turned around in his seat. His smile grew. Kennedy walked over to them.

"Hello," she said. "So, Maurice, how're you feeling?"

Maurice's smile didn't lose any of its joyful luster, but it did wane a little bit. "Still fighting exhaustion," he said. "And a little bit of awkwardness."

His eyes flitted around the sanctuary, glazing over a few of the people. Kennedy wondered if he had spoken to anyone other than herself and Felicity.

"I reckon the last time you were in this church was when Mom and Isaiah got married," she said.

Maurice nodded. His smile then waned completely. "I've got bigger worries than my own health and social status," he said. "Kennedy, I do hope that my surgery . . ."

"Won't be for nothing?" Kennedy's eyes welled with tears. "Yeah, me too."

She sat next to Maurice. "Thank you," she said. "Thank you anyway."

She wiped her eyes and looked up at Felicity. She forced a smile. "How're you doing?"

"As fine as I'll ever be," Felicity said. "I've been so worried about my brother. I'm so glad all of you are safe."

She turned her smile to Maurice. "And it sure is nice to see Maurice again. I'm so happy that you found Jesus."

Maurice's smile came back. "Me too. And I'm happy for you and Jonathon."

"Thank you," Felicity said. "It is good to see you again. You know, maybe you should come back here. To Pine Lodge."

Maurice's smile waned again. "Marilyn said that to me not long ago," he said. "It is a little tempting. I mean, I'm quite happy in Prescott. I got to start over with my life there. I guess I'm just a little worried that others in Pine Lodge won't share your attitude."

He twiddled his thumbs. "So, what's your baby's name?"

Felicity ran a hand over her orb-shaped belly. "Still trying to figure that out."

"You haven't come up with a name yet?" Kennedy said.

Felicity chortled. "It's harder than you think it is," she said. "Oh, Kennedy, Billy wanted me to ask you something."

Kennedy stared at Felicity. Expectation welled in her gut.

"He spoke to Pastor Cameron," Felicity said, "and Billy was wondering if you would be willing to play something on the piano for us to start the vigil."

"Billy did what?" Kennedy could feel her heart's nervous pumping in her ears.

142

"He says you don't have to if you don't want to," Felicity said. She smiled. "He was too shy to ask you himself. He just said that he wanted to hear you play."

Maurice elbowed Kennedy. He had that knowing smile on his face again. Kennedy didn't know whether the blushing of her cheeks or the churning of her stomach burned more. She glazed over the sanctuary for Billy. She spotted him standing near the stage with Aaron, Wesley, and Gunnar. Her heart flitted, and a little smile inched its way across her face. Billy then looked over at her. Kennedy tore her eyes away.

She couldn't find it in her heart to refuse Billy's request.

"I . . . I have something," she said. "I wrote a song in college. I've got it memorized. I suppose I can play it."

"You wrote a song in college?" Maurice said.

Kennedy nodded. "It was just an assignment for one of my music classes. So, should we get started?"

"Of course," Felicity said. She turned and rushed over to Pastor Cameron. She whispered in his ear. Pastor Cameron clapped his hands to get everybody's attention.

"Miss Kennedy has agreed to begin our prayer vigil with a song on the piano," he said loudly.

Kennedy almost regretted her decision. All the same, she walked over to the piano and sat on the bench. Everyone gathered around the piano. And, of course, Billy had to stand right next to her. Hopefully her nerves wouldn't hinder her performance. She warmed up her fingers with a scale and arpeggio. She didn't have her sheet music with her. But she didn't need it. Not with the very notes she had written herself still etched in her mind's eye.

The music began its soothing effect on her after only a few notes. She could almost feel the atmosphere around her simmer, as though neither her nor any of the people surrounding her had a care in the world.

Even more, the lively melody filled her with hope. It felt as though God himself was steadying Kennedy's anxious heart as she played.

The applause ensured that there was not a single beat of silence when she finished making her music. Kennedy looked at her mother and Marilyn. Their smiles matched the cheerful looks in their eyes, as though Kennedy's song had healed Isaiah at that very moment. She turned her gaze to Maurice. He was grinning from ear to ear like a proud father.

A proud father figure, perhaps.

Finally, Kennedy forced herself to look at Billy. His face was plastered with awe, relief, joy, and love.

Yes, love.

"Beautiful, Kennedy," Pastor Cameron said.

"Yes, very!" Maurice said. He grasped Kennedy's shoulder and gave her a gentle shake. "And you say you composed that?"

Kennedy nodded.

"What's your title?"

"Oh." Kennedy smiled sheepishly. "I have no title."

"You know," Maurice said, "I reckon I might. I was thinking of my favorite psalm while you were playing, Kennedy. Psalm 18. We both have known God's deliverance from our enemies. And I still remember your favorite phrase from that psalm."

"You do?" Kennedy's eyes widened.

"Of course I do. Swiftly on the wings of the wind."

Kennedy's smile grew. "I like it. Yes. My title will be 'Swiftly on the Wings of the Wind.'"

Billy laid his hand on Kennedy's other shoulder. "And it's perfect," he said.

Just then Pastors Cameron and Logan called everyone over to the front pews. Kennedy sat with her family in the very front. She saw Billy and Felicity sit with Maurice in the pew just behind them.

Pastor Cameron stood up front. He was no longer smiling. His downcast eyes were on Kennedy and her family.

"Thank you, everyone," he said, "for gathering here tonight for this prayer vigil for Caitlin and her family. In his epistle to the Galatians, Paul calls us to carry one another's burdens and so fulfill the law of Christ."

Kennedy blinked to keep the tears at bay. At least this was just a prayer vigil and not a funeral.

"Just as Christ bore all our burdens on the cross," Maurice said.

Pastor Logan smiled. "Indeed," he said. "And you have lived out Galatians 6:2 by donating part of your own liver to Isaiah. Now we will pray that your sacrifice will not be in vain. Let's all bow our heads. Those of us who want to pray can jump right in. Start us off, Cameron."

Pastor Cameron began praying. Kennedy opened one eye so she could glance over at Maurice. Pastor Logan made a good point. He really had shared the burden of Isaiah's illness. More than that, to be honest. He was empathetic to Kennedy. He too knew the horrors of abduction.

Kennedy couldn't help but smile. If Maurice did ever come back to Pine Lodge, perhaps he would attend this very church? That thought was enough to lift her spirits a little bit.

Nicole's voice interrupted her thoughts. Kennedy listened to Nicole pray. Her soft voice reminded her of the time she had first met Nicole in the Lonely Pine Eatery. How quick Nicole was to pray for her then. She too had always been good at helping Kennedy bear her burdens.

And then there was Billy. Her knight in shining armor. His armor surely would've helped him bear some burdens! Just looking at Billy made Kennedy's heart flutter. She grasped her curls. At least Billy had his eyes closed. Kennedy quickly closed her own eyes and made herself listen to the prayers.

All too soon Pastor Logan was finishing a closing prayer. All eyes opened. Hugs and smiles were exchanged. Kennedy and her family were approached by a line of people wanting to shake their hands and give them encouragement. Kennedy and her sisters formed a group hug with Darcy, Rachel, Sierra, and Susannah. Then Wesley took Marilyn aside and kissed her cheek. Kennedy focused her gaze on Billy. Her own cheek longed for his lips.

"I loved your song, Kennedy," Nadia said. "Your sisters told me that you performed it for your college recitals. I wish I could've been there, but at least I got to hear you play it tonight."

"Thank you," Kennedy said.

Nadia gave Kennedy a hug, then she turned and went out the doors. It wasn't very long before everyone else started trickling out the doors. Already several cars were leaving the parking lot.

Kennedy felt a tap on her shoulder. Her gut lurched when she saw Billy behind her. Her cheek tingled with excitement.

"I know it's hot right now," Billy said. "I mean, I just wonder if we'll have another nice evening later. You know, cooler."

"Yeah?" Kennedy didn't know what else to say. She was too focused on his lips and her desire to feel their moisture cooling her cheek.

R-RING!

Kennedy saw Jonathon pull his cell phone out of his back pocket. He held it up to his ear. "Hello? Robert. What—"

Jonathon's face fell. Kennedy and Billy eyed one another.

"I'll tell them!" Jonathon's voice was suddenly urgent. "You be careful!"

Kennedy's gut flipped as the sheriff turned toward her and Billy. All eyes were turned to him.

"The deputy sighted Abner Munoz nearby!" Jonathon said.

Gasps erupted. Victoria and Jessica ran to Mom's side.

"He also thinks he spotted Horace Cobb and a few other people," Jonathon added. "Everyone, get in your cars and get away from here."

Mom immediately ushered Victoria and Jessica to Uncle Oliver's pickup. Uncles Oliver and Edward, Aunt Thelma, Aaron, and Darcy had already got in. Kennedy ran outside to catch up with her family.

BANG!

Marilyn and Felicity screamed. Jonathon spun around to face the hedges alongside the churchyard. He drew his gun.

"Show yourself!" he shouted.

Tense silence answered him. Kennedy didn't dare move a muscle. She eyed Maurice. She had a horrible hunch that his recent surgery was not the reason for his pale face.

BANG!

A windshield shattered. Kennedy gawked at Pastor Logan's car.

"Take cover!" Jonathon yelled.

Billy grabbed Kennedy's arms. The two of them, followed by Marilyn and Rachel, raced inside the church.

"What are we doing?" Rachel said. "We need to drive away, not run around in here!"

"Your dad's gonna have a hard time with that," Billy said. "We need to hide. Come on."

He led the three girls to the basement. Kennedy heard the gunshots ringing outside. Then a bunch of yells. What the heck was going on out there?

CRASH!

Glass shattered. Kennedy spun around. She, Billy, Marilyn, and Rachel froze right where they stood.

"What was that?" Kennedy whispered. Her wide eyes were fixed on the hall.

"Hello-o-o-o! Miss Kennedy!"

Kennedy's muscles tensed. Horace Cobb. He was in the church.

"Come out, come out, wherever you are!"

Now Kennedy felt queasy. Mort Kane was inside too.

"Come on, don't be shy!"

The queasiness went up a notch. Ernesto!

"How many of those guys broke in?" Rachel hissed.

Kennedy clung to Billy.

"We know you're here!" Horace called. "Awfully rude to not greet your guests. We made quite an entrance too. Got a laceration or two on our hands and faces, we do."

Blackness started to overtake Kennedy's vision. She took a deep, silent breath, but she still stumbled back. Billy caught her. He dragged her backward. Kennedy regained her composure and stood up. Billy mouthed to the girls to follow him. The foursome ran back the way they came.

They only made it halfway up the stairs.

"There you are!"

Kennedy shrieked. Horace, Mort, and Ernesto stood at the bottom of the stairs. Billy held out his arms in front of the girls.

"Stay behind me!" he said.

Horace ran up the stairs after them. Marilyn and Rachel's screams almost shattered Kennedy's ears. She was too busy trying not to faint. But Horace never did draw near to her. Billy grappled him by the shoulders and pushed him backwards. Horace let out a yell as he tumbled down the stairs, colliding into Mort and Ernesto at the bottom.

"Ouch! Watch it!"

"Get off me!"

Billy herded the girls to the sanctuary. But Kennedy could still hear Horace's heavy footsteps tramping up the stairs. Then his angry voice.

"Mort, run around and cut them off!"

"They're coming!" Kennedy squeaked.

"No!" Billy hissed. He grabbed Kennedy's arms and looked her in the eye. "If they wanna abduct you, they'll have to go through me first! Now come on!"

The four friends raced across the sanctuary and to the door to the right of the stage. They ducked into the women's dressing room. Billy closed the door and shoved a large box in front of it.

"I don't know how long that'll hold," Marilyn said.

"We're trapped," Rachel said. "There's no way we'll get out of here now!"

147

Kennedy wanted to plop onto the chair and let the nausea fade away, but she doubted she and her three friends even had a few seconds to spare. Then her eyes rested upon the rectangular hole in the wall. The hole that led into the tunnel under the baptismal basin.

Just on the other side of that tunnel was the men's dressing room. And just outside the men's dressing room? There was a door that led outside to the back parking lot.

"Guys!" Kennedy said. "We've got to take the tunnel!"

She pointed to the hole.

"Perfect!" Marilyn said. "We might be able to get out that way! Or just hide!"

"You girls go." Billy rummaged through the box in front of the door and pulled out a large net. "Good thing we always save this after our crazy Wednesday night games."

"What are you—?"

Rachel shut her mouth when footsteps reverberated from the hall. Billy snapped his fingers at the girls and jutted his finger toward the hole. Marilyn and Rachel crawled through the hole. But Kennedy stayed put.

"Billy, please come!" she said.

"Don't worry, I will follow you," Billy said. "Just go. Go!"

Kennedy turned and climbed into the hole. She heard the door open. Then Ernesto give a startled yell.

"You stupid boy!" the criminal shouted. "Get this net off me or else!"

Kennedy clambered deeper down the tunnel. She ducked to avoid the beam. Once again, it reminded her of Starwood City's undertown. How she had to sneak through those underground halls and rooms after escaping from the counterfeiters, her captors. But at least in the undertown she had been able to run. This tunnel almost felt like a wooden airduct.

She heard clambering behind her. Much to her relief, Billy was in the tunnel and kneeling in front of the hole. He seemed to be pulling something toward the hole. Kennedy peeked over. She saw that Billy was pulling the chair over to the hole. He spun on his knees and grinned at Kennedy. He waved his hand, motioning for her to keep moving.

A door slammed against a wall. Kennedy froze. So did Billy and the other two girls. They exchanged horrified looks but stayed silent.

"Where are those youngsters?" Mort's voice said. "You said the boy ran in here, Ernesto!"

"He did!"

"Then how did he just vanish into thin air?"

"I don't know. Ow! Hey, watch my hair, Cobb!"

"Hey, do you want me to get you untangled or not?" Horace snapped. "I can't believe you let a young man throw a net over you."

"He ambushed me!"

"Mort, get over here and help me with this net!"

Kennedy heard receding footsteps. The men grumbled for a few minutes.

"Finally!" Ernesto said. "What do we do now?"

"Maybe the kids went through the window?" Mort said.

"Does that window look like it's been opened to you?" Horace demanded.

"Those kids are sneaky! Let's just look outside."

"Hey, who gives the orders here, buster? Get a move on."

More receding footsteps. Billy nodded at the girls. The four friends began moving again. In seconds Kennedy was crawling out into the men's dressing room after Marilyn and Rachel. Billy came out after her. He tiptoed over to the door and inched it open. He peeked out, then he nodded at the girls. The four friends tiptoed out. Billy leapt to the door just in front of them and opened it. They ran outside and around the yard, not stopping until they reached the front parking lot.

"Nobody's here!" Rachel said. "They all must've driven off."

"But your dad wouldn't leave without you!" Billy said.

"Or Mom without me and Marilyn!" Kennedy added.

"What's that?" Marilyn asked.

Kennedy looked to where her stepsister was pointing. She gagged at the sight of the tiny, crimson red puddle on the sidewalk in front of the door.

"Blood," Marilyn wheezed.

Kennedy turned away. That was when she spotted Maurice and Felicity squatting next to Billy's truck. Maurice looked up and smiled a little, but Kennedy could still see the fear in his eyes. He waved at them. Billy and the girls dashed over to them. Kennedy was startled to see Felicity in tears.

"Hurry!" Maurice said, standing up. He opened one of the truck's doors. "Into the truck! Billy, you need to drive!"

"What happened?" Kennedy demanded.

"Oh, Kennedy," Felicity said, "Jonathon was shot!"

Kennedy felt like she had been shot too. "And my mom?"

Felicity choked back a sob. "Your mother . . . she was taken by Ruben and Winifred!"

Chapter Eleven

A Redemption Story

SOMEHOW KENNEDY MANAGED not to throw up. But she was still frozen on the spot. Her eyes fell on Maurice. Anger joined the horror in her gut.

"Every time you appear," she said, pointing a finger at him, "the criminals are not far behind. They always seem to find you no matter where you are. Why? Why is that? Is it just a coincidence?"

Maurice's eyes widened in shock. "Kennedy," he said, "you can't really mean that."

"Then why is everyone else gone?" Kennedy demanded. "It can't be just a coincidence, everything that has happened since the day you showed up at the Hamiltons' house! You went to Gunnar's apartment, and Abner followed you there! Then you went to Myra's house, and Abner attacked me and Billy right in her yard! Now we are under attack here at the church right after a prayer vigil! Where are those crooks taking my mother? Where is my uncle? The rest of my family? Were Victoria and Jessica kidnapped too? And where is Jonathon?"

"Stop it, Kennedy!" Felicity said. "Your aunt drove Victoria and Jessica away to find Robert and get him to go after your mom. Your uncle and Pastor Logan are getting Jonathon away. They will meet the ambulance."

"Alright, no more idle standing around!" Maurice said. "We need to get away from here now! Into the truck!"

"I'm not going in there with you!" Kennedy seethed.

"It's my truck," Billy said, "so I'm driving. Maurice can't do any driving anyway. Come on!"

Kennedy wouldn't budge. The rising fear in her gut forbid her from getting into the pickup. Billy and Maurice grabbed her arms and dragged her forward.

"Hey, let me go!" she said.

"We'll let you go when you're in the truck!" Billy said.

He and Maurice hauled Kennedy into the backseat. She was further pulled forward by Marilyn and Rachel, who at the same time were helping Felicity climb inside. Maurice slammed the door behind Kennedy and rushed around to the passenger seat. Billy got into the driver's seat and locked the doors.

Kennedy heard the sound of glass doors smashing. She saw Horace, Mort, and Ernesto running out onto the sidewalk in front of the church's main entrance.

"GO!" Maurice yelled.

Billy shifted into gear. The pickup flew backwards just as a gunshot rang outside. Kennedy shrieked and ducked, her arms over her head. But no windows or tires had been blown out. Billy jammed forward and drove out of the parking lot at a wicked speed.

"What are we gonna do now?" Rachel asked.

"We'll meet up with Gunnar, Tiana, Alec, and Susannah," Felicity said. "Gunnar called me earlier. He said Alec and Susannah are with him and Tiana. They ran into some issues when two of the criminals tried to attack their vehicle on the road."

"Sheesh!" Billy said. "Talk about desperate!"

Kennedy knew desperate alright. She turned her glare away from Maurice and out the window. At least it didn't seem that the three criminals were following them in another car.

But what if Maurice were to pull out a gun hidden on his person? What if he were to force Billy to drive to some hideout in the countryside? She had to think up some sort of escape plan for her and the others, just in case. Could they jump out of the pickup if they needed to? But then again, if they found the hideout, maybe Kennedy could find and rescue her mother.

Her mother. Oh, her poor mother. Was she alright? What would those felons do to her? Where could Ruben and Winifred be taking her?

And what about poor Felicity? She was so pregnant. She was in no shape to fight off any criminals.

Oh, how could Billy and the others have allowed Maurice to take them away right now?

"Hey, Fel," Billy said, looking up at the rearview mirror, "why didn't you drive off with someone else? Like Mrs. Connolly?"

"I tried to grab a getaway ride," Felicity said, "but I was so terrified from the gunshots. I didn't want my tummy to get hit by a bullet."

She rubbed her round belly. "So in my panic, I just ducked behind your pickup. Maurice shielded me. He never left my side."

A twinge of guilt hit Kennedy. She glanced at Maurice.

"I would sooner have let them shoot me than a vulnerable pregnant woman," Maurice said.

"But you had surgery just days ago," Marilyn said.

"Didn't matter to me."

Billy smiled meekly. "Thanks for keeping my sister safe," he said.

Kennedy's guilt increased when she saw the humble relief in Maurice's gray eyes. She twirled a few strands of her hair. Maybe she had been too hasty in her accusations. Maybe Maurice never was trying to lead the criminals to them.

"I'm a Christian now," Maurice said, "and I ain't gonna let any of those crooks lay a hand on any of you. Not this time."

"Yeah," Marilyn said with a smile. "For a moment, I shared Kennedy's, um, concerns. But now I know that you truly have found Jesus, Maurice. Your testimony is so inspiring."

"Well, it all started with Kennedy's letter."

Kennedy gaped at Maurice. "My letter?"

Maurice smiled at her. He didn't look like she had lashed out at him only minutes ago. "Yes. Shortly after I went to jail, I got your Christmas letter."

"Oh." Kennedy almost forgot about that Christmas letter.

"I couldn't believe your forgiveness," Maurice said. "After I betrayed you so horribly, you still wrote me a letter for Christmas when I was new in jail. I kept it all these years. Even now, it lies in my apartment in Prescott. It brought me a lot of joy that Christmas. Enough joy and relief to cope with the guilt. Why, it was the first joy I had felt in a long time, even before I first met up with Horace Cobb and his gang. But what struck me most was that in your letter, you said that you would pray for my salvation. I was touched. But I was also too nervous to try to come to Christ. I didn't have a Bible. I hadn't read the Bible in ages at the time. I did not know if Jesus would be willing to accept me after all the terrible things I had done. The only thing I felt I could do was promise myself that I would be on my best behavior while in prison. It paid off. I actually made friends with the prison staff and even a few other prisoners. I even befriended Barney Chambers. You know, one of Horace's old gang members. Then, sometime during the summer of 2013, we got a visit from a prison ministry group."

"My dad was among them," Rachel said with a proud smile.

"He sure was. Logan and I hit it off almost immediately. I just loved listening to him share the Gospel with everyone. But even as we talked for the first few times, I was still too nervous to come to Jesus. Logan assured me multiple times that Jesus could take my sins away. He gave me my very own Bible. I read it every day since I got it. I had such a hard time putting it down. For a year, Logan paid me many visits. Sometimes he would bring Rachel with him on his visits. I always loved seeing Rachel. She reminded me of you, Kennedy."

Kennedy lowered her eyes, but her smile didn't falter. She felt Rachel elbow her arm.

"Oh!"

Kennedy jerked her head around at Felicity's gasp. All eyes turned to the pregnant woman.

"Fel?" Billy said. "Sis, are you okay back there?"

"Yeah, I'm fine." Felicity clutched her orb-shaped belly. Her smile became a giggle. "I thought I felt my baby moving around in here. For a moment there, I was a little worried about some telltale contractions."

She heaved a big breath. "I'm so over this pregnancy."

"Yeah, I get that, Felicity," Billy said, "but just for the time being, can the kid wait a little longer?"

Felicity, Marilyn, and Rachel burst out laughing. Kennedy smiled herself, though she did share Billy's concerns. Now was the last moment for Felicity to go into labor.

"Perhaps," Felicity said. She turned her smile to Maurice. "I didn't mean to interrupt your story, Maurice."

"It's no problem," Maurice said. "Where was I? Ah, Rachel and her father visiting me in jail, yes. We had our own Bible studies. Even our guard enjoyed hanging out with us and studying the Word. Oh, I can still hear the laughter we often shared during our Bible studies. I felt a little more courage every day. Then, sometime in 2014, I was finally ready. And I told Logan that I was ready. Logan and Rachel led me to accept Jesus Christ."

Kennedy's smile became an awed grin. Maurice's eyes filled with more joy and sincerity with each word he spoke.

"It didn't end there. My testimony inspired so many of the other prisoners. Including Barney. And then, due to good behavior, my jail sentence was shortened. It had already been a fairly short sentence since I had turned myself in in the first place. I got out of jail in the summer of 2016. Logan helped me find a job and a nice apartment in Prescott. I didn't need help finding a church. I had chosen his church long before I got out of prison."

His eyes met Kennedy's once again. "Your letter was the first seed to be planted in my heart," he said. "Then Logan came. I had more seeds planted. And our numerous Bible studies made for excellent watering and care of those seeds. And then God gave the growth. I thank Him and praise him so much for that."

Tears stung Kennedy's eyes. How could she have not seen the change in Maurice sooner? It was obvious now that there was no way he had joined back up with Horace Cobb and his new gang. After everything she had seen, how could she have thought such things? Why, Maurice had donated part of his liver to Isaiah. If that wasn't proof enough of his changed heart, then nothing was. What was left of her anger was replaced by embarrassment; after all, she had falsely accused Maurice of treachery in front of Billy and the others.

"Oh, Maurice," Kennedy said, "I'm sorry. I shouldn't have accused you of leading those crooks all over the place."

"It's alright, honey. You were just in a panic. And honestly, I can't blame you for having those kinds of thoughts. I forgive you."

Maurice's words and warm smile soothed Kennedy.

BANG!

Screams. A blowout. Kennedy thought her eardrums burst. Horror washed away all soothed feelings.

"Don't look now!" Rachel said. "But we've got company!"

Kennedy looked over her shoulder. A red pickup tailgated them. Maverick hung out of a window, pointing a gun forward.

Ruben and Winifred sat in the driver and passenger seats.

"Mom must be in that truck!" Kennedy exclaimed.

"Those crooks gave me a couple of flat tires!" Billy said. He swerved the truck onto another road and drove under a large sign. "But we're at Old Dodge Park. We'll have to try taking cover here!"

"Are you crazy?" Rachel shouted.

"Don't worry, we just might outnumber them!" Maurice said. "Look ahead, everyone!"

Kennedy turned her gaze to the windshield. Much to her surprise, she saw two other pickups pulling in front of them. Gunnar and Alec sat in the driver and passenger seats of one pickup. Wesley was driving the other.

The three trucks met in the parking lot. Kennedy jumped out. She stared in shock when she saw Darcy, Victoria, Jessica, Aaron, and Sierra get out of Wesley's truck.

"What are you guys doing?" she demanded. "I thought you were with Aunt Thelma!"

"We met the ambulance for Jonathon," Victoria said. "Aunt Thelma wanted Gunnar and Aaron to take us girls away while she tries to contact Robert."

She heaved a big breath. "We know about Mom," she said, her voice breaking.

"Oh, Kenny," Jessica wailed, "what are we going to do? How can we help Mom?"

"No time for chitchat!" Maurice said. "We all need to stay together! Come on, everyone into the park!"

"Follow me!" Kennedy said. "I know where we can find a bunch of weapons!"

She led everyone to the Wild Western town. They ran past the horse stables. Kennedy paused for a split second; she knew that Sunshine was in one of those stalls.

The group ducked into the alley near the saloon. Luckily the back door was unlocked. Maurice herded everyone inside, then he locked the door behind him.

"Alright, Sis!" Victoria said. "Show us the weapons!"

Kennedy and Billy had everybody gather around the boxes and shelves. Each person grabbed a weapon. Kennedy slung a bow over her shoulder and attached a quiver of arrows to her belt. She also picked up a holster for a gun.

"I don't think we've got much in the line of actual bullets," Darcy said. She finished attaching a silencer onto her gun. "Most of these cartridges are filled with blanks."

"We'll just have to make do with what we've got," Susannah said. "Even if we shoot blanks, we might be able to fool those crooks into thinking we're armed."

"Smart thinking," Maurice said. "Alrighty, here's what we'll do: the guys and I will take the front lines. You ladies stay back here and guard Felicity. She's in no condition to fight. Just make sure that she at least has a loaded gun on her person."

Felicity raised her hand to show off her pistol. Kennedy's wide, anxious eyes flitted from Maurice to Billy. "But I want to be next to you guys," she said.

"You're their primary target," Maurice said. "I'm not letting you in their sight."

"Yeah, Ken," Billy said, "please, stay and protect my sister. She needs you more than me and the guys do."

Kennedy couldn't miss the pleading look that filled Billy's eyes. She nodded. "Alright."

"And someone needs to call Robert!" Wesley said.

Sierra whipped out her cell phone and began dialing.

CRASH!

Kennedy whirled around. She felt all color drain from her face. Felicity lay flat on her side on the floor, having apparently tripped over a box and knocked over a vase, its flowers and water spilled on the floor.

"Fel!" Billy exclaimed. "Are you alright?"

He kneeled by his sister and grabbed her hand. But Felicity struggled to even sit up. Kennedy felt sick; was she okay? And was the baby in her big belly okay?

Felicity moaned. "Billy," she murmured.

Kennedy ran to Felicity's side and slipped her hand under her arm. She and Billy raised Felicity onto her feet. It was then that Kennedy saw the clear water dripping down Felicity's legs and onto the floor.

She gasped.

Felicity let out a sudden wail. She clutched her belly.

"What's wrong?" Tiana exclaimed.

"That fall broke my water!" Felicity said. She released an agonized yell. "My baby . . . she's coming!"

Chapter Twelve

Shootout at the Fort

KENNEDY FELT LIKE she was going to faint. And she had no doubt that Felicity felt like fainting too. Why, judging by the horrified looks that filled each and every eye, everyone probably felt like fainting!

"Of all the rotten timing!" Victoria said.

"I'll say!" Wesley said. "Billy, why did your sister have to go into labor at the worst possible moment?"

"Dude, seriously?" Billy retorted. "Come on, the lot of you, lend me and my sis some helping hands!"

Wesley and Aaron ran out to the hallway and pushed a cushioned chair into the room. Billy and Kennedy eased Felicity to it. She plopped down with a moan. Tiana and Susannah grabbed a few cloaks from the costume shelf and threw them over Felicity.

"My battle plan still stands," Maurice said. "It's imperative that you ladies shield Felicity now."

"Good luck, guys!" Rachel said.

Kennedy gazed after Billy and Maurice as they led Aaron, Gunnar, Wesley, and Alec out of the room. Maurice wasn't in any better condition to fight than Felicity. And six against ten? What odds did her friends have?

Felicity's pained groaning snapped her back to reality.

"Jess, you're the science queen," Victoria said. "What do we have to do?"

Jessica kneeled by the couch and held Felicity's hand. "Uh, Felicity, just breathe," she said.

"I'm breathing!" Felicity wheezed.

"And try not to scream too loud," Rachel said. "We don't wanna alert our favorite felons to our spot."

"It's lucky we're all back together, eh?" Victoria said.

"Lucky?" Kennedy said. "Lucky! We're surrounded by those crooks. How did every one of you end up at the entrance to Old Dodge Park anyway?"

"Like we said earlier," Darcy said, "we met the ambulance on the road. Our trucks had been staying close together since we left the church. Anyway, Pastor Logan and my dad went with your aunt and uncle to the hospital with Jonathon. Gunnar, Aaron, and Wesley said that they would get us girls away. Then we met a few of those thugs on the road. We ended up here where you and your crew so happened to be at. Like your sister said, lucky."

Darcy leaned forward. Her voice dropped to a whisper. "I'm afraid to say that Jonathon's in a pretty serious condition."

Kennedy nodded glumly. She gave Felicity a sympathetic look. Would the baby get a chance to meet her father?

"And what about Maurice?" Darcy said. "Everywhere he is, the criminals show up. Are they really just following him?"

"Hey," Kennedy said defensively, "I had those thoughts too. But I know now that he's truly on our side."

She smiled a little. There was not a shred of doubt in her mind as to where Maurice's loyalties lay.

"Alrighty, Ken," Darcy said, "if you trust him, then I reckon the rest of us should too."

A thud from the hallway made Kennedy spin around. She gawked at the door, as though it might burst open with unpleasant and unwelcome visitors. The only move Kennedy could make was lifting her pistol.

"Incoming!" Susannah hissed.

Sure enough, Kennedy's fear came true. Screams filled the room as Abner Munoz barged in. He pointed his gun at the girls. Rachel jumped in front of all the girls and held up her own pistol.

"Don't come any closer!" she yelled. "Or I'll shoot!"

"Oh, please, please hurry!" Sierra yelled into her phone. "We were just found by one of the criminals! You must—hello, are you still there?"

Sierra gaped at her phone as if it had suddenly caught fire. Kennedy's stomach flipped. What happened now?

Abner's sneer added an extra layer of ugly to his face. From her peripheral vision, Kennedy saw Tiana's face go pale. Jessica had to grab her shoulders to steady her.

"I ain't afraid of a bunch of young ladies," Abner said. He turned his sneer to Felicity. Kennedy winced when she saw the evil twinkle in his cold eyes.

"What have we here?" he said slyly. He twirled his gun in his hand. "A pregnant woman in labor? Now that's what I call an added bonus to a room of cowgirl hostages."

"Don't go anywhere near her," Kennedy snapped. "Tell me what Ruben and Winifred have done with my mother!"

"Yeah!" Victoria said. "Speak up, bucko!"

Abner rolled his eyes. "Your mother is fine," he said. "They haven't harmed a hair on her pretty little head. She's just another hostage for us. Now do step aside, ladies, and y'all better stick your dainty little hands in the air."

He took a step toward Felicity. He clicked his gun. Felicity screamed. "Get away from me!"

Kennedy's arm shot up.

BANG!

More screams. A startled yell from Abner. But no blood on his skin. It wasn't even his gun that had been fired. Kennedy was holding up her own gun, having left a bullet-sized hole in the wall.

"Get out!" she shouted. "Or my next bullet won't miss!"

Abner lunged at Kennedy. But she whacked him across the head with her gun. Abner fell at her feet. Kennedy backed off. But the former cattle rustler was only dazed. He turned and began to crawl toward Felicity. Kennedy snatched a sword and hit Abner's head with the hilt. Abner fell limp onto the floor.

"Whoa!" Tiana exclaimed. "Nice one!"

Kennedy nodded at Felicity. Her gaze was filled with relief and gratitude.

"Sierra," Rachel said, "what happened with the phone call?"

"Robert was cut off," Sierra said. "I heard him screaming on his line. He may have been attacked by one of those goons!"

"Drat! That's bad. What did he say before he was cut off?"

"He did say that help's on the way."

"We should still move," Kennedy said. "Just in case any of those other crooks come along."

"Can Felicity move?" Marilyn asked.

"I think so," Jessica said. "She hasn't been in labor for long."

She and Victoria took Felicity's hands and gently raised her to her feet. As soon as everyone left the room, Kennedy shut the door. The girls took Felicity down the hall. They came to a wider dressing room. Victoria and Jessica had Felicity sit on the sofa. Susannah and Rachel pushed a desk in front of the door.

"Now we must really be quiet," Rachel said.

Kennedy's mind refused to be quiet. Yes, Sierra did say that help was on its way. But would it get here soon enough for Felicity? What if more of the criminals came their way?

Kennedy thought back to Maurice's words. She was their primary target.

Maybe if she left, the criminals might be too distracted chasing her, thus leaving Felicity alone.

Kennedy pushed the desk away from the door.

"Hey!" Susannah said. "What are you doing?"

"I'm going to keep every one of those scoundrels away from Felicity," Kennedy said.

"But those scoundrels are after you!"

"Exactly." Kennedy looked at the other girls. "The guys are outnumbered. We may have dealt with Abner and one of the thugs may be tackling Robert, but that still leaves eight more of them. And who's to say that Abner hasn't recovered and is looking for us? The rest of you stay with Felicity."

"No!" Victoria said. She stomped right up to her sister. "I'm going with you."

"And so am I!" Marilyn said.

"Ditto!" Rachel said.

"It's too dangerous!" Kennedy said.

"Try stopping me and your sisters."

"And what about Felicity? She needs all the protection she can get!"

Marilyn glanced in Felicity's direction. "We truly do care about her and her baby," she said. "But you need protection too. If Abner is looking for us and he sees you out in the hall—"

"Then I can lead him away from Felicity."

"No, *we* will lead him away from Felicity."

Kennedy sighed. She turned her gaze to Jessica, Susannah, Darcy, Sierra, and Tiana. "The rest of you stay here with Felicity and keep her safe," she said. "As soon as we leave, put the desk back in front of the door. And don't move it unless it's one of us. Call any of us if you have any problems."

Kennedy inched the door open. The door's creaking made too much noise for her. She peeked out into the hall. It was empty. She signaled to Victoria, Marilyn, and Rachel to follow her. As soon as Kennedy closed the door, she heard the sounds of a lock clicking and the desk being pushed back.

The four girls tiptoed as fast as they could. Kennedy was almost sure that they would bump into Abner. Every creak made by the girls' footsteps almost sounded like Abner coming down the hall. Kennedy stopped at one corner to peek around. Seeing that the coast was still clear, she led the girls onward. They came to a pair of double doors. Kennedy opened the right door and peeked in at a backstage area.

Then Victoria threw her finger onto her lips. The four girls froze. Kennedy heard heavy footsteps echoing from the hall behind them. Somehow, she was able to keep her shaky breathing silent.

"Hello, girlies."

That simple whisper was enough to make Kennedy scream and spin around. Her stomach dropped. Abner stood at the end of the hall.

Victoria grabbed a vase from a niche in the wall and threw it at Abner. He ducked. The vase flew over his head and clattered on the floor behind him.

"You missed me!"

Victoria grabbed a picture frame and threw it. Once again, Abner ducked. But he had just stood back up when Rachel threw another frame at him. And that frame hit him right in his face and knocked him off his feet.

"Hurry, get in here!" Kennedy said. She and the other girls rushed through the door. Kennedy made an attempt to slam it shut, but Abner bashed himself against the door just as Kennedy heard the doorknob click. Even so, she felt Abner's grip on the doorknob on the other side. She tightened her own grip on the knob. Victoria ran to her side and threw herself against the door.

"Go, go!" Kennedy said to her sister.

"There's no way you're gonna be able to hold back that thug all by yourself!" Victoria said.

Kennedy pushed her sister away. "Just trust me!" she said. "Now go, hide!"

Victoria, Marilyn, and Rachel ran past the crimson curtain onto the stage. Kennedy let Abner shove the door open against her. Then she whacked his head with the butt of her gun. Abner let out a loud groan and fell flat on his stomach. He still groaned a little as Kennedy darted past him.

"Guys!" she hissed as she ran onstage. "Get down!"

Victoria crawled into a trunk. Rachel jumped off the stage and ducked behind the bar. Kennedy and Marilyn hid behind the piano.

Abner's footsteps, still heavy but now awkward as though he was stumbling, echoed across the stage. Kennedy held in a shaky breath. She felt like she was in some sort of action chase scene in a

Western play in this saloon. If only this moment was simply a play! She only hoped that Abner would not look behind the piano. She and Marilyn should've chosen a better hiding place!

Abner moaned in pain. Peeking out from behind the piano, Kennedy saw him rub his head. He stumbled to the steps. For a split second, Kennedy thought he was going to fall down. But he just wobbled off the stage and to the front door, still rubbing his head. He slammed the door behind him. After a moment of tense silence, Kennedy, Victoria, and Marilyn came out of hiding.

"You must've done a number on him, Ken," Victoria said in a hushed voice. "Didn't even bother to look for us."

"Yeah, and I'm glad for that," Kennedy said.

"Where's Rachel?" Marilyn asked.

"Over here!"

Kennedy saw Rachel running out from behind the bar. She was holding a butcher knife and a rolling pin.

"Uh, what are those for?" Victoria asked.

Rachel smiled sheepishly. "Who says a few more weapons won't be handy?"

"But you've got a gun in your holster."

"I know, but I wanna be extra prepared."

"Well, the butcher knife I understand," Marilyn said, "but the rolling pin?"

"Uh, yeah," Rachel said, waving the pin in her hand, "have any of you guys watched any TV at all? These bad boys make great weapons."

Marilyn took the rolling pin from Rachel's hand and stared at it. She tapped it against her palm a few times. "Alright, I think I see what you mean."

"Alright, we've got extra weapons," Victoria said. "Let's just get out of here before Abner decides to come back."

The girls walked toward the front entrance. Even though Abner wasn't in the building anymore, Kennedy still felt that the cacophony of footsteps was way too loud. She stopped and turned around, her eyeballs glazing over the saloon's dining area. Not a sound made her jump. She then tiptoed to the window and peeked out.

"I don't see Abner anywhere," she said. "We need to get out of here before he does come back. Or any of those other goons, for that matter."

The girls rushed out of the saloon and ducked behind the railing of the porch. Kennedy scanned the town for Abner. He was nowhere in sight. Just up ahead, Kennedy saw the Wild Western fort. And standing right at the top of that fort were Maurice and Billy, their rifles aimed out at the open air.

"Let's go!" Kennedy said. She, Victoria, Marilyn, and Rachel ran off the porch and made their way toward the fort.

"There she is!"

Kennedy gulped at the sound of Horace's voice. She forced her legs to run faster. In seconds the four girls were approaching the front doors of the fort. Kennedy waved up at Maurice and Billy. Even from way below, she saw their astonished faces.

"What are you doing?" Billy shouted.

"Coming in and joining the battle!" Kennedy shouted back. She opened the door of the fort and ran inside, the other girls close on her heels. Marilyn and Rachel slammed the doors shut. Maurice and Billy ran down the stairs to the ground. Wesley, Aaron, Gunnar, and Alec surrounded them.

"You girls should be back at the saloon with my sister and the others!" Billy said.

"Where are the others?" Maurice demanded.

"They're still at the saloon," Kennedy said. "We had two run-ins with Abner there. After the first one I figured that I should get away from Felicity and make sure our enemies leave her be."

"By keeping them distracted with you?" Gunnar said.

BANG!

Marilyn let out a shriek. All eyes turned toward the doors.

"Alright, let's not waste more time arguing," Maurice said. "They're coming back for another attack. You girls stay close to us."

Maurice led everyone to the stairs. His increasingly heavy breathing with every stair he took didn't escape Kennedy's notice. Color drained from his face with every wheeze he gasped. But he still took his position on the watchtower.

Kennedy stood next to Billy. He gave her an encouraging smile, which Kennedy returned. At least she was fighting with him by her side. Her eyes wandered to the town. What a magnificent view she had from up here near the top of the fort. She could see the entire little Western town, the miniature golf course, the outdoor swimming pool, everything. From almost every direction, the bluffs loomed over all of Old Dodge Park itself. Why couldn't

Kennedy simply be enjoying this beautiful view with Billy, and not battling her old enemies?

"Here they come!" Marilyn said in a hushed voice.

Kennedy's eyes floated down to the ten familiar figures marching toward the fort. Horace was in the lead. Abner was right behind him, walking next to Grey. Kennedy let out a sigh of relief. At least Felicity and the other girls were safe.

She wiped sweat from her forehead. Was it nerves or the unbearable afternoon heat making her sweat? Maybe both. She had to be in a much hotter situation than any summer afternoon in the desert could beat down upon her.

Her eyes wandered to Ruben and Winifred. The criminal couple. The woman who had once kidnapped her. Now she and her ruthless husband had kidnapped her mother. Her fear skyrocketed just glaring at them. If they were here, then where was her mother? Was she okay? Surely she wasn't lying somewhere dead, was she? And was Robert okay, wherever he was? If he was hurt, who would come to their aid?

"RYAN!"

Kennedy felt like her every muscle locked into their tensest mode. She glared down at Horace and pointed her gun at him.

"I'm right up here!" she yelled.

Horace sneered up at her. He put his hands on his hips.

"Think you're safe in that nice big fort?" he said.

"Where is my mother?" Kennedy shouted. "What have you done with her?"

"Yeah, fess up, you creep!" Victoria added.

"Hey, hey, hey, just calm down, girls!" Horace said, raising his hands. "Your dear mother is just fine. Other than terrified, of course. Well, more for you than for herself. But, my dear Kennedy, can we not talk negotiations? Perhaps I'll tell Ruben and Winifred to release your mother and bring her here if you agree to cooperate with me."

"Hey, you're not fooling anybody!" Billy screamed. "You are not taking Kennedy! You'll have to go through me first!"

Horace's sneer turned into an ugly glare. He whipped out his gun and fired. Kennedy screamed and ducked, her arms around her head. She smelled a faint whiff of burnt smoke just above the spot where she lay rolled up.

"That was a warning shot!" Horace said. "The lot of you are surrounded! Give yourselves up, or else it won't be the fort that gets the next bullet!"

Maurice responded with his own gunshot. The criminals let out a cacophony of yells and hit the ground. But none of them looked like they had been hit. Horace jumped to his feet. He gave Maurice a menacing glare, then he spun around to face the other criminals.

"Give them the fight of their lives!" he shouted. "But bring Kennedy Ryan to me!"

The criminals raced toward the fort, and Kennedy heard them pounding against the doors. Maurice and Alec led Billy, Wesley, Gunnar, and Aaron down to the ground. Kennedy took a step toward the stairs, hands clenching her weapons. But Marilyn grabbed her arm and pulled her back.

"What the heck are you doing?" she said. "You heard what Horace said! You're safer up here!"

"But they'll be outnumbered!" Kennedy said. "Without us, it's six to ten! But with us, it's ten to ten!"

She tore her arm from Marilyn's grasp. Victoria and Rachel were already flying down the stairs. Kennedy was not far behind them. And Marilyn was right behind her.

Just as the girls reached the ground, the doors of the fort burst open. The criminals flooded in. Maurice stood in front of his group, his arms wide. He pointed his rifle at Horace, who in turn was pointing his gun at him.

"The lot of you will pay for everything you've done to us," the former bank robber said.

"Oh, so it's not just Kennedy?" Maurice said. "Figures. She had a lot of help."

"Oh, she was the ringleader all those times before. So she's still our number one target. Surrender her. Now."

"Never!"

Maurice fired. Grey let out a sudden yell and dropped to his knees, gripping his arm, blood dripping onto the sand. Octavia looked away, her face pale.

"My patience is running low!" Horace seethed. "And so are your chances! Hand Kennedy over to me now or else I'm sending a volunteer shooter here to blow her mother's brains out!"

Kennedy's heart nearly stopped beating. She had to get to her mother! And, based on what Horace just said, was she nearby?

"Then I'll fire at your volunteer shooter before he can even run two feet from this fort!" Maurice said. "He'll never get a chance to get close enough to Caitlin!"

"Yeah, none of you are getting away from us that easy!" Aaron added.

"So be it!" Horace said.

He fired. So did Maurice. Then he charged at the gangsters. Alec, Billy, Aaron, Wesley, and Gunnar were charging right behind him. Victoria let out a screech and rushed after Winifred. Kennedy ran after her sister. Winifred raised her gun to at Victoria. Victoria kicked the gun out of Winifred's hand. Winifred yelped, grasping her hand. Kennedy snatched up Winifred's gun.

"That's for kidnapping my mom!" Victoria said. "And also for kidnapping my sister months ago!"

Winifred lunged at Victoria. Kennedy sprung at Winifred and whacked her neck with the gun. Winifred turned her attack to Kennedy. She threw out her fist. Kennedy grabbed that flying fist and twisted Winifred's wrist, causing her to fall to her knees, yelling in pain.

"You made a horrible mistake!" Victoria said triumphantly. "Kidnapping Kung Fu Kennedy!"

Kennedy kicked Winifred's side, further knocking her over. Then she pulled Victoria away. She saw Rachel and Marilyn fighting Octavia. Octavia tried to hit Rachel in the face, but Rachel conked her head with the rolling pin. Octavia squatted, grasping her head, giving Marilyn the chance to tackle her to the ground.

"Come on, Ken," Victoria said, "what are we doing standing around while our friends are fighting?"

"I don't see Ruben anywhere," Kennedy said.

"So what? One less guy for us to tackle."

"No, Victoria!" Kennedy said fiercely. "Horace said that if I didn't surrender, he'd send someone after Mom. So what if he's already sent one of these thugs out of the fort? Like Ruben?"

Victoria's face turned white. Her wide eyes darted over to the fighters.

"We need to find Ruben and follow him," Kennedy said. "If we do that, we'll find out where Mom's being held. Then we can try to save her."

"We won't try," Victoria said. "We will save her. Come on!"

Everyone was probably too occupied with their fighting to notice the two sisters sneaking out of the fort. Kennedy didn't even shut the door behind her.

"Kenny," Victoria said, "how will we find Ruben and get to Mom on time?"

Kennedy's eyes fell upon the nearby horse stable. "We ride. Come on!"

The girls ran to the stable. Despite the fear churning in her stomach, Kennedy grinned when she came across Sunshine's stall. The golden palomino mare nickered with happy recognition.

"Sunshine!" Kennedy ran her hand over the mare's nose. "I need your help!"

She entered the stall and grabbed a curry comb hanging on the wall. She only gave Sunshine a few quick brushes; time was of the essence, after all.

"I got saddles!"

Kennedy peeked out of the stall. Victoria was running over, carrying two saddles and blankets. She dumped them in front of the stall. Kennedy grabbed one saddle and blanket. She threw the blanket over Sunshine, then she hooked the saddle on and attached her bow and quiver of arrows. She threw herself onto the mare's back and rode out of the stall. Victoria met her in the middle of the long row of stalls, riding a black-and-white horse. The two sisters rode out of the stable.

"I hope we didn't waste too much time," Victoria said.

"Me too!" Kennedy said. "Hey, look, there he is!"

She pointed. Just beyond the low wooden fence, Ruben was racing across the asphalt road and toward a tall wooden signpost that led out of the Western town. He looked over his shoulder, then suddenly picked up his pace. Kennedy and Victoria took off after him. Their horses jumped over the fence. Despite the advantage of riding horses, the girls did not catch up with the speedy Ruben. He had already run through the exit and was scrambling up a hill.

"We can't lose him!" Victoria said.

"And we won't!" Kennedy said. She goaded Sunshine into a faster run. With each step Sunshine took, Kennedy felt like her heart was on fire, a fire hotter than the afternoon sun beating down on her head. She lost her father years ago. She may or may not lose her stepfather. But she was not going to lose her mother!

The two horses scampered up the hill. Ruben stopped at the top of the hill and pointed his gun at them. Kennedy whipped out her own gun. She and Ruben fired at the same moment. Two misses. Kennedy and Victoria had to soothe their frightened horses. Meanwhile, Ruben disappeared over the hill. Kennedy and Victoria rode up the hill. The sisters grinned.

A truck sat on a dirt road near the bottom of the hill. And Mom was sitting in the passenger seat of that truck.

Ruben walked toward the truck, his gun still in his hand. Victoria pulled her own gun out of her holster. Then her horse sped down toward Ruben.

"Vic!" Kennedy yelled.

Ruben spun around. Before he could react, Victoria rode past him and whacked his head with the butt of her gun. He fell to the ground.

Kennedy rushed Sunshine down the hill. "Vic!" she said. "I say, that was really good!"

Victoria grinned and twirled her gun in her hand. "A girl's gotta do what a girl's gotta do. Now come on, let's get Mom out of that truck. I'm sure it's awfully hot in there."

Victoria slid off her horse and dug her fingers through Ruben's pockets. She pulled out some keys and ran around to the other side of the truck. Kennedy turned Sunshine so that she was facing the truck. She smiled back at her mother's relieved and joyful smile. Mom raised her left hand in a happy wave. Her right hand was raised up, handcuffed to the handle just above the passenger door. Kennedy was more than ready to remove those handcuffs from her mother's wrist and wipe the tears from her eyes.

BANG!

The windshield shattered. Kennedy and Victoria screamed. Kennedy looked down at Ruben; he was still unconscious.

"Kennedy!" Victoria said. "Gang leader at twelve o'clock!"

Kennedy's head whipped up at the hill. She felt like she was going to faint right off of Sunshine's back.

Horace was riding a black horse down the hill.

Kennedy pointed her gun at him. "Stay back!"

Horace just laughed. "Have you finally accepted my terms, Miss Kennedy?" he asked coolly.

"Maybe," Kennedy said in a hard voice.

"Maybe?" Horace said. "What's that supposed to mean?"

Kennedy heard a car door shut. She saw Victoria crawling in the back seat of the truck. Horace spun around. He let out an enraged yell and tried to open the driver's side. But it was locked.

"You can't get them now!" Kennedy said. "But you can try to get me!"

And with those words she turned her horse around and rode off.

Chapter Thirteen

A Harrowing Horse Ride

SUNSHINE CANTERED UP the hill. The green brushes rustled and snapped under the beating of her hooves, as if the ground itself understood the urgency of the situation. Kennedy squinted at the rays of the late afternoon sun. The last thing she needed was for the sun to blind her.

She glanced over her shoulder. Horace was riding after her. Kennedy goaded Sunshine into a faster run. She tightened her grip on the reins despite her sweaty palms. She wiped her palms on her jeans, but it did little good; her jeans were damp too.

She looked back again. Horace was closer than he had been just a minute ago. Kennedy whipped out her gun and pointed it upward. She fired one shot. She smiled when she heard Horace's startled yell. He seemed to be slowing down.

Kennedy steered Sunshine down into a canyon. The rock walls towered over her, casting shadows on the sandy orange floor. A wind rushed through the canyon, adding its eerie howls to the eerie shadows. The canyon went deeper. And darker under those shadows. And yet, despite the shadows and the wind, Kennedy still felt beads of sweat soaking her curls and sliding down her face. She coughed as dust rose from beneath hooves. Dust and specks of dirt clung to her dry, cracked lips. Dirt tickled her nose, making her want to sneeze. Her sweat mixed with the dirt on her cheeks. She spat onto the ground to rid herself of the taste of mud grinding on her teeth. She licked her lips. The tip of her tongue captured a drop of salty moisture.

The wind whipped her hair, throwing curly strands in front of her face. The wind also whipped the sagebrush and grass on the ground, as if making the vegetation goad her into riding faster. Kennedy's mouth felt drier than the desert around her. She smacked her lips, but it brought little relief. Her mouth evaporated again. Her throat was sore from the parching dryness. Was that a hint of nausea that just passed through her head? The heat must be getting to her. She couldn't be getting lightheaded right now! She breathed deeply. Sheer determination forced her to ignore the dizzy spells and push forward. Her hands, still slippery with sweat, shook with the desire to loosen their grips on the reins. Then her foot nearly slipped out of the stirrup. Kennedy slid her foot back in and tensed the muscles in that foot to keep it in. Her toes tingled.

A tumbleweed bounced past, as though it was racing the wind and horse. But it didn't get far; the tumbleweed got caught on a small cactus. Even the wind wasn't able to free it from its spiky prison.

The shadows did little to relieve her from the scorching heat. Her deep breathing became panting. Kennedy looked up and narrowed her eyes at the random reflection in the near distance. It looked like water. Could it be water? No, of course not. She had been to this area before. Everyone in Pine Lodge knew that there was no water in this spot in the bluffs. And as her horse drew closer to that spot, the reflection dissipated like sand in the wind. A simple mirage, just as she had suspected. She still wished for water.

The only thing more unbearable than this heat was her dire situation.

BANG!

Kennedy screamed despite her parched throat. Sunshine let out a frightened whinny and picked up her pace. Kennedy took another look over her shoulder. Horace was once again in sight. But this time he wasn't alone. Ruben, Winifred, and Ernesto were riding behind him on their own horses. Just that sight alone was enough to turn Kennedy's nausea up a few notches.

"Come on, Sunshine!" she said. "Faster!"

She patted Sunshine's neck. She guessed that her mare was every bit as thirsty as she was. Maybe even tired. The mare was the one running, after all. Kennedy couldn't let dehydration take either of them now. Not with four criminals in close pursuit!

But Sunshine picked up her speed. And so did the wind, which felt so good on Kennedy's sweaty face. She then saw the tumbleweed fly past. She had to smile a little bit to see that it had escaped from its cactus captivity and was flying once again in the wind.

Kennedy was riding swiftly on the wings of the wind.

She suddenly felt better. And braver. She looked up at the sky. She believed that God was watching over her and protecting her. And her mother. And Felicity and her baby. And all the rest of her family and friends.

Kennedy reached for her own gun and pointed it back at the criminals. But she wasn't startled by a bang when she pulled the trigger. It was just a measly click that startled her.

She was out of bullets.

Yet a gunshot still pierced the air.

Suddenly Sunshine neighed in fearful agony. She reared up and kicked her front legs.

"Whoa, Sunshine!" Kennedy said.

But Sunshine didn't listen to Kennedy. She glanced over her shoulder. She felt queasy at the sight of blood spilling down the mare's flank. Sunshine reared even higher.

Kennedy lost her grip on the reins and fell backwards. She landed flat on her back. She heard Sunshine whinny in horror, then retreating hoofbeats.

"No!" Kennedy screeched. She jumped to her feet. But the mare was already far ahead, cantering as fast as her pained hump would let her.

Kennedy spun around. Those criminals had the advantage of horses. And she had no bullets left in her gun.

Though, she still had her archery set. It must've fallen off Sunshine's saddle. Surely that had to be better than nothing!

Kennedy tore the bow from her shoulders. She nocked an arrow to the bow. She aimed at the criminals. Breathed deeply, then released the arrow. It flew with the wind toward the four criminals. Winifred screamed and halted her horse. Ruben ducked his head.

"Don't stop, you idiots!" Horace yelled. "You're on horses and she's not! Get her! Don't let her get away!"

Kennedy whirled around and made a dash for it. She raced down the canyon, then she made a sharp turn and began climbing up the rocky wall. She reached the top and ran down the hill as fast as her legs would carry her. Her heart walloped her chest; it may have been beating even faster than she was running.

She ducked behind a huge boulder under a cottonwood tree. Kennedy nocked an arrow to her bow, then she peeked over the boulder. She saw Silver River flow through the area and meeting up with Yavapai Creek.

Her heart sank.

She recognized the area before her. It was the exact same area where she had first seen Horace Cobb and his old gang. It was this area where Kennedy, Billy, and Susannah had first spied on Maurice's meeting with that gang.

It was the place where it had all began.

"There she is!"

Kennedy shrieked as she swung around. She shrieked again when she saw Horace and Ernesto running toward her. She leapt to her feet. But Horace and Ernesto reached her before she could even run one step. Horace grabbed her arms and yanked her backwards. In mere seconds he ripped the bow from her hands and took out every arrow from the quiver and tossed them away. He wrapped one arm around her waist and clamped his hand over her mouth. She tried to pry his hand away, but Ernesto snatched her arm. His grip hurt her wrist.

Ernesto sneered as he pushed his gun against her neck. "So you thought you could get away from us, eh?" he said. "You escaped from me and my gang once. But you won't this time."

"Indeed," Horace said. His voice shook with gloating glee. "Nothing will keep me from my revenge against you, Miss Kennedy, I intend to make sure of that. Now, Ernesto, you do the honors and bind her."

Kennedy whimpered when she saw Ernesto reach for a roll of duct tape and a coil of rope attached to his belt. No, not again! She struggled in vain. Horace held her still while Ernesto tied her wrists together in front of her and slapped a piece of tape over her mouth. Then the two men dragged her down the hill.

It happened again. She was a captive once again. And her horror only increased when she saw Winifred and Ruben leading the horses along the edge of the creek. The criminal couple greeted Kennedy with cruel smirks.

"We must have a record," Winifred said coolly. She tickled Kennedy's chin and toyed with her curls. "Kidnapping you twice? I must say I'm proud of me and my team."

Hot tears stung Kennedy's eyes and slid down her cheeks alongside the sweat.

"Alright," Horace said, "enough dillydallying. I've waited a long time for this moment."

He closed his eyes and took a deep breath. His lips curled into a sneer as he opened his eyes back up. Those beady eyes made Kennedy feel like a helpless mouse cornered by an enormous hawk.

"Now you will pay for all that you have done to me in the past," he said.

He raised his gun. It clicked. Kennedy shut her eyes.

BANG!

Kennedy barely heard her own weak whimper. Winifred's screech pierced the air as she fell to her knees.

"Winnie!" Ruben yelled. He dropped his gun and ran to his wife. She grasped her bleeding arm.

Kennedy would've gasped if she could have. That gunshot couldn't have come from Horace's gun!

"LET HER GO!"

Horace turned around, still clutching Kennedy. Her eyes shot up in astonishment when she saw Maurice standing on a low ledge, his gun straight on Horace.

"Let her go," Maurice seethed, "or my next bullet will not miss your thick skull!"

Horace's glare could've been a bullet itself. "Like I'm gonna throw away my chance for revenge!" he shouted. He sneered again. "But I'm glad you got here. You're just in time. I did want you to see your dear, precious Kennedy receive her punishment from me, old friend."

Kennedy heard two guns click. Her heart was hammering so much against her chest that it might've been shooting off its own bullets. From her peripheral vision, she saw Ruben carry Winifred away toward the horses. The couple got on one horse. Ruben rode away, leading the other horses. Oh, if only Kennedy and Maurice were able to grab two of those horses and flee themselves!

"Come on!" Horace shoved his gun against Kennedy's head. "I ain't got all day! Drop your gun, buster! Or your charming young cowgirl gets it!"

"Yeah!" Ernesto said. "Come on, Carr! You're outnumbered and you know it! We'll give you only ten seconds to drop your gun before Horace shoots the girl!"

Maurice's glare didn't lower, but he did lower his gun. He sighed, then he threw it to the side.

"Alright!" Maurice lifted his hands. "I did what you wanted me to do! Now let Kennedy go!"

Horace's only response was a smirk. "My old pal Maurice," he said. "you've always been so complacent under my command. Like when we first teamed up, remember? Oh, yes. You were more than happy to follow any order I gave you. As long as you got what you wanted. I miss the old Maurice Carr."

"That was then," Maurice said. "This is now. Like I told you the day you and Ernesto abducted me, I'm redeemed. I am not that man anymore! Now release Kennedy!"

Horace's glare returned. He threw Kennedy to the side. She flopped on the ground by a large boulder. She scooted herself up. Ernesto and Horace walked closer to the ledge on which Maurice stood, but Kennedy couldn't fail to notice that Horace still had his gun pointed back at her.

"No," he said. "No, you're not that man anymore. Pity. You would've made a fine criminal. I would've been proud to have called you one of my gang members."

"But now you are soft!" Ernesto said. "And still complacent. You dropped your only ammunition for this young lady you adore."

"Exactly!" Horace said. "But I still want my revenge. Against Kennedy. And against you!"

Kennedy squeezed her eyes shut. But the tears of fear were too strong for that.

"Psst!"

Kennedy whipped her head around. Relief overcame nearly all of her fear.

Billy was squatting next to the rock, his finger upon his lips and his other hand gripping a gun. Kennedy eyed the two criminals. Luckily, they were still distracted with Maurice. But now, Kennedy could see a glint of hope in Maurice's eyes. And that glint met her eyes. She turned her watery eyes back to Billy. He was still smiling at her as he slowly reached his hand out to her.

"Hey!"

Kennedy whirled her head back around. She whimpered. Horace and Ernesto had their guns fixed on her and Billy now.

"What do you think you're doing, boy?" Horace said. "Oh, I see, you're the brave cowboy rescuing the damsel in distress. Well, not on my watch!"

Billy's battle cry was louder than the shot that rang from his gun. Horace dropped his own gun, howling as blood spurted from his hand. Ernesto had jumped back.

"Cobb!" he said urgently.

"It's just my hand," Horace said, but his voice was shaking with agony.

"Just your hand!" Ernesto said.

"And maybe it won't just his hand a minute from now!"

Ernesto spun around. The duct tape over her mouth barely stopped Kennedy from smiling. Maurice's gun was once again in his hand.

Come on, Horace," Ernest said, "we gotta get out of here!"

"NO!" Horace roared. "I am so close to my revenge!"

He stretched out his good hand, attempting to reach his gun on the ground. But Ernesto dragged him away in the direction Ruben and Winifred had gone. Horace was kicking and screaming while Ernesto dragged him into the thin forest.

Maurice stared at the trees for a moment. Then he waved at Billy and disappeared from the ledge. Billy scooted in front of Kennedy and grabbed her shoulders. He pulled her forward. His hands went up to her cheeks. Just feeling his hands made Kennedy's cheeks warmer. Billy removed one hand to peel the tape from her mouth. His other hand remained on her cheek.

"Kennedy," he said. "Are you alright?"

Kennedy's parched and sore throat was too tight to speak. Tears streamed down her cheeks as she nodded. She gazed into Billy's beautiful blue eyes filled with fear and sympathy. Oh, she was worried that she would never see those soft eyes again. She wanted to embrace him. If only her hands weren't bound!

But Billy embraced her. A powerful but gentle wave of solace and safety flooded her entire being and settled her heartbeat. She melted into Billy's comforting embrace.

"Hey, hey, hey. It's okay." Billy's whisper was a soothing enchantment. "You're okay, Kennedy. I'm here, I'm right here. Me and Maurice both. You're safe now."

Kennedy finally managed to control her shaky breathing. A gentle breeze wiggled her curls. Billy let go of her and fingered the ropes around her wrists. "Let's get you untied," he said.

"Y-yes," Kennedy stammered. "Thank you."

Her eyes lowered down onto her wrists. It seemed like she went under a trance just watching Billy toy with those ropes. The touch of his fingertips was such a soft comfort on her wrists. So much better than the tight, scratchy ropes. But even the tightness of the ropes was helpless to hinder the rapid thumping of her pulse.

Billy unraveled the ropes with ease. But whereas the ropes fell off Kennedy's wrists, Billy's fingers remained. Kennedy looked up at him. She didn't break eye contact with him even while she rubbed her fingers over her wrists.

"I'm sorry if I scared the rest of you," she said. "It's just that Victoria and I were just riding out to find Mom."

"I know," Billy said. His fingers began massaging Kennedy's palms. "Aaron had gone after the two of you. He and Victoria saved your mom, and all three of them got back to Old Dodge Park safely.

Victoria told us everything that had happened. Maurice, Aaron, and I came after you on horses. And we found Sunshine. Aaron took her back to the park while Maurice and I searched for you."

His voice began breaking. "Oh, Kenny! I just can't tell you how relieved I am that we found you in time! If you had been hurt or killed . . . I would never have been able to handle that."

He tightened his grip on her hands as he lifted her to her feet. Then he wrapped his arms around her as he pulled her close.

"I am not missing my chance to confess now," he said. "Not after everything that's happened to you. Kennedy . . . I love you."

Kennedy's meek smile became a broad grin. The broadest grin that she probably ever had in her life.

"And I love you," she said.

She didn't stop herself. She couldn't stop herself. She lifted herself up onto her tiptoes and pressed her lips against Billy's. They were every bit as sweet as she always imagined them to be. She felt Billy's lips form a smile against her own.

"Alright you two lovebirds!"

Kennedy broke away from Billy. Maurice was leading two horses toward them. Judging by the knowing grin on his face, he had to have witnessed the kiss between the two of them. Kennedy's cheeks burned. She eyed Billy; she wondered which of the two of them had the redder face.

Maurice's grin didn't falter. He just handed Kennedy's lost bow and bunch of arrows to her. She took them gratefully.

"Gotta hang onto your weapons," Maurice said. "Oh, and I found your empty gun and reloaded it too. Not with many bullets, though. Didn't have a lot on me."

Maurice handed the reins of the sorrel horse over to Billy. "This is a mighty strong gelding," he said. "You and Kenny can ride him back."

"Back?" Kennedy said.

"Yes." Now Maurice's grin went away. "There's still trouble at the park. We're not out of the woods yet."

His smile returned as he wrapped his arm around Kennedy. "But at least Billy and I got you out of your woods."

"Yes," Kennedy said. "Thank you."

"Of course. Now come on, we have no time to lose."

Chapter Fourteen

High Dusk

OLD DODGE PARK was quiet. Eerily quiet, even for a park that wasn't yet open for business. Oh, why this unsettling silence? Why couldn't this current situation be one filled with the excited and happy chatter of tourists exploring this park?

Kennedy sat in front of Billy on the horse, her wistful gaze roaming the park. The sun was just beginning to set in the west. A beautiful dusk was approaching. If only it was a romantic sunset into which Billy and Kennedy were riding!

And even the eerie silence just had to be shattered by a gunshot.

Maurice threw his hand up. Billy's horse stopped. Kennedy raised herself up a little.

"No surprise they're still here," Maurice said darkly. "Let's try to get back to the fort."

The threesome rode through the alleys of the log buildings. Kennedy almost expected another shot to ring through the air. But they made it to the stable with no trouble. Maurice slid off his horse and walked around to Billy's horse. He placed his hands around Kennedy's waist.

"Alright, Kenny," he said, "I'll help you down. Careful now."

Kennedy was sort of reluctant to let Maurice pull her away from Billy. Once she was on her feet, Billy slid off the horse himself. Maurice led the two kids to a back door of the fort. As soon as they walked through, they received what seemed to be a crowd of a welcoming committee. No, more like a joyful mob.

"You guys are back!" Aaron exclaimed. "Man, were the rest of us going beside ourselves with paranoia!"

"Aaron!" Kennedy hugged her cousin. "Where's my sister? Where's my mom?"

"They're right over here, Ken," Aaron said. He held out his hand to the crowd behind him. Kennedy thought she was going to burst with joy when she saw her mother running over with Victoria, Jessica, Marilyn, Darcy, and Uncle Edward. Kennedy embraced her mother.

"Oh, Mom!" she said. "You're back with us! You're okay!"

"And so are you, my dear girl!" Mom said. Her happy tears fell onto Kennedy's shoulder. "We're all back together again."

"Not to mention that Robert finally got here!" Jessica said.

"What?" Kennedy said. "He did?"

"Yeah! And so did Nicole! She brought backup! We've got the National Park Service! NPS Law Enforcement Rangers! And a few of them took Felicity to the hospital. The rest of us ran here to meet up with everyone else."

"Wonderful!" Kennedy said. "Now we have the high ground against those thugs."

"Well, they don't give up easily," Uncle Edward said. "NPS is scouring the entire park."

"But even so, we still outnumber those goons, don't we?"

"We don't have that much backup," Wesley said. "Not only did some of them take Felicity away, but some of them ran to the hills when we told them about a few of the thugs chasing after you. Not to mention that Robert was injured. He was attacked by Earl while on the phone with Sierra. That's why it took so long for him and the NPS to arrive. They had to help him first. Earl had handed the poor guy a good clonk on the head and did a number on his ankle."

Kennedy winced. Sudden yells from outside the fort made her wince even more.

The doors burst open. Once again, the mob of criminals came flooding in. There were only five of them this time. Earl was walking backwards, firing bullets at the open doors. Kennedy raised her eyes in surprise when she saw Robert and Nicole following Earl, shooting their own guns. Despite his limping left ankle, Robert was moving swiftly.

Maurice, Uncle Edward, Alec, Wesley, Gunnar, and Aaron raced to the fight. Gunnar instantly attacked Abner. Billy grabbed Kennedy's arm.

"Come on," he said, "I'm getting you and your family out of here."

"But our friends!" Kennedy said.

"Billy's right, Kennedy," Mom said, "we must leave."

Kennedy allowed Billy to pull her away. Her mom, sisters, Marilyn, Darcy, Susannah, Rachel, Sierra, Tiana, and Nicole were right behind them. Billy led everyone to a closed door near a corner.

He opened it and left all the women out, then he closed the door behind him. They rushed through an alley and toward the saloon.

"Kennedy!"

Kennedy froze. Ernesto.

"I'm still coming! I'll find you!"

Kennedy felt like her heart plummeted deep down into her gut, accompanied by a flash of nausea shooting up into her head.

"Do not listen to him, Kennedy!" Mom said, her voice full of panic.

"I can't let any of those lawbreakers get you again, Mom!" Kennedy said.

"Where are you, you sneaky little brat!" Ernesto shouted.

Nicole and Billy jumped in front of the group. Billy held his arms out. "All of you stay back!" he said. "Try to take cover!"

Mom yanked Kennedy to the saloon's porch. All the other girls scattered too. Kennedy ducked behind a barrel. She nocked an arrow to her bow.

"Are you armed, Mom?" she asked. Mom lifted her shirt a little, revealing a gun in a holster attached to her belt.

Billy's battle cry startled Kennedy. Her jaw dropped when she saw Billy wrestling Ernesto.

Marilyn's terrified scream pierced the air. Kennedy gaped in horror. Octavia had cornered her stepsister on another porch!

"No!" Mom said. "Marilyn!"

Kennedy jumped up and ran toward Octavia. Victoria and Jessica ran to her side.

"GIRLS!" Mom screeched. "No, no, no! Get away from that woman!"

The three sisters paid their mother no heed. They attacked Octavia from behind. Kennedy whacked her across the back with her bow. Jessica punched her arm. Octavia stumbled back, then she lunged at Victoria.

"YAAAA!"

Rachel dashed toward Octavia, waving her butcher knives above her head. One knife slashed Octavia's cheek. Octavia turned her own attack onto Rachel. Victoria swung her own knife. The tip grazed Octavia's elbow. Then Mom pounced on the former cattle rustler, pinning her down.

"Don't you dare lay a finger on my daughters, you wicked crook!" she screeched.

"You tell her, Mom!" Victoria said.

Nicole pushed her way through the girls and kneeled by the dazed criminal. Mom stood up to let Nicole handcuff Octavia. The criminal lady was too stunned to resist.

"Good fight, girls!" Nicole said as she yanked Octavia to her feet. Victoria whooped and pumped her fists. With a laugh, Rachel copied her actions.

CRASH!

Kennedy yelped and spun around. Now she felt sick.

Billy lay unconscious on the ground. Ernesto raised his gun and pointed it at him.

Kennedy screamed. Then she jumped.

"No!"

She hardly heard her mother. Her sole focus was on aiming her arrow at Ernesto. She breathed.

She released the arrow.

In seconds it was lodged in his shoulder.

Ernesto wailed. He slumped down on his knees, clutching his bloody shoulder. He heaved a big breath. Then, with a pained but defiant glare, he snapped the arrow in half. He turned his glare to Kennedy. Then he raised his gun again.

She didn't know how fast she ran. Nor did she care. All Kennedy cared about in that moment was reaching Ernesto just in time to whack the bow across his head. He fell over on his side, dropping his gun. Kennedy snatched up the gun and whomped the butt of it on Ernesto's temple. He slumped again, his eyes blank.

Billy groaned.

Kennedy gasped. She stepped over Billy. His eyes fluttered open. He looked up at Kennedy in surprise. She smiled and held out her hand. Billy took it. Kennedy raised him to his feet.

"Are you alright?" she asked, not letting go of his hand.

Billy nodded. He rubbed his head. "Guess we're saving each other's lives today," he said.

Kennedy chuckled. "I reckon so. But what do you expect? We love each other. We confessed as much."

She leaned forward and kissed him. Oh, the feeling of his lips locking with hers once again was so soothing.

"Uh," Jessica said, "am I really seeing that?"

Victoria let out a snigger. But Kennedy didn't care that her sisters were laughing at her.

"KENNEDY RYAN!"

Kennedy ripped herself away from Billy. If she had felt ill at Ernesto's yell earlier, then this yell would surely take the cake.

Horace stomped out of an alley. His evil glare was fixed on Kennedy. Not even the bloody bandage wrapped around his hand seemed to bother him.

Did Horace ever give up?

"Get behind me, Kennedy," Billy hissed.

"No," Kennedy said in a hard voice. "I am going to protect everyone. No one else is going to get hurt on account of me."

Despite Billy's pleas, she ran from him and stood near the center of the little Western town, several feet away from Horace. He appeared so tall. Even his shadow was a giant. The rays of dusk shone eerily on him, making his appearance extra menacing.

Old Dodge Park may be an imitation Wild Western town. A simple tourist attraction. But this moment was very real. And it felt surreal. Like a typical, cliched Wild Western movie. It brought back those awful memories of her first showdown with the criminal who stood before her.

This was no doubt the most terrifying thing that had ever happened to her. Even more terrifying than being kidnapped.

Kennedy and Horace raised their guns at the same time.

"Think you are a heroic cowgirl from some Wild Western movie?" Horace laughed. "You make a fine female version of John Wayne. I actually kind of like it. Too bad it had to be you. It's a pity my thirst for revenge clouds my admiration for your grit."

He fired. Kennedy yelped in alarm, but she felt no bullet graze her skin. She ducked behind a barrel and fired at Horace. But he still ran toward her. Kennedy clicked the trigger of her gun. Nothing happened. Once again, she was out of bullets.

Yet another gunshot pierced the air.

Kennedy peeked out from behind the barrel. But Horace was spinning around where he stood, a confused look in his eyes, every bit as confused as Kennedy felt.

"COBB!"

Kennedy jumped to her feet. Her mouth hung open. There was Maurice, running toward Horace with his gun.

"Hurt her," Maurice seethed, "and I will make sure that my next bullet hurts you!"

Maurice stood in front of Kennedy. "Give up, Horace!" he said. "Just give up! The deputy's here and so is a nice crowd of park police! They've already arrested most of your cohorts!"

"NO!" Horace bellowed. "I WILL NOT GIVE UP! I REFUSE TO GIVE UP UNTIL I HAVE MY REVENGE!"

Kennedy winced. He looked like a total madman. More like a madman than Kennedy had ever seen him.

He ran, screaming at the top of his lungs.

Two simultaneous gunshots.

Maurice's eyes went wide.

And only he was groaning in pain. He clutched his bloody abdomen while he collapsed to his knees.

"Maurice!" Kennedy shrieked. "No, no!"

She tried to grab Maurice's shoulders. But he fell flat on his side on the ground. He lay almost perfectly still, coughing up dust, his breathing a heavy labor.

Kennedy slowly lifted her head. Anger filled every fiber of her being. Anger hotter than the desert itself. First Horace had her stepfather poisoned. Now he had shot her father figure.

The light breeze that she hardly noticed at first seemed to pick up, as if joining her in her anger.

Horace's triumphant cackle rang through the hot air. He twirled his gun in his hand. Kennedy leapt to her feet and dashed toward the criminal. Billy was right on her heels. Horace let out another laugh as he pointed his weapon at Kennedy.

"Now nothing will stop me from killing you, my dear Miss Ryan!" he said.

But Kennedy already had an arrow nocked to her bow. And she fired it.

The arrow flew swiftly on the wings of the wind.

It lodged itself right into Horace's forehead.

A tiny yelp from the criminal, and a gasp from Billy behind her. Horace's face went blank, and his eyes wide with shock.

Then he fell silently backwards.

A tense silence took over the atmosphere. The only sounds Kennedy heard were her heavy breathing and the soft wind.

"Kennedy."

She turned around. Billy had dropped his gun and had his arms wide. Kennedy threw her bow on the ground and fell right into Billy's embrace. They wrapped their arms around each other as tight as they could. Kennedy hardly noticed as everybody else began gathering around.

"Maurice!" Nicole shouted.

Kennedy tore away from Billy. Yes, Maurice! She kneeled by the unconscious man. The sight of crimson blood oozing from his stomach made her turn her queasy head away. Tears stung her eyes as she closed them.

"He needs immediate medical attention!" Nicole said. "I'll call an ambulance!"

Kennedy felt strong hands slip under her arms and lift her onto her feet. She opened her eyes to see Billy holding her.

"Don't look," he said. "You're pale enough as it is. Come on, let's get you home with your family."

"But what about the other thugs?" Kennedy asked.

"They've been apprehended," Billy said. He pointed. "Look over there."

Kennedy faced the direction Billy was pointing. Robert was handcuffing Ernesto. The deputy handed him over to a few police officers, who wasted no time in leading him away. Then Robert turned his attention to the comatose Horace. He winced at the sight of the former bank robber.

"They've all been arrested," Billy said. "It's okay, Kennedy. You're safe now. For real this time."

Kennedy smiled feebly. Yes. She was safe once again. It was all over.

Billy led Kennedy over to her family and friends. She had nothing else to do but let herself collapse into one enormous group hug.

Billy was the first to reach his sister's room. Kennedy and her sisters were close on his heels. Kennedy smiled broadly when she saw Felicity lying in the bed, holding her newborn baby. And Jonathon was standing next to the bed, upheld by a crutch and his leg in a cast. Robert stood next to the sheriff.

"Billy!" Felicity said. She let out her hand to her brother. "I was so worried about you!"

"I'm okay," Billy said. "Are you okay? Is my niece okay? Oh, and Jonathon, are you okay?"

"Yes, yes," Jonathon said with a laugh, "my wound wasn't that serious. I just need to take it easy for a while. But I am a little disappointed that I had to miss my daughter's birth."

"But at least she's fine and healthy," Felicity said. "And I got to finish my delivery here instead of at Old Dodge Park."

Jonathon leaned forward to kiss his wife's head. Robert had to hang onto his arm so he wouldn't stumble.

"So, Deputy," the sheriff said, smiling at Robert, "I heard a few great things about your police work."

Robert smiled sheepishly. "Just doing my duty," he said.

"You went above and beyond!" Jonathon said. "You fought despite a bump on the head and a twisted ankle."

"Yeah, you didn't let that sore ankle stop you from your swift fighting moves," Victoria said.

Robert shrugged. "Could be my last name. It is Swift, after all."

Everyone laughed.

"Oh, speaking of that word, *swift*," Felicity said, turning her smile to Kennedy, "Jonathon and I finally agreed on a name for our daughter."

"You have?" Kennedy said. "Do share!"

Felicity's smile broadened. "We chose to name her Camira. The name means 'of the wind'. After all our recent ordeals, it was so appropriate to name her after your favorite catchphrase in Psalm 18."

Kennedy nodded. "It's perfect," she said. "And what's her middle name?"

"Oh, yeah, can't forget that," Jonathon said. "Kennedy."

"What?" Kennedy lifted an eyebrow.

"Yes," Felicity said. "Kennedy, you saved me from Abner in the saloon. So of course I thought we should name her after you. Meet Camira Kennedy Shea."

Kennedy put her hand over her heart. Her loving gaze fell back to the baby girl in Felicity's arms.

"I love it!" Billy said. "The perfect name for my niece. You chose wisely, Fel."

Mom patted Kennedy's shoulder. "I'm so proud of you," she said. "You protected mother and baby."

Kennedy smiled back at her mom. Just then Mom's phone began ringing. Mom took one look at the screen. Her smile faded, but she only gave Kennedy a quick nod and left the room. Kennedy stared after her.

"Ken?" Felicity said. Kennedy turned back around. Felicity sat up a little. "Would you like to hold her, Ken?"

Kennedy smiled and reached out her arms. The baby cooed up at her and reached her tiny fingers to Kennedy's nose, as if Camira already knew how special Kennedy was to her.

But her joy had to fade when the thought of another special someone crossed her mind.

"If nobody minds," she said, "I . . . I want to see if I can find Maurice."

"Of course we don't mind," Felicity said.

Kennedy handed the baby to Victoria and left the room.

"Excuse me," she said to the woman at the desk, "but where is . . . where is Maurice Carr?"

The receptionist looked up at her. "He's still in emergency surgery," she said. "And he won't be receiving visitors for a few days. I'm sorry, dear."

Kennedy's shoulders slumped. She just nodded. "I get it. I really hope he'll make it. I mean, he just had surgery days ago. Got part of his liver removed."

"Yes." The receptionist's voice was soft. "I heard everything. It is truly amazing. And we are glad to have the old Maurice Carr back after all these years. I'm sure the whole town will be talking about it."

Kennedy felt a hand on her shoulder. She looked up at her mother's excited grin.

"What's up, Mom?" she asked.

"I have wonderful news," Mom said. "I just got a call from the hospital in Phoenix."

Kennedy's eyes widened. Did she dare let her hope up this high? "Isaiah?"

"Yes, honey. He's finally making a good recovery. He woke up and he's alert. They'll let him out of their ICU in a few days, then he will come home."

Tears of relief sprung from Kennedy eyes, and joy from her heart. She hugged her mother. Over Mom's shoulders, she saw Marilyn's gleeful face.

Lord, you healed Isaiah. You saved all of us. Thank you!

Well, not quite all of them. Maurice's condition was still questionable. Would God heal Maurice too?

The nurse opened the door. "He's ready to be discharged, Mrs. Wilson," she said with a smile.

Kennedy had never seen her mother grin so broadly in her life. She didn't doubt that her own grin was identical. As were the grins of Marilyn, Victoria, Jessica, Uncle Edward, and Darcy.

Victoria and Jessica almost barged into the room, earning themselves a gentle chiding from the nurse. Kennedy saw Isaiah sitting up in his bed. And he was wide awake. His familiar smile was back. So was the joyful twinkle in his eyes.

"Oh, Daddy!"

Marilyn rushed up to her father and hugged him. Her tears streamed down her cheeks. Isaiah laughed and patted her back.

"My Marilyn," he said, "how wonderful it is to see you."

Kennedy's eyes welled with tears. She leaned in to hug her stepfather. She and Marilyn made room for Victoria and Jessica, then Mom, then Uncle Edward and Darcy.

"Are all of you okay?" Isaiah asked. His eyes met Kennedy's. "I hope that my illness was not too terrible?"

"Are you kidding, Dad?" Victoria said. "It was horrible! So horrible! Me, Ken, and Jess absolutely hated going through the nightmare of a sick father for a second time, and Marilyn was just devastated. But we are so glad that you pulled through it and beat that mushroom poisoning!"

"Thanks to Maurice Carr," Kennedy said softly.

Isaiah nodded. "Yes, I heard everything. The criminals. The adventures you had. And Maurice."

He laid his hand on Kennedy's. "How are you doing? I'm sure that everything was pretty traumatizing?"

"It sure was," Kennedy said. "I was captured a second time. But Billy and Maurice saved me right away."

"Uh, second time?" Isaiah glanced nervously at Mom.

"Yes, Mom knows about my kidnapping in Starwood City. I was so scared when Horace, Ernesto, Winifred, and Ruben caught me again in the bluffs. But it's all over now. Every one of those thugs has been arrested."

"Well, Horace sort of," Victoria said. "It's amazing that your arrow didn't kill him, Kennedy."

"Yes, very much so," Kennedy said. "But I heard that he'll have permanent brain damage."

"Which means he won't be bothering us ever again," Mom said.

"I hate to break up this lovely family reunion," the nurse said with a smile, "but we still have to get Isaiah discharged."

"Oh, yes!" Mom said. "We want to take him home."

Kennedy grinned. Yes, she desperately wanted to bring her stepfather home.

The lobby of the Pine Lodge hospital was quiet. Kennedy fidgeted in her seat. She settled a bit when Billy touched her hand. At least, her body settled, but not her pulse.

"We'll see him soon, Ken," Billy said.

"I know." Kennedy's eyes wandered to the piano standing in the middle of the lobby. Just the thought of playing on it relaxed her a bit more. Nobody would mind.

"I'll think I'll try the piano," she whispered to Billy.

The twosome walked over to it. Kennedy sat on the bench and tapped a few keys. Oh great, now her fingers were beginning to freeze. What should she play?

Her mind wandered back to Maurice. Then she thought of that song she wrote in college.

The song that Maurice had named.

Perfect.

Her fingers were released from their tension. They glided across the keys. The music created a comforting air around her and Billy. Her thoughts never left Maurice the entire time she played.

She finished too soon. Just then a nurse came over to her. Kennedy stood.

"Kennedy," the nurse said with a smile, "that was lovely."

"Thank you," Kennedy said. "I wrote that song. It's called 'Swiftly on the Wings of the Wind.'"

"That's a nice title."

"Maurice came up with it."

"Yes, Maurice." The nurse's smile faded. "I just came over to tell the two of you that you can go into his room now. But he's still unresponsive."

Kennedy's smile faded too. Billy clasped her hand. The two friends didn't let go of each other's hands as they walked through the hallway and into the hospital room.

Indeed, the bedridden Maurice didn't seem to realize that he had a couple of visitors. An oxygen tube covered over half of his face, and his eyes were shut. His breaths were almost unnoticeable.

"The surgery was a little difficult," the nurse said. "We are keeping a close eye on him."

She sighed. "Every one of us recognized him. It's nice to have him back."

"Home?" Kennedy whispered.

The nurse nodded. She went to the door. "Let me know if you need anything."

Kennedy nudged Maurice's hand. It barely budged.

"Maurice," she whispered, "I don't know if you can hear me, but thank you for taking that bullet. You put your life on the line for me. Again."

She closed her watery eyes. "Isaiah's home," she said. "You would be so happy to see him again. Your sacrifice for him wasn't in vain. Thank you for your liver for him. His recovery was such a miracle. I just . . . I just hope God gives you the same miracle."

Billy wrapped his arm around Kennedy. At the same time, Kennedy thought that she felt Maurice's fingers squeeze against her hand.

Cheers erupted when Kennedy and her family entered the restaurant. Kennedy couldn't stop turning her head in different directions. This place was crowded. She wondered if every resident in Pine Lodge was in this restaurant.

She smiled at her stepfather. His smile was beautiful.

"It's wonderful to be back here," he said. "I'm so glad that I could see my restaurant again. Glad that I can still be its owner and manager."

"So is everyone else, Dad!" Marilyn said.

The counter was reserved for Kennedy's family. She sat on a stool in between her parents. Victoria and Jessica were instantly distracted by their friends. And Kennedy was distracted when she saw Billy and his parents sitting with Jonathon, his parents, Felicity, and the new baby girl. Kennedy jumped from her stool and ran over to them.

"Billy," she said, "I'm so glad your family could make it."

"Me too!" Billy hugged Kennedy and kissed her cheek. She didn't rub it. She waited so long for Billy's kiss upon her face.

"How's Camira?" Kennedy smiled down at the baby, who was smiling back and reaching her tiny hands up.

"Just the sweetest granddaughter ever," Pastor Cameron said.

"Hey, come on, Ken," Billy said, "your other friends wanna see you."

The twosome ran over to Rachel, Nicole, Aaron, Gunnar, Wesley, and Robert. Nicole greeted Kennedy with a hug.

"I'm so happy for how everything turned out for everyone!" the ranger said.

"Me too," Kennedy said. "Oh, Nicole, thank you for all the backup you brought to the park."

"My pleasure," Nicole said. "And my duty. But more of my pleasure. Always glad to help a friend in need."

"And I finally got full confessions from the other crooks," Robert said. "They all had teamed up shortly after their jailbreaks. They agreed to try to get revenge on Kennedy."

Billy ruffled Kennedy's hair.

"So Earl disguised himself and used the fake name Roman Hughes," Nicole said, "so he could infiltrate this restaurant. Those crooks had many plans. Earl agreed to try to set your house on fire. That didn't work, thank heavens. But the very desperate Horace wanted to have plenty of backup plans."

"Such as a bear trap?" Kennedy said darkly.

"Yes," Robert said. "I already told Aaron here about it. He was pretty spooked."

"Can you blame me?" Aaron said.

"The backup plans are also why Horace had a few of his cohorts break into GCU and steal the death cap mushrooms," Robert said. "Earl was horrified when Isaiah ate them. He meant for either Kennedy or Marilyn to eat them. So he tried again. But he did not count on Victoria's mushroom knowledge. That threw all the plans into chaos."

"I remember," Kennedy said.

"Grey knew all about Maurice's whereabouts," Robert said. "He still has those computer skills."

"And they kept attacking because Horace insisted," Nicole said. "They wanted to give up. But not Horace. And, well, we know the rest of the story."

"Yeah!" Rachel said. "How could we not?"

"Jonathon was so proud of you, Robert!" Gunnar said. "You are an awesome deputy!"

Robert smiled shyly. "Thanks, man."

Kennedy glazed over the dining area. People were taking turns hugging Isaiah. Tiana and Sierra were laughing with Victoria, Jessica, Marilyn, and the Grant twins. Susannah and a few other waiters and waitresses were taking orders.

But there was still something missing. Kennedy longed for Maurice's presence among the celebrations.

Despite the happy chatter, Kennedy heard the front door's bells jingle. She turned around. And gasped. There were a few other gasps, then silence overcame the place.

Maurice Carr was wobbling into the Lonely Pine Eatery. He looked up. His smile was timid. Sheepish. Uncertain.

Kennedy didn't bother to hold back the tears. She rushed up to Maurice and hugged him, though still careful not to knock him over.

Applause filled the entire restaurant.

Maurice chuckled. "My Kennedy," he said. "Surely you did not think a gunshot wound was gonna stop me from coming to your family's celebration party?"

Kennedy sniffled. "I was so worried about you!" she said. "Billy and I visited you in the hospital, but you were still in a coma. I don't think you knew Billy and I were there."

"Oh, but I had just enough consciousness to hear a familiar piano song being played," Maurice said. "When I finally woke up, I thought it was just a dream. The nurse assured me that it wasn't."

He ran his hand over Kennedy's curly hair. He sniffled and turned his head up. "It is good to be back here," he said.

"I know I'm glad you're back!" Kennedy said.

And everyone else was too. Maurice was greeted by a mob of people eagerly waiting to shake his hand, to reunite with him, to congratulate him, to say welcome back to him.

And among the first people to greet Maurice was Isaiah.

"My old friend," Isaiah said, his voice breaking, "I hear that I owe my life to you. Thank you."

Maurice embraced Isaiah. "You're so welcome, old friend."

"Come on," Isaiah said, "sit with our family."

Kennedy was just about to follow Maurice and Isaiah back to the counter, but Billy stopped her.

"Hey," he whispered, "uh, you know, since we couldn't go to Phoenix for that art festival . . . should we try another date?"

Kennedy grinned. "Most certainly," she said. She smiled at Marilyn and Wesley, then at Alec and Nicole. Now she too could enjoy the love of her life. But for this moment, she and Billy would enjoy their date with their family and friends.

"Look!" Billy said, pointing. "There's Sunshine!"

Kennedy grinned. Her golden palomino mare was running as though she had never been shot in the flank. Just like Maurice and Isaiah, Sunshine had made a great recovery. Kennedy waved at Victoria, who was riding Sunshine. Victoria waved back.

After the horse-riding show, Kennedy and Billy walked to the stables. They found Victoria tending to Sunshine. As soon as she met Kennedy's eyes, she waved and beckoned them over. The palomino mare nickered happily as Kennedy drew close. Kennedy ran her hand over her horse's nose.

"How's the happy couple?" Victoria asked.

Kennedy laughed. "Wonderful. You sure look like you're loving your new job here."

"Of course I am! It's only been a few days and I just adore working here at Old Dodge Park! I've got a great boss and great coworkers and great pay!"

"Vic," Billy said, "may we borrow Sunshine and another horse? I really wanna take Kennedy out on a ride in the bluffs."

"Sure, my boss won't mind."

"Hey, thanks!" Billy said. He ran into a nearby stall. Victoria handed Sunshine's reins to Kennedy. The mare let out an excited nicker.

"Oh, I feel you, Sunshine," Kennedy said. "It's so good to be back with you."

"She'll be back on the ranch before you know it," Victoria said. "Hey, gotta get back to work. Have fun!"

She gave her sister a quick hug and ran out of the stable.

Billy came over with a buckskin gelding, a horse Kennedy recognized as Buckaroo from her uncle's ranch. The two friends took the horses outside and brushed and saddled them. As soon as they climbed onto their horses, they rode out of the stable. In minutes, they reached the bluffs.

"It's a great day for a ride!" Billy said. "Feel that breeze! It's so refreshing from the sun!"

The wind ruffled Kennedy's hair. She loved it. She gazed at Billy. He was more handsome than ever.

Billy returned her gaze. He then halted his horse and slid off. Confused, Kennedy copied his actions.

"What're you doing?" she asked.

Billy didn't reply. He just smiled and grabbed Kennedy by her shoulders. He leaned in and kissed her lips.

She smiled too. She pulled away. "I love you, Billy."

"I love you too, Kennedy," Billy said. He grinned. "Hey, let's have a horse race!"

"Oh, you're on!"

Kennedy and Billy clambered back onto their horses. They laughed as they rode off.

They rode swiftly on the wings of the wind.

About the Author

Photo credit: Elise Williams, eMarie Photography, https://emariephoto.com/

Alicia Layne Thomason is an author, poet, and musician. She graduated from Montana State University Billings in December 2021 with a Bachelor of Arts in English and a Bachelor of Arts in Music. Alicia lives in Billings, Montana. Her website is alicialaynethomason.com.